THE STORY OF BUCKHORN

Center Point
Large Print

Also by Lauran Paine and available from
Center Point Large Print:

Night of the Rustler's Moon
Iron Marshal
Six-Gun Crossroads
Dead Man's Cañon
Lightning Strike
Reckoning at Lansing's Ferry
The Drifter
Winter Moon
The Texan Rides Alone

THE STORY OF BUCKHORN

A WESTERN DUO

LAURAN PAINE

CENTER POINT LARGE PRINT
THORNDIKE, MAINE

This Center Point Large Print edition
is published in the year 2018 by arrangement with
Golden West Literary Agency.

The text of this Large Print edition is unabridged.
In other aspects, this book may vary
from the original edition.
Printed in the United States of America
on permanent paper.
Set in 16-point Times New Roman type.

ISBN: 978-1-64358-035-7 (hardcover)
ISBN: 978-1-64358-039-5 (paperback)

Library of Congress Cataloging-in-Publication Data

Names: Paine, Lauran, author.
Title: The story of buckhorn : a western duo / Lauran Paine.
Description: Center Point Large Print edition. | Thorndike, Maine :
    Center Point Large Print, 2018.
Identifiers: LCCN 2018042970| ISBN 9781643580357
    (hardcover : alk. paper) | ISBN 9781643580395
    (paperback : alk. paper)
Subjects: LCSH: Western stories. | Large type books.
Classification: LCC PS3566.A34 S75 2018 | DDC 813/.54—dc23
LC record available at https://lccn.loc.gov/2018042970

THE STORY OF BUCKHORN

BUCKHORN

A WESTERN DUO

TABLE OF CONTENTS

The Valley of Thunder

I

They hoorawed the town Saturday night, broke two front windows at Sabin's saloon, shot out the carriage lamps on each side of the livery barn's front entrance on their wild charge out of town, nearly ran down old man Harriman who was blind and who lived with his old, white-muzzled dog in a shack at the south end of town, and one of them shot and killed the old dog. It was enough, Ray Teller said, when after church on Sunday morning the simmering anger of the townsmen came to a head out front of the church after the minister had preached a sermon about godless men who had no regard for the rights of others. But they had not needed the sermon; they were silently angry even before they went to church. Nor was it an isolated instance; since the riding season had begun about two months earlier, hoorawing range men had burst into Dunnigan, scattering pedestrians, swaggering the plank walks, spoiling for trouble even when they had not been drinking, and deliberately intimidated people, most of whom did not go armed—merchants, workmen, clerks, people who did not in many cases even own guns.

Last night it had been the men from George Luckner's Rafter Ranch, but the week before it had been a combination of range men from Will Kershaw's Arrow Circle Ranch and John Bailey's Mexican Hat. Frank Sabin stood glumly in his black suit listening to Ray Teller and the others, reluctant to speak because as soon as he did someone was going to place part of the blame on his saloon. He'd heard it before; if he did not sell them liquor, they would not run wild. But this morning with the summer sun lying like a benediction over the immense expanse of Thunder Valley, and its town of Dunnigan, people were subdued; all they had to do was walk homeward from the churchyard and gaze upon the wreckage, as well as old Harriman's dead dog in the center of the road at the lower end of town. The women went along, some with children showing shiny faces, slicked-down hair, and scuffed but recently oiled shoes. The men stood in tree shade in their church-going dark suits, quietly discussing things, and no one said a thing about Frank Sabin's saloon until the town blacksmith, burly Ray Teller, asked Charley Bennett if the town council couldn't pass an ordinance about selling whiskey to anyone, not just range men, between, say, 8:00 at night and perhaps midnight.

Charley was a balding, thick man who wore a massive gold watch chain across his big middle every day of the week at his general store, not just on Sunday like the others standing out front of the church. Charley Bennett had been a town councilman seven years, longer than any of the others who served. He looked directly at Sabin as he said: "I don't believe it'd work, Ray. They'd buy bottles before closing time, and go out into the roadway and do their drinking. The only way I can see to limit their drinking would be to do it across the bar. Right, Frank?"

Sabin was a dark-eyed, dark-complexioned man slightly under average height, powerfully muscled and beginning to gray at the temples. He had been a widower for eleven years, and when he had first arrived in Thunder Valley fifteen years earlier, he had cowboyed for Luckner, then had served a term as town marshal. He looked at big Charley Bennett and said: "If I tried that, Charley, they'd tear my place down, and maybe wreck the town. And you're laying something on me . . . or any one man . . . that no one man can do."

Clinton Whitney who worked at the smithy for Ray Teller, a large, brawny man, younger than the others, said: "Where I grew up in Nebraska, they had the same trouble . . . irresponsible range riders runnin' roughshod over folks. They set up a town law enforcement committee . . . the storekeepers and hostlers and so forth." Clinton paused, then said: "Folks stood behind the town marshal."

The men looked at the ground, or at the front

13

of the empty church, but not at one another until Frank Sabin spoke. "I know Tom as well as any of you. I like him and respect him. We're standing out here beating around the bush. Tom Anderson is just too old. He's been talking them out of it for twenty years, but one of these days he isn't going to be able to do it, and one of them with a snoot full is going to kill him. You think it's my saloon . . . I'll tell you what I think, and I don't like to say it, but unless the town council fires Tom as marshal and brings in someone to replace him who is at least thirty years younger, and hard as iron, it's not going to matter if we form a town protective association or not."

Charley Bennett fondled his massive gold watch chain, still looking at the ground. "Another talk with Luckner and Bailey and . . ."

Frank Sabin flushed. "Aw, hell, Charley," he said in disgust. "That doesn't work. How many times have folks from town gone out and talked to those fellers? I'll tell you something I've heard across my bar a dozen times . . . they send their riders to Dunnigan to let off steam, and joke about hoorawing the town. No, it's got to be something a lot more drastic than talk."

Clinton Whitney pulled loose his string tie because his neck was always too large for any shirt he bought, and he could stand the discomfort for an hour or so each Sunday morning, but that was all. As he tugged the tie and collar loose, he said: "Old Harriman's dog last night . . . someone's little kid next week or the week after, or maybe someone's wife."

The others knew this, had mentioned it among themselves now and then, and had shaken their heads about it, but that was all they had done. Now having it brought up, after last night, was different, especially after Frank Sabin's bluntness. Charley Bennett looked around. "We've got a council meeting tomorrow night. I'd like to see you fellers there. You got all day today and all day tomorrow to think of a solution."

Sabin gently shook his head at Charley Bennett. "There's nothing to think about, Charley, and holding meetings isn't going to do anything but stall things. Gents, they'll be back next Saturday night. Hell, I can replace my busted windows, the chairs and tables and backbar bottles . . . it'll cost money, but I can do it . . . only, what do I do next Saturday night, or the Saturday night after that . . . until someone gets killed, or maybe several folks get killed? Yeah, I know you're all at home having supper or in bed, so you're safe, but there are men working around town, at the stage company's corral yard, or down at the livery barn." Frank paused, and the others waited without looking at Sabin. "Get rid of Anderson, Charley. I'll be sorrier than any of you to see him leave, but unless he goes, someone's blood

15

is going to be on our heads because we *know* what should be done, have known that for a year at least, and haven't done a damned thing about it."

Bennett reddened. He could be spiteful; he was not often that way, but he could be. Now he looked at Sabin and said: "It's the whiskey, Frank."

Sabin looked straight back from his black eyes. "Charley, it's *not* the liquor! It's letting them chouse the town so long that they do it naturally. The liquor helps, but if they didn't get it from me, they'd still get it. It's not liquor, Charley, it's a . . . gutless town council."

Instantly Ray Teller moved to break up the little unscheduled discussion by saying: "All right, Charley, we'll think on it and be at the meeting tomorrow night. Frank, let's head on down the road."

Bennett stood gazing after the departing figure of Frank Sabin, fondling his gold watch chain, angry-eyed and red. Clint Whitney scuffed in the dust, then muttered something about having to get down to the café for breakfast.

Teller, walking with Frank Sabin, said: "Sooner or later someone was going to say the wrong thing. It always happens."

Sabin looked at the taller man. "Ray, for Christ's sake it's the truth. You know it's the truth. I'm standing right here to tell you that

16

unless they replace Tom, you or me or someone's kid or woman is going to stop a bullet."

"Accidentally, Frank, those range men don't really . . ."

"Frank, if you get killed accidentally or on purpose, you're just as dead, aren't you?"

They stopped in front of the saloon. The blacksmith gazed at the scattered window glass, the broken chairs and bottles that had been hurled through the windows. He straightened a little and gave Sabin a slap on the shoulder. "I'm sorry," he said, and walked briskly on southward.

Frank fished inside his baggy black church-going coat, came up with a cigar, bit off the end, and lit the thing, then stood considering the wreckage he had to clean up, and shook his head, because he was not thinking of the wreckage, or the financial loss, he was thinking about that entity he had described out front of the church—the gutless town council. He knew perfectly well he was right; so did Ray Teller and the others, but since nothing had been done in over a year, since last riding season in fact, it probably would not be done now, either. He said a fierce word and went inside to shed his coat and get to work cleaning up the saloon.

II

Sabin was wrong. In fact, when he arrived at the fire house where they held the council meetings and looked around for Marshal Anderson, Clint Whitney leaned and whispered: "They fired him. He left about ten minutes ago."

The room was full, something that rarely happened. Charley Bennett was presiding, something he did very well and clearly enjoyed doing. He was a little pompous; maybe it was justified; his general store was the most lucrative and flourishing business in town, and if it meant much in a place like Dunnigan, he was a leader. The business before the council when Frank had arrived was the procurement of a replacement for Tom Anderson. Only one townsman stood up and said—"You shouldn't have fired Tom until you had a man to take his place."—which was what Frank Sabin was thinking, although actually whether old Tom was on hand next Saturday night or not would not make much difference. It hadn't before.

Frank had put in a long day both yesterday and today, and someone had over-stoked the potbellied big stove, so the room was too hot. Frank left early in order to avoid being embarrassed by falling asleep.

The following morning when he encountered Ray Teller at the café having breakfast, Ray said the council had decided to send forth enquiries for Tom's replacement. That was all they could do. Frank ate his breakfast, went back to inspect the clean-up he'd accomplished, found it satisfactory, and put on a pot of coffee atop the iron stove over near the north wall of his place of business. An old gaffer called Bailer arrived, guiding old blind Josh Harriman, and Frank brought them a deck of cards near a front window where heating sunlight came through. There was only one deck they could use; Frank and old man Harriman had worked over it with a leather punch last winter forcing raised spots so Josh Harriman could tell what cards were in his hand by feeling the spots, and counting them.

When old Bailer, a wizened, raffish, dark man who also lived in a shack at the lower end of town came to the bar for two cups of coffee, he leaned and said: "Had to get him out, Frank. He was just settin' in there, rockin'. That old dog was his family. Maybe if you could pour a small jolt in his cup?"

Sabin put the whiskey in the cup and smiled at Bailer, then poured whiskey into the other cup as well, and winked.

Later, two yardmen from the stage company corral yard came over for beer. One of them was a half-breed of some kind, a stalwart, black-eyed

19

man with lean features. When Frank brought their glasses, the half-breed said he knew a man who could replace Tom Anderson. Frank was not particularly responsive; everyone would have a man to recommend. He told the half-breed to go down to the general store and talk to Charley Bennett, and later, after the yardmen had departed, Frank dug out an old newspaper, spread it atop the bar, put on his glasses, got a cup of black coffee, and settled down to a quiet time of relaxing. The man who did carpentering around town would not be along until late afternoon to replace the broken front windows. There was never much trade in the morning or early afternoon, and even the nights during the week were usually quiet because his trade was pretty well limited to townsmen on week nights.

Clint Whitney came in later in the afternoon, while the glass was being installed in the broken windows, and drank beer while watching the carpenter.

Frank, catching Whitney's look, nodded and said: "Yeah . . . until next time."

The brawny younger man leaned on the bar. "Glass is damned expensive, isn't it?"

It was *very* expensive in Wyoming, especially in as distant and isolated a place as Thunder Valley where everything came overland by freight wagon, and glass required very special handling every mile of the way. "Yeah, but if I boarded up the front wall solid, it'd be darker'n hell in here, and besides that I couldn't see out."

"Did you ever go to the cowmen to pay, Frank?"

Sabin snorted. "Yeah. It's the same as going to the devil for a rosary."

Clint considered his empty glass, then said: "I got a cousin named Mitchell . . . Hugh Mitchell . . . we always called him Mitch. I was goin' to mention him at the meetin' last night. He's been a gun guard on bullion stages and a deputy sheriff in Nebraska."

"For Tom's job?"

"Yeah."

"Did you mention him to Charley Bennett?"

"No. You think I should?"

Frank leaned on the bar top. "Could he handle it? You've seen what happens here. I think it's maybe got past the stage where even Wild Bill Hickok or Wyatt Earp could do it alone, Clint."

"Mitch could handle it, Frank."

Sabin shrugged. "Then go tell Charley. Lord knows we've got to have someone, and damned soon." Sabin was gazing at his new window when he said this.

An hour later Charley Bennett arrived at the saloon. He looked worried; he had reason to look that way. The only thing customers had been discussing all morning had been the fact that

21

Tom Anderson had loaded his property aboard the southbound stage and left town, which meant there was no lawman for Dunnigan township now, and, as Charley told Frank over a beer, that man who had complained last night about firing Tom before the council had a replacement for him was going around town saying the councilmen, and Charley in particular, had been derelict in their duty. Then Charley said: "Clint Whitney was by the store a while back. He's got a cousin down near Evansville he told me could do the job."

Frank nodded and remained silent.

"Evansville isn't too far. We could get him up here by Friday . . . if he'd come. Clint says he's managing a freight line down there."

"Did you write him?" Sabin asked.

Bennett fidgeted. "I was going to. Maybe I'll do it this afternoon."

Frank bobbed his head in the direction of the front wall. "Those two pieces of glass cost me nine dollars. Getting 'em installed was another dollar and a half."

Bennett turned briefly to look at the windows, then faced forward again. He understood the dry implication. "I'll write him this afternoon," he said, and left the saloon.

That evening when Sabin's usual customers began arriving, they all admired the new windows, and inevitably someone asked how long

22

Frank thought they would last. Someone at the upper end of the bar offered to wager a silver cartwheel they would go the way of the former windows come Saturday night. No one offered to cover the bet.

It was a quiet night; mostly, the unmarried men around town played poker and drank their beer from pitchers. The married men usually drank a couple of jolts of whiskey, then lingered until their consciences bothered them, and departed.

Frank closed up at 10:00, heard the last stage leaving town, and went out front to suck in fresh night air and look up and down the roadway. There were new lights on opposite sides of the livery barn's doorless big front opening, and old man Harriman's dog had been removed.

Tuesday went the same way as did Wednesday, quiet, orderly, but with an increasing undercurrent of tension as the weekend came closer. There was betting around town about Frank's replaced windows, but nothing was mentioned to Frank about this until Ray Teller and his helper, Clint Whitney, came by Wednesday night for a drink after work and said the betting was heavily against the windows being in place next Sunday morning. Ray also said several range men had been down at the trading corrals out behind the livery barn when some of the betting was taking place, and they had offered twenty-to-one odds to anyone who cared to put up cash, that the windows would *not* be in place by Sunday morning, which meant of course that the betting, and the fact that it was under way, had by now got beyond town to the cow outfits.

Ray said: "Board 'em up, Frank."

Sabin leaned on the bar, gazing at his new windows. Boarding them up would not do it; bullets would rip through the planking and still break the glass. But there was something else. Boarding up his windows bothered Sabin; it was a little like begging. He refilled the glasses for Clint and Ray, then said: "No, but this time when they bust them, someone's going to regret it a long time."

Teller and his assistant blacksmith considered Frank's face and let the topic pass, turning next to discussing the prospects for rain, a safe subject with anyone in range country, even with town dwellers, because if the cattlemen suffered, so did the economies of the towns.

After Frank closed up Thursday night, barred the front door, then washed glasses, and had his one drink of hard liquor of the day, as a nightcap, he meticulously dried his hands, removed his bar apron, and reached beneath the backbar, brought forth a sawed-off, ten-gauge scatter-gun, broke it, extracted both loads, and went to work cleaning the ugly weapon. Every man had a limit. Frank Sabin had never turned his back on a fight in his life, nor had he ever gone looking for one. He was satisfied that Charley Bennett and the other councilmen would not be able to do anything by Saturday night; he did not blame them for this exactly. He blamed them for not having done something long before, but right now his windows had become objects of personal, *very* personal concern. People around town were amused at the prospect of Frank's having them shot out again. Frank was not amused.

He reloaded the ten-gauge, set four more loads on end beside it under his backbar, then went to bed. He had no illusions about the odds. The range riders did not arrive in Dunnigan on Saturday nights except in large numbers. But enough was enough.

He did not have a troubled sleep, and in the morning, when he opened up and saw the morning stage entering town from the south, he watched it with the same impersonal curiosity he had watched the same coaches enter town every morning for years.

He swept the place out, flung a bucket load of dirty water into the roadway to dispose of scrub water while simultaneously keeping down the dust, then he went down to the café for breakfast.

The place was full. It usually was, early in the morning. A brute of a big, bearded freighter was hunched over his platter, shoveling food in with both hands. He looked more like a pirate than a freighter, and the townsmen on both sides of him were leaving plenty of space for the shockle-headed, bearded big man to eat.

Frank finished and went out front to light his first cigar of the day. Across the road the jailhouse looked abandoned and empty. It saddened him to think of Tom Anderson being gone after so many years. They had been good friends, but friendship was not enough under the present circumstances. Still, as he turned to walk back to the saloon, it troubled him a little to have been the one who had insisted that Tom be replaced.

When he walked into the saloon a rangy, raw-boned man was leaning there, looking at the backbar shelves. He was not a young man but neither was he very old. Frank guessed his age to be perhaps thirty-five, maybe a year or two different one way or the other. The stranger had light blue eyes, a bronzed complexion, and nodded as Frank went behind the bar to tie on his apron, but did not smile as he asked for a glass of beer.

When Frank returned with the glass, the rangy man said: "Strange thing. I've been all around Thunder Valley, bringing cattle in and taking them out . . . but that was years ago . . . and this is the first time I've ever been in Dunnigan."

Frank made a reasonable assumption from this that the raw-boned, bronzed man was a range rider. He said: "It's not a bad town. Most of the time. The winters are mild. Summer riding season is a little different."

The rangy man's light eyes showed irony. "So I've heard," he said quietly, and lifted his glass to half drain it. As he put it down, he said: "Where do I find a man named Charles Bennett?"

Frank hung fire over his answer. "Down at the general store. He owns it. Mind if I ask your name?"

The rangy man drained his glass and shoved it aside as he answered. "I don't mind, mister. My name's Hugh Mitchell."

Frank nodded his head in confirmation of the thought that had come to him moments before. "Mister Mitchell, Charley Bennett'll almost always be at the store this time of day."

Hugh Mitchell dropped a coin beside the glass, nodded, and departed. Frank watched him cross the room and shove past the spindle doors, then let his breath out in a rattling sigh. Mitchell had looked like a confident, capable man. From what Clint Whitney had said, Mitchell was probably about as capable a man as the Dunnigan town council was likely to find, but it was still, in Frank Sabin's opinion, a situation no solitary individual could handle regardless of how tough or fast or willing or mean he could be.

He was pumping up three beers for a trio of itinerant range men when Charley came briskly in from the roadway. Frank finished with his customers, then went to the lower end of the bar where Charley was tapping impatiently. Bennett said: "We just hired a new marshal."

Frank said: "Mitchell? He was in here a while ago looking for you."

Charley stopped tapping. "He looks to me like he can do it. He's been a lawman before. We had to agree to pay him a lot of money, though. Twice what we paid Tom."

Frank said: "Charley, if he can do it by himself, he's a miracle worker. If they get him, Charley, it'll be just that much harder for the next man . . . and for us. I'll tell you what I'm going to do tomorrow night to the first son-of-a-bitch that shoots out my windows. Blow him apart with my ten-gauge. And I think it's up to the council to make damned sure there are some men around wearing guns to back up Mitchell. Charley, enough is damned well enough. Dunnigan's taken all any town's got to take. You agree with me?"

Bennett looked at Sabin and let his eyes slide off to settle upon the distant potbellied big old cast-iron cannon heater.

"Charley?"

"Yes, I agree. I'll talk to the other council members."

"Bull crap! You go get Clint and Ray and a couple more men, tell them to stay armed tomorrow night. Tell Mitchell they'll back him up. We've got a cellar full of talk. Let's try something different for a change."

Bennett was red in the face as he leaned back from the bar to meet Sabin's black, steady stare. Then he turned and marched out of the saloon, and Frank shook his head and spoke aloud: "He won't do it."

The range men up the bar finished their beer, dropped coins, and asked the way to the Luckner Rafter cow outfit. Frank impassively gave them the proper directions and also watched them walk out of his saloon.

III

Hugh Mitchell returned to Sabin's saloon late in the afternoon. The only other customers were two hostlers from the lower end of town, and when they saw Tom Anderson's dull, old dented badge on the stranger's shirt front, they stared, then they huddled close to whisper back and forth.

Frank brought a beer for Mitchell without being asked, set it up and said: "What did they tell you around town?"

Mitchell did not touch the beer glass. "About the same thing my cousin told me. They raid the town every Saturday night."

"Yeah. Did they tell you it's not just three or four of them?"

Mitchell nodded. "Riders for the big outfits . . . Luckner, Kershaw, and Bailey."

"Mister Mitchell, one man . . ."

"Mitch."

"Mitch, one man can't do it. We don't have a town committee to help out, but . . ."

"I talked to Clint. He'll be around tomorrow night. Maybe by then I can find another man."

Frank nodded and leaned, gazing out a front window where a dusty, stained, fiercely bearded big range rider rode to the tie rack and swung wearily to the ground. Frank's interest did not remain on the range man because Mitchell said: "I guess the marshal they fired was getting long in the tooth."

Sabin's response was philosophical. "We all do, eventually. Tom was a good man. It's sad to see an old friend wear out. They would have killed him sooner or later."

The bearded, powerfully muscled rider walked in, ranged a look around, then approached the bar, placed a big, scarred fist on it, and said: "Barman, a glass and a bottle."

As Frank turned away, the bearded stranger turned hard black eyes upon Mitchell. "This goddamned country is hot," he said. "I've been dry as a cornhusk for forty miles."

Mitchell faintly smiled. "It's summer."

The big man wagged his head about that. "They told me Wyoming was cold in winter and never hot in summer. They sure lied, didn't they?"

Frank set up the bottle and glass. Before drinking, the cowboy beat off dust in tan clouds with a disreputable old hat. His hair was black and curly, like his beard, and except for his forehead, which was almost indecently white in comparison to the bronzed, weathered hue of the rest of his face, he seemed dark, almost as dark as Frank Sabin.

Mitchell watched the big man down his whiskey, then said: "Forty miles?"

The range man nodded.

"And you just tie up your horse out front?"

The implication was clear; the horse needed care more than its rider.

The cowboy considered his whiskey bottle for a time before turning slightly toward Mitchell. "No, I watered him south of town, and as soon as I've had one more jolt, I figure to take him down to the livery barn. Marshal, you hadn't ought to chouse a man when he's got to town dry as a plank and hungry."

Mitchell showed that faint smile again. "The horse is hungry, too, friend, and I wasn't chousing you. I just happen to like horses."

The bearded cowboy continued to lean, facing Mitchell. He tapped the bar top with his fingers for a moment. Frank Sabin knew all about these situations. He moved over to refill the cowboy's glass as he said: "The third one's on the house."

31

The cowboy sighed, loosened his stance, and faced forward. He downed that drink, too, then he turned without another glance at either of them and marched out.

Frank took away the bottle and glass. When he came back, the new town marshal was leaving. Frank leaned and put a perplexed gaze upon Mitchell's back. Those tired, bone-dry, dirty, and dusty riders never walked into a saloon in a good mood. Mitchell had to have known that. Frank sighed and looked out his new windows.

Outside, the day was waning. The heat was still out there, a harbinger of hot days ahead, and a fine-looking, graying man, a little thick in the girth but big enough to carry it well, walked his horse past the saloon. There was a sinewy, youthful range man riding alongside. He grinned broadly and jerked a thumb. The handsome older man nodded and half smiled back. "New windows. They sure are nice and shiny, Cuff."

The cowboy laughed.

Marshal Mitchell was out front of the livery barn when those two horsemen turned in, swung down, and the younger man called for a hostler while the handsome older man pulled off his riding-gloves and tucked them under a shell belt with a filigreed sterling silver buckle, keeper, and tip.

The hostler came, recognized the handsome man, and said: "Howdy, Mister Luckner." Then took the horses down into the shadowy runway. Luckner and his range rider strolled away, leaving Hugh Mitchell gazing after them briefly, before entering the barn in search of that powerfully muscled, bearded range man.

He was out back using one of the public corrals, probably because he could not afford having his big brown horse stalled. He was forking meadow hay over the topmost stringer when Mitchell came over and said: "Nice horse."

The cowboy finished pitching hay, grounded the fork, and leaned on it as he impassively studied Hugh Mitchell. Finally he said—"Yeah."—and started to turn away.

Mitchell said: "What's your name?"

The bearded man slowly turned back, black eyes softly glowing. "My name is Walter Landon. Marshal, maybe I got the wrong feeling about you, but as far as I know there was no call for you to follow me down here, unless you're one of those town marshals who likes to peck at newcomers to your town, and if that's the case, don't do it with me."

Mitchell leaned on the corral stringers. Ten feet distant upon the opposite side of the corral Walter Landon's big horse was making the pleasant sounds horses make when they are eating.

"Yeah, I followed you down here, Walt, but not to peck at you. Today is my first day in this town, too."

Landon thought that over. "And you become town marshal in one day?"

"Yeah. They fired the one before me. I've done this before, not in Wyoming but other places. The reason I followed you down here . . . do you figure to hire on with one of the cow outfits beyond town?"

Walter Landon nodded his head. "Yeah, but not for a couple of days. I come a hell of a ways. I'd like to just set a little, get washed off, and eat a ton of someone else's food."

Mitchell said: "I need a deputy."

Walter Landon stepped over to the stringers, also, to lean. "You need a deputy. Are you just talking or are you offering me a job?"

"It'll pay more than cowboying. Yeah, I'm offering you a job."

"Marshal, I've never been a lawman. I've tangled with a few of them. No, I think I'd rather keep to open country." Landon's low, broad forehead wrinkled. "It looks like a decent, quiet town to me. What'n hell would you need a deputy for?"

"I don't think it stays quiet on Saturday. Especially on Saturday night."

Landon's frown disappeared. "I see. What the hell, a few fellers come in from the cow camps to let go a little."

Mitchell straightened up. "Have a good stay," he told Landon, and walked away.

If Hugh Mitchell had known Dunnigan as well as his cousin knew it, he would have been able to feel the undercurrent. People looked at him, some nodded, none spoke, and all hurried past. The news had already spread over town that there was a new town marshal wearing old Anderson's badge. Some shook their heads. A few surreptitious bets were made, and this time not on the fate of Frank Sabin's windows.

Clint Whitney met Mitchell out front of Teller's smithy and shook his head. "The damned town is sort of holding its breath, Mitch. For a Friday, it's quieter than it usually is."

Mitchell let that pass, and said: "The feller at the saloon . . . what's his name?"

"Frank. Frank Sabin."

"Decent, Clint?"

"Yeah. Frank's a damned good man. Like I told you, they busted hell out of his place last Saturday night."

Mitchell stood looking up the shadowing, sunglow-tinted roadway. "I tried to hire us a feller a while back."

"No luck?"

"No. You got a shotgun to go with your belt gun, Clint?"

"Yeah. Ray's got a big old twelve-bore," replied Whitney. "I'll have it tomorrow evening."

"We still need another man," mused Mitchell, watching a stalwart half-breed cross from the

35

stage company corral yard toward the saloon. Clint looked up, recognized the man his cousin was eyeing, and said: "Not him. He'd do it, but he broke his right arm at the elbow last winter. It's a little stiff."

"Got any recommendations?" asked Mitchell, swinging his gaze back to Whitney.

Clint thought a moment, then sighed and wagged his head. "Not in town. Mitch, those stockmen got folks buffaloed all to hell."

Mitchell squinted at the lowering huge red disc hanging inches above the western rims of Thunder Valley and said—"Suppertime."—and walked away.

Clint went back into the shop scowling, and Ray Teller, who was washing up in the clinker bucket, faced around. "Are you going to help him tomorrow night?"

Clint nodded and raised his eyes. "Ray, even with shotguns I don't know . . . two men. They're saying around here that the range men consider Frank's windows as a sort of personal challenge."

Teller straightened up to shake water from his arms and hands. "They'll all come, for a damned fact. Every man who can make it, anyway. Clint, I think I'll go talk to Charley Bennett. At first I didn't think much of it, but now I'm beginning to feel different. If they'd just shoot out the damned windows, we could take up a collection around town and buy a pair of new ones for Frank. If

36

your cousin braces them . . . You lock up. I'm going up to talk to Charley. Good night. See you in the morning."

Ray Teller rolled up his shiny old mule-hide apron, flung it aside, and walked briskly from the shop. Like most people, Ray disapproved of the things that had been happening in Dunnigan; he wanted changes made, and he fully realized there would have to be changes made. He even felt militantly indignant, but last Sunday when he'd expressed himself out front of the church was a long time ago. This was Friday, one day away from trouble. He knew trouble was coming, suspected that it might be very bad trouble, and, almost a week after expressing himself forcibly out front of the church, Ray's resolve was still strong, something *did* have to be done, but he was beginning to be afraid, too.

Charley looked harassed. He frowned slightly when Teller entered the store, then signaled to the old man in black cotton sleeve protectors who worked as a clerk around the store to mind things, and Charley took Ray to his dingy little office behind the bolt goods shelves. As he closed the door, Charley expressed himself irritably.

"All I've heard this week is complaints . . . why didn't the council hire a man before we fired Tom. Today, it's different. Why didn't we hire a gunslinger to replace Tom." Charley went to his squeaky desk chair, sank down, and leaned back,

37

leaving the town blacksmith to take the only other chair in the room, a small, wired-together ladder-back chair without arms. As Teller eased down, he blew out a rough breath.

"Clint's going to help Mitchell tomorrow night. Two of them with belt guns and shotguns."

Charley ran a tired hand over his face. "And Frank. He told me he wasn't going to let 'em blow out his windows without making them regret it. Those god-damned windows!"

It wasn't the windows, they both knew that, but Charley had been on his feet all day, it was getting close to suppertime, and the week-long recriminations were not sitting well with him, either.

"I been wondering," Ray began quietly. "George Luckner was in town today."

"Yeah, he came by for the mail and some other stuff."

"He's a reasonable man, Charley."

Bennett's eyes swung. "Now," he said, emphasizing the first word, "you're beginning to get some sense."

Ray ignored that. "I've known George Luckner, John Bailey, and even Will Kershaw for a long time. They don't want a battle between us and them. Sure as hell someone will get killed. This blasted thing is getting completely out of hand."

Bennett was wearing a faintly cynical expression. "Ray, any time last week . . . I mean this

38

week up until today . . . we could have gone out and talked to Bailey, Kershaw, and Luckner. I *told* you fellers out front of the church last Sunday. I've been saying so at the council meetings . . . reason with the ranchers, let 'em see our side, and what's happened? Frank's as good as told me I was afraid of the stockmen, among other things he said to me." Charley moved and the chair squeaked. "Ray, Tuesday or Monday we could have done it. Friday . . . and those damned range men cocked and primed and looking forward to coming to town tomorrow to shoot out Frank's windows . . . it's just too damned late."

Teller rubbed a blue bruise on one arm; the most experienced and careful blacksmith who ever lived never went a full week in his life without getting at least one bruise, commonly more than one, and very often injuries worse than bruises. He continued to rub the sore place as he spoke. "All right. Then we've got to do something besides set here and leave it up to Clint and his cousin."

"Such as?" demanded Bennett, looking closely at Ray Teller. "Arm the town, turn out everybody with guns? Ray, the range men would burn this place to the ground."

Teller stopped massaging his sore arm and faced Bennett. "You want to let just those two face Luckner's, Bailey's, and Kershaw's range men?"

"There won't be just those two. Frank'll be in it with his damned backbar scatter-gun."

Ray sat a moment regarding Charley Bennett, beginning to believe he should not have come up here at all. Charley was a good civic leader, an experienced town councilman, a successful merchant, even a good talker, but this upcoming business would require someone who probably did not possess a single one of those attributes. Ray arose. "Well, I'm going to see if I can't at least scare up a couple more men, otherwise it's going to be plain murder."

Bennett also rose. As he went to hold the door for the town blacksmith, he made his final statement. "Ray, Clint said his cousin could handle this. Mitchell told me how he'd worked as a lawman before. Why don't we just let him handle things? He was recommended real high by Clint, remember?"

Ray studied the other man's round, unlined face for a moment, then turned and walked out of the store.

IV

Sabin's saloon did not have many customers Friday night. Old Bailer came along to snag a drink from the dregs bottle Frank kept under the bar, and into which he poured whatever his patrons left in their glasses. Old Bailer said Josh Harriman was in his shack, rocking back and forth in his chair in the dark.

"Misses the dog," Bailer confided, watching Frank fill his shot glass. "Him and that dog . . . did you know he had that dog so's it'd tell him when it was safe to cross the road? It'd watch, and, when it was safe, it'd bump old Harriman's leg with its nose. Danged smart dog, Frank. But I don't know . . . I go over and set and talk, and part of the time he just sets in that damned rocking chair without even answerin'."

Frank pushed the dregs bottle over the bar. "Take it along, and mind you see that he gets at least part of it."

That bearded big range man came in wearing clean clothes that were just as threadbare as the ones he'd arrived in Dunnigan wearing, and he had washed until his nose and cheeks shone. He smiled at Frank, so evidently he had eaten, too, because his mood was much better tonight. As he accepted the bottle and glass, he looked around. "Where's the marshal?" he asked.

Frank had no idea. "Not in here. Maybe over at the jailhouse."

Walt Landon leaned on the bar, staring at Frank. "Did he just come into town today?"

"Yes."

"And they hired him on as marshal the same day?"

41

Frank made a swipe of the bar top with his sour rag. "Yeah, but he didn't just happen to be riding through. He's got a cousin works down at the smithy. The head of our town council wrote for Mitchell to come up for the job."

"Mitchell."

"Hugh Mitchell. Folks call him Mitch."

The big cowboy carefully filled his glass and put the bottle aside. "Just how big are the cow outfits in this valley, mister?"

"Three of them are big. There are maybe six or seven that are a lot smaller. Mostly the little ranches are in the far foothills; sort of starve-out ranches. But the big ones own or control thousands of acres, run upward of maybe six, eight thousand cattle, and hire on eight or ten riders each season, and winter through with maybe three or four men. Are you looking for a riding job?"

Landon threw back his head, dropped the whiskey straight down, and said: "Yeah. But not for a day or two. Maybe Monday or Tuesday I'll go scouting around." Walt Landon made a piratical grin at Frank. "All I've heard around town, at the livery barn, out front of the general store, over at the pool hall is that the devil'll be riding in here tomorrow night to raise hell and prop it up. I don't want to miss that."

Frank did not smile. "You finished with the bottle?" When the bearded man nodded, Frank turned abruptly and walked along his bar to the shelf where the bottle had come from, and did not return.

Southward and upon the opposite side of the road Hugh Mitchell was swearing because his predecessor at the jailhouse office had not cleaned ash from the wood stove for a long time. It was packed in the lower bin like lead, and he had to scoop out three scuttles full and pack them across the back alley before he could get enough draft to make a decent fire, and all just to heat some coffee atop the stove.

There was fine gray dust in the air, too, that settled over everything. So Mitch had to dust the scarred, old, battered desk and the chair in front of it before he could sit down and wait for his coffee to boil.

When he was finally comfortable a gnome-like, darkly weathered old man popped his head in from the roadway, smiled from ear to ear disclosing some snags of teeth, but not very many of them, and sidled inside to stand by the open door as though he expected to need a swift route of withdrawal. He said: "My name's Bailer. That's not my real name, but it's close enough. You'll be Mister Mitchell, the new town lawman."

Mitch pointed. "Have a seat, Bailer. Is something wrong?"

Bailer perched upon a wall bench. "Well,

Mister Mitchell, I got a friend. Blind feller name of Josh Harriman. He had an old dog. It was all he had. He had it trained so's it'd keep him from getting rode down or run over when he crossed the road. It's dead."

Mitch arose to go see if the coffee was hot. It wasn't, so he turned just as Bailer said: "Range men shot his dog last Saturday night. The trouble is . . . Harriman won't leave his shack now. It worries me. I set with him as much as I can, and boil his gruel and all, but now he's got to where he won't hardly even eat."

Mitch returned to his chair and slowly sat down. "Who shot his dog?"

"I don't know. It was them range riders who choused the town last Saturday night. I got no idea which one done it. Maybe they don't even know, they was shooting guns and racing out of town and hollering and all. You know how them things are when fellers got a snoot full."

Mitch said: "What do you want me to do, Bailer?"

"Maybe talk to Josh. He's old, which is bad enough, I can damned well tell you, but not being able to see and all, he set an awful lot of store by that old dog."

Mitch considered the sinewy old man with the incredibly lined face. "Where did you get the name Bailer?"

"Oh, years back I was a buffler hunter. I was a

44

lot of other things, too, Mister Mitchell." For a moment the old man was silent, his lively eyes studying Mitchell's face. "Well, once I was the best shot in the whole danged Fourth Cavalry." Bailer jumped to his feet, embarrassed. "Anyway, I'd sure take it kindly, if when you was down at the south end of town, you'd stop by and see if you can get my friend to eat, and walk out in the sunshine a little."

After Bailer had departed, Mitch finally got his cup of black java—and he then made another discovery. His predecessor had not washed out the jailhouse coffee pot in a long time. Even fresh coffee tasted like the floor of a Mexican barracks.

Just before full night arrived, he took his bedroll and saddlebags to the rooming house, hunted up the slatternly woman who ran the place, and hired a room. She made the only straightforward remark to him anyone had made, although a lot of people had been thinking it all day. As she showed him a ground floor room on the south side where the one window opened on Dunnigan's main road, she looked up and said: "Mister, you don't have to pay in advance. From what I've heard, you won't need the room after tonight anyway."

He paid her for a week, slung the bags on a chair, tested the bed, unrolled his bedding atop it, then got his razor and some other things including

45

a gray towel and went out back in search of the wash house.

Later, he lay in darkness, listening to a late stage wheel into town from the east, then to a baying hound, evidently someone in town kept lion or bear dogs, and heard a man's deep-down profanity. The hound stopped his noise at once, and Mitchell rolled up onto his side to sleep.

In the morning there was a filmy overcast, which usually presaged rain, but not for a day or two. The sun shone through the overcast in a diffused way, so the heat did not arrive until about midmorning, and by then the film was dispersing, so maybe it would not really rain after all.

Mitchell went to the café, ate, heeded but ignored the strong silence around him where other early risers were also eating, and crossed to the jailhouse to fire up the cleaned stove and put the pot back atop it. As bitter as the coffee was, he was not accustomed to anything better.

Frank Sabin walked in looking solemn, but Frank never showed much expression. The mood, though, was clear when he spoke as he sat down. "In my business a man usually waits all week for Saturday. It's a saloon man's best day. But this is one Saturday I don't look forward to."

Mitchell went to test the coffee. It was hot, so he drew off two cups, wordlessly handed one to Sabin, took the other one back to the chair with him, and sat down, eyeing the saloon proprietor. "Do they come all in a bunch?" he asked.

Frank shook his head. "No, it'll start before supper, a couple of them, maybe three or four, and they'll tank up at the bar and others will drift in. By eight o'clock they'll all be here. Some of 'em have to come from farther off than others." Frank tasted the coffee, looked down into the cup, then leaned and put the cup aside. "You got any help?"

"Clint, from Teller's shop. I could use another good man, though."

Frank dryly said: "You could use the whole damned Sixth Infantry." Then he arose. "I ought to tell you . . . the first son-of-a-bitch who points a gun at my windows tonight is going to get one hell of a surprise. I got a ten-gauge under the bar."

Mitchell arose, too. "I'll be up there. Let me handle it . . . if I can." He smiled without a shred of humor. "But it's your saloon and your windows."

Frank left, and Mitchell made a round of the town, more to let people know he was there than because he expected to find anything in progress that would be illegal. Then, with hours to kill, he walked as far southward as the livery barn, watched them whip-breaking a spoiled horse in a round corral out back, and sauntered down among the half dozen tar-paper shacks beyond where

47

the plank walk ended. Three of the shacks were windowless, doorless, and clearly abandoned. The way he knew which shack belonged to old Harriman was by the ropes tied from the porch to the broken front gate, and from the front porch along the edge of the shack where there was a deeply worn patch going out back somewhere.

He knocked, listened, knocked again, and when there was still no response, he opened the door and looked in. The shack was a regular boar's nest; it was untidy, unclean, and dark. He saw the man sitting in an old rocking chair and stepped inside as he spoke, saying his name and who he was. The old man was large and at one time had been powerfully built. Now he was old and loose, and although he heard everything Mitchell said, the only indication that he had heard, or even that he was alive, was the gently rocking of the chair. Mitch went over, pulled up a crate, and sat down. Harriman turned his head slightly at the sounds but still did not speak. Mitch said: "When your dog was killed . . . did you hear them yell any names?"

Harriman did not speak; he only shook his head and continued gently to rock.

Mitch went to a window and pried it open; the place smelled sour. He then returned to his crate and said: "Did Bailer make your gruel today?"

Harriman nodded this time, and finally faced in the direction of the other man's voice, and spoke:

"Yes, but don't you know Bailer can't make gruel worth a damn?"

Mitch laughed, and old Harriman showed the faintest shadow of a smile. Mitch said: "Want me to roll you a smoke?"

Harriman fished in a shirt pocket and brought forth a shaggy plug of chewing tobacco. "Smoking'll kill you, Marshal. Anyway, it don't savor to a man like a good cud. Care for a chew?" When Mitchell declined the offer, old Harriman returned the plug to his pocket and, peering in the direction of his visitor, said: "Bailer told me they're going to try and kill you tonight."

"That's the talk, I guess, Mister Harriman."

"Marshal, I wasn't always blind. Once I could see as good as you can. I'll tell you something about what you're up against. George Luckner thinks to humor his riders by letting them raise hell in town. The other cowmen do the same, but Mister Luckner's the worst. He don't like Dunnigan nor the folks in it. He indulges his men. Marshal, he's got six men in his riding crew. How many you got?"

"One, but I've been through something like this a time or two before."

Old Harriman began shaking his head. "Not at those odds, Marshal. Not very often anyway, or you wouldn't be setting there now." Harriman stopped rocking. "I was in the Indian wars. When we won, it was because we snuck up on the

49

bastards, then jumped up yelling and scattered 'em like quail. But if we rode up in plain sight like soldiers do, they'd usually give us hell. You don't wait, Marshal. When those sons-of-bitches come into town, you jump up and go at 'em right away."

Mitchell arose, patted the old man's shoulder, and said: "Mister Harriman, that's exactly what I figure to do. Quick, hard, and fast, and, when it's over, I'll come down and tell you how it went. Now you do me a favor."

"Yeah, I know. Eat Bailer's damned gruel. By God, Marshal, that man's the worst cook I ever run across."

"Eat it anyway."

Harriman lifted a frail, large hand. "Shake on it," he said, and as Mitch reached the door and looked back, the old man was rocking again, but now in the gloomy interior of his shack it was possible to make out a faint, frail smile.

Mitchell had not covered a hundred feet before Bailer stepped from behind a nearby shack and called over, then came scuttling. He said: "I didn't expect you down here so quick, Marshal. In fact, I didn't figure you'd be anywhere near the lower end of town today . . . this is Saturday."

Mitchell considered the perpetually weather-stained old lined face. "He told me he'd eat."

Bailer lifted aside one part of his old coat to show a depleted whiskey bottle. "If he don't eat,

by God, I'll send him to sleep with this stuff."
Bailer let the coat drop closed. "Marshal . . .
anything I can do? I mean later on this evening."
"Stay out of the road, Bailer."

Mitchell strode back up in front of the livery barn, saw three men who had been talking turn slowly and watch him pass by. It did not require any special gift to guess what those men had been discussing.

Up in front of the jailhouse that big, bearded range man named Walt Landon was leaning on an overhang upright, whittling on a scrap of wood using a Barlow knife with a wickedly honed blade. As he passed, both nodded to the other. Landon went back to his thoughtful whittling and Marshal Mitchell entered the jailhouse to select and inspect the shotgun he was going to be carrying the next time he left the jailhouse.

V

The afternoon passed slowly. By 3:00 there was no traffic in the roadway, and by 4:00 mothers had called their children inside. Charley Bennett stood with his clerk at the window of his store, gazing unhappily out where thin shadows were beginning to puddle across the road-way. The old clerk said: "We won't do no more business today, Mister Bennett." Charley's retort was brusque. "Go on home, Sam. No sense in both of us staying here."

When Charley was alone, he went to his cubbyhole office, rummaged for a bottle in his desk, took two healthy swallows, replaced the bottle, and dropped down at the littered desk.

Someone entering from the roadway made the doorbell jangle, and Charley got heavily to his feet. The customer was a large, bearded range man Charley had never seen before. As Charley walked to the counter where the range man was standing, he cast a furtive glance out front, but there was no one out there, no cow outfit horses at the rack.

The big man said: "You got a box of Forty-Five slugs?"

Charley turned woodenly to take a box down from the shelf. He looked out front again, with a queasy sensation in his stomach. As the cowboy dug out some money, Charley said: "Do you work around the valley?"

The big man counted out payment very carefully before answering. "No. Over in Cedarville that same box of slugs sells for two bits less."

Charley made a small deprecating gesture. "Our freight costs are high. On everything."

The bearded man walked out with the box in his fist, and Charley waited a discreet moment, then returned to the front window to look left and right. There were no riders in sight and no horses

52

tethered up by Sabin's saloon. He decided to lock up for the night.

Down at the livery barn four men were standing in a group out front near an unkempt cottonwood tree, only occasionally talking, for the most part watching the upper roadway.

Ray Teller had made a dozen mistakes since morning at things he could normally do in his sleep. By noon he was ready to roll up his apron and put up his tools. By midafternoon, with a strong, troubled urge to talk to Clint, he went out back where Whitney was installing new boxings in a heavy wagon for one of the foothill cowmen, sat on a horseshoe keg, and said: "Are you nervous?"

Clint looked up. "Yeah."

"I am, too. I've been thinking today . . . by God, I'm going to round up some folks around town, and whether the town council likes it or not, we're going to form a protective committee. This is damned foolishness, a town that's buffaloed by a bunch of range riders."

Clint had two boxings wedged into the hubs and rolled up the third wheel to work on. He did not speak, which was probably just as well since Ray's agitation had made him talkative. Clint worked and listened, and when he eventually had all four wheels ready for their axles, he paused, leaning on a fore wheel, and said: "You mind if I leave when I'm through here?"

Teller mopped his sweaty neck. "No. Go any time you want to. Tell Mitchell I'll be down here with my carbine. I never was a good shot, but maybe the noise'll scare 'em." Ray stood up, grinning. As he was passing back inside, he turned and said: "See you in the morning."

Clint bolted the wheels into place. Normally they would pull the wagon to make sure the boxings were not too tight, then remove the wheels and lather both axles and boxings with grease. He set the bucket of thick black grease in the wagon bed, then went to a trough to scrub. He had an occupation at which it was impossible not to be dirty by the end of any working day. He scrubbed hard and methodically, then went inside for his shirt and jacket and hat, and for the first time since he had been working for Ray Teller there was a gun belt and holstered Colt hanging from the same peg. He finished getting ready, looped the tie-down thong around his leg and knotted it, then walked out front into the quiet, empty roadway, on his way across to the jailhouse. A bony-tailed, slab-sided dog was foraging along store fronts, and down in front of the livery barn there was a small knot of men standing by a big tree talking, but there was no roadway traffic and no people sauntering the plank walks.

At the jailhouse, when Clint walked in, Hugh Mitchell was cleaning a scatter-gun at the desk with his hat shoved back, a cup of coffee at his elbow, and his holstered Colt and belt lying there, also waiting to be cleaned and inspected.

Mitch looked up. "There are three other shotguns in the rack," he said, and looked back down at what he was doing.

Clint crossed to the wall, selected a weapon, and brought it back to the desk to clean and oil it. His cousin said: "I already cleaned it and plugged in fresh loads. Nothing else to do this afternoon. I cleaned every weapon in the rack." He smiled a little, a tough, hard smile. "You stay outside the saloon, over across the road. I'll stay inside."

Clint scowled. "Nothin' 's goin' to happen in the road, Mitch."

"That's exactly where it's going to happen, Clint. They're not going into the saloon." Mitchell's pale eyes rested steadily on Whitney. "If one of 'em goes for a gun, blow him off his horse, and don't stop firing until they're trying to get turned to head back out of town. In a mess like this, you can't hesitate. When the shotgun's shot out, drop it and use your handgun. And move. Every time you fire, move."

Clint listened, wiped a sweaty palm down the outer seam of his trousers, and nodded.

Mitch finished cleaning and recharging the twelve-gauge and put it aside as he reached for his six-gun. "They'll be on horseback," he said, speaking matter-of-factly. "We're going to try and catch them before they get down. There's no way under the sun to shoot straight off a scairt horse. But if they get down"—Mitch paused to gaze at his cousin.—"they'll get among the buildings and we'll lose."

Clint nodded, and arose to go stand at a front wall window, looking out where daylight was lingering, but softly mellow now. Mitch arose, belted the holstered Colt into place, tied it to his leg, made several adjustments, then picked up the shotgun, reset his hat, and walked to the door. As they were leaving the jailhouse, he said: "You remember now. You'll be across the road. Get into a doorway but keep watch. The first sign of dust you see, whistle. I'll be in the saloon. We're going to get the sons-of-bitches between us."

They walked northward, did not see a person although a number of people saw them, and up where Mitch veered off in the direction of Sabin's saloon, he said: "When I let go, you do the same . . . and don't stop as long as there's one left in the roadway or until you run out of slugs."

Clint watched Mitchell cross to the saloon and enter, then turned to find a recessed doorway. The one he found belonged to the building that housed the saddle and harness works. There was a man inside, leaning on a counter, white to the eyes and absolutely motionless. Like a lot of other surreptitious watchers, he was frightened all the way down to his boots, but he had no intention of missing any of this.

The saloon was empty. Even the old men who habitually played cards where sunlight coming through a window would warm them were not there. Frank Sabin was not wearing his bar apron and there was a bottle and a glass in front of him at the bar. When Mitchell entered, Frank motioned. "Take one. Just one."

Mitch walked to the bar, pushed the bottle and glass aside, and said: "You got a bar gun?"

Frank raised it, and Mitchell considered the sawed-off barrel. "You've got to be close to make much of an impression with that."

Sabin placed the gun gently atop the bar. "I figure to get close. Do you figure to be in here? Wouldn't being outside where you can watch the road be better?"

"Clint's out there. He'll whistle."

"It'll be dark directly."

"Frank, for something like this they'll quit early. Some of them won't even head for the home place. They'll ride directly to town."

Sabin accepted that. "Yeah." Then, revealing his inner thoughts, he also said: "Damn' fools. I'll tell you something, Mitch. I've been around cowboys most of my life. They're a bunch of kids with men's bodies."

A keening whistle sounded from the roadway. Mitchell looked straight at Frank Sabin, and crookedly smiled. "I'll be in your doorway. Be careful where you aim that blunderbuss."

Frank watched Mitchell go to the door and halt just inside it, shift his shotgun to both hands, then peer over where Clint was, before shoving past the spindle doors to halt with them at his back.

Dusk was coming. It would not arrive for perhaps another half hour, but out across Thunder Valley visibility was impaired. Clint had been unable to see dust; by the time he whistled he was watching horsemen.

Mitch saw them, riding all in a tight bunch and dropping from an easy lope to a steady walk as they came down within a couple of hundred yards of the first buildings at the north end of town. He guessed that there were four, maybe five or six of them. When they had reached the northernmost buildings, he could count them. There were six, and they were riding heads up, relaxed in their saddles, but erect, and when they came down into the silent, empty roadway, one man out front turned his head and said something. If anyone answered him, Mitch could not determine it.

Mitch had plenty of time to make his judgments. That man out front was wide-shouldered, narrow-hipped, and long-legged. He had a jaw that was too thick and heavy for the rest of his face, like a bulldog. Mitch watched him especially.

The riders angled toward Sabin's tie rack and did not see Mitchell until he took a forward step and swung the scatter-gun with both hands, low. They were drawing rein when Mitch spoke.

"If you want to stay in town, shed your guns. Now!"

The six range men sat motionlessly, staring. Mitch allowed them a couple of seconds, then dragged back both hammers of the shotgun and spoke again: "Or start shooting!"

The thick-jawed man's face darkened. He deliberately and slowly turned his head, looking elsewhere. He probably did not see Clint across the road in that dark doorway. He turned back, leaned, spat, then raised just his eyes. "Put that gun down," he said very distinctly, "and get out of the way."

Mitch tipped up the barrel and tugged one trigger. The explosion was deafening. Startled horses shied and whirled, men cursed, and the thick-jawed man had half his body twisted away when he drew with his free hand while simultaneously fighting to control his terrified mount. Mitch lowered the shotgun and fired his second round. The thick-jawed man was half lifted from the saddle by tearing impact. He went over the horse's head into the dusty roadway. That explosion completely terrified two of the horses; they bogged their heads and bucked as hard as they could. Two men went sprawling, rolling and scrambling to avoid being trampled.

From across the road Clint stood at the edge of

the plank walk and fired at a wiry young cowboy who was holding his six-gun high, aiming toward Mitch. Two-thirds of the blast struck the cowboy; the lower pattern of shot hit his horse in the rump. The horse whirled, reared high, and went over backward. When he fought back up to his feet, he stepped on the inert man who had been atop him, then fled northward up out of town, running as hard as he could.

From southward somewhere, probably in the vicinity of Charley Bennett's store, a rifle roared, its sound totally different from the six-guns and shotguns out front of Sabin's saloon, and a red-headed range man threw up both hands, dropped his cocked Colt, and went down the off-side of his horse like a stone. He had been hit between the eyes by a bullet almost as large as a man's thumb.

One range man was still atop a horse. He dropped his six-gun and was using both hands on the reins to get his horse untracked when Mitch yelled to him: "Get down, you son-of-a-bitch!"

The cowboy hunched far over and hooked his mount hard with both spurs. The horse was finally ready to run. Clint fired his last shotgun charge, and dirt, stones, and dust exploded five feet in front. The horse planted down both forelegs, hard, and shied. His rider went off sideways, landed flat on his back, and was stunned. Then the horse whirled and raced down through town southward, stepping on and breaking both reins as he raced away.

Mitch leaned aside the shotgun, drew his Colt, and walked down into the roadway. The stunned man was floundering, but the pair of men who had been bucked off and had lost their six-guns in the process were sitting fifteen feet apart, staring in disbelief. When Mitchell walked up and said— "Stand up!"—they both obeyed without taking a step or making a sound.

Clint walked over to the stunned man, reached, got a fistful of shoulder cloth, and one-handedly hoisted the dazed man to his feet, then gave him a violent shove toward the other two. They caught him and supported him.

Mitch picked up guns, held them by trigger guards on the fingers of his left hand, stepped past the man with the bulldog jaw who was dead, and gestured. Clint herded the three survivors in the direction of the jailhouse.

Frank Sabin was in his saloon doorway, holding that sawed-off shotgun, looking out where three dead men lay sprawled. The descending dusk softened the sight, the air smelled foully of burned black powder, and the roadway was torn and churned where terrified horses had fought to break away.

Frank looked southward, caught a glimpse of a wispy, wiry silhouette near the dogtrot between the general store and the building next to it, recognized the shape and the way the man moved as he ducked from sight carrying a long-barreled, big-bored old rifle, then disappeared. Frank said: "Bailer . . . I'll be damned."

VI

They were Luckner's men from the Rafter outfit. They sat in the jailhouse office under orange lamplight completely speechless. Mitch went over each of them for hide-outs, then told them to empty their pockets into their hats and tell him their names. He wrote down each name, then drove them like sheep into the cell room and locked them up.

When he returned, Clint was just coming in from the back alley. They exchanged a look. Mitch went searching for a bottle of whiskey, which he found in a cluttered lower desk drawer, poured half a cupful of lukewarm coffee from the pot on the stove, filled the rest of the cup with whiskey, and handed it to his cousin.

Clint sat down, drank half the cupful, then blew out a ragged big breath, and gazed steadily at the roadway door while Mitch took the three hats with their contents to the back room to place them on a shelf. As he was returning, the roadway door opened and the bearded, powerfully muscled range rider named Walt Landon walked in and said: "You ain't finished, Marshal. There's four more coming into town from the west." Landon walked to the wall rack and stood like a man making a purchase, finally selected one of the remaining three shotguns, broke it to check for loads, then snapped it closed and turned, smiling through his full beard.

"It happened too fast," he said, "I couldn't buy in before, but this time I can."

Mitch considered Landon, then shrugged. There was not a lot of time if another crew was entering town. He switched his attention to Clint Whitney. "You all right?" Clint nodded and stood up with his shotgun. Mitch said: "You better reload, Clint. They don't even make good clubs if they're empty."

Walt Landon handed Whitney four loads and they waited until the scatter-gun was recharged and Clint had dropped the other two shells into a pocket, then they left the jailhouse, with the lamp still burning.

Landon was brisk. "Same way?" he asked as they were crossing the nearly dark roadway. "Him on the west side of the road, you in front of the saloon?"

Mitch was looking northward for a sighting of riders when he answered: "Yeah. Maybe it'll work again. How many did you say there were?"

"Four," stated the bearded big man, "and I'll get northward on the same side of the road as you, up by the Land Office . . . behind them."

Mitch halted ten yards from the saloon. The dead range men were gone. From up ahead in the murky gloom Sabin's voice came dryly: "I lugged 'em inside and covered 'em."

Landon went northward to a recessed doorway, smiling as though he enjoyed things like this. Clint was across the road in the harness shop doorway again, never in his life farther from smiling, and, as Mitch reached the saloon doors where Frank Sabin was standing, the older man cocked his head in a listening position, so Mitch told him another four were on their way. Frank looked up where the sound was audible and softly said: "Bailey or Kershaw, if they're coming in from the west."

Mitch said: "Go back inside, but keep watch. I might need you."

Sabin returned past the spindle-doors with his scatter-gun, considered getting a drink from that bottle still standing alone on the bar top, then turned his back on it and moved away from the doors as the sound of shod hoofs striking roadway hardpan reached him.

Mitch was almost in total darkness when the horsemen walked their animals down the murky roadway. He could distinguish booted Winchesters this time. Luckner's riders had not been carrying saddle guns. These men seemed hesitant, as though they might have expected to meet other range men in Dunnigan, which they probably had. They stopped behind a bulky rider wearing a coat that was unbuttoned and hanging loose on his rangy frame. The distance was too great for Mitch's shotgun. He remained like stone, waiting for them to come closer. Eventually they did, rode within a few yards of Sabin's tie rack, and this time, when they halted, a man said: "Jess, I don't like this."

Mitch moved into sight away from the doors and slung his shotgun toward them with both hands. "Shed your belt guns." He did not raise his voice.

The four horsemen looked steadily at him. One man raised both hands to his saddle horn, perhaps to have them in plain sight. Another man, adorned with a droopy cavalryman's mustache, leaned slightly, peering at Mitch. "Who are *you?*" he asked.

Mitch did as he had done before; he hauled back the dogs of his scatter-gun. "Get rid of those guns!"

Northward up the plank walk where he was invisible to the horsemen Walt Landon did the same; he cocked both barrels of his weapon.

Mitch tipped up his barrels, aiming straight at the man with the droopy mustache. "You've got a second," he said.

The range man straightened back, hung like that a moment, and behind him a rider said:

"Leave it be, Jess. There's another one out front of the harness works."

The range riders dropped their six-guns, and sat like statues. Mitch gestured. "Get down. Step away from the horses. Keep your hands in sight."

Again he was obeyed. Landon walked heavily from the plank walk to the roadway, approaching the range riders from the rear. Clint, too, started toward them. Mitch remained where he was, holding his shotgun at the ready. When Landon came up, he hooked his weapon over an arm and roughly pawed the range riders for additional weapons, then he scornfully said: "Bunch of old women. Bunch of chicken guts." He accompanied this with a rough shove, and the pushed man whirled and swung. The fist caught Landon high on the shoulder. It was like a signal. Landon dropped his shotgun, gave a roar, and waded in. The other men did not move except to crane around, watching. Landon was not a fighter; he was a battler with the physique and temperament for it. The cowboy hit him five times to each blow Landon landed, but when Landon connected, the cowboy staggered. He was wily, though. By maneuvering his opponent, he got the cowboy with his back close to the tie rack. The man was supple and fast on his feet, and he knew now that he could not trade blows with Landon. His mistake was not to understand how close his back was to the tie rack. He hit Landon on the cheek, on the jaw, and got all his weight behind a pivoting blow from the shoulder that would have dropped almost any other man. It caught Walt Landon over the heart and did not even rock him back.

Landon called the cowboy a fighting name and drove at him. The cowboy gave ground, his back touched the tie rack, and too late he realized his peril. Landon rushed him, struck him up alongside the temple, sent the range man's hat sailing, made his head snap far back, and, as the cowboy sagged, Landon battered him to the ground.

Mitch waited until Landon was moving back, turning toward the other three range men, and said: "Herd 'em to the jailhouse."

Landon stood poised to attack the other three, grinning widely. As Clint nudged the remaining men away, Landon blew out a breath, looked down, caught hold of the battered man, hoisted him like a sack of grain, flung him over one shoulder, then squatted to retrieve his shotgun, and followed the others.

Mitchell grounded his shotgun and briefly watched. From just inside the doors Frank Sabin spoke. "You don't need the Fourth Infantry, Mitch. You got that feller."

At the jailhouse the unconscious man was taken by Walt Landon to a cell and dumped on the floor. When Landon returned, he was still grinning as he went after some coffee.

Clint addressed the lanky man with the mustache. "Jess, Rafter's already been here. You know Sheridan, their range boss? He's dead and so are two others."

The mustached man called Jess looked around at Mitch without a word.

Mitch went to his desk and sat down. "Put the stuff from your pockets in your hats and tell me your names and who you work for."

Jess obeyed first, stepped to the desk, and said: "Jess Delaney. I'm top hand for Mister Kershaw of Arrow Circle. These fellers also work for Mister Kershaw." Mitch finished writing and pointed to a wall bench. When he had finished with all three of them, he asked the name of the beaten man, wrote that down, too, then stood up. "You're lucky," he told them, and gestured. "Stand up." He took them to the cells and locked them in, too. As he was standing there, looking in, he said: "Jess, who else is coming?"

The top hand refused to answer. He turned his back to the cell front and went over to sit down upon the edge of a wall bunk, looking disbelievingly out at Hugh Mitchell.

Clint retrieved his laced coffee from the bench where he had put it before leaving the jailhouse the last time, drained the cup, and almost at once got good color back. He stared at Walt Landon.

Mitch took the hats to the same shelf in the back room where he had placed those other hats, returned, and shook his head a little at Walt Landon. "Why the hell did you do that? You didn't have to."

Landon did not disagree at all. "Thing is, Marshal, just getting disarmed and locked up don't really do it. But those fellers won't forget a good beating, will they?"

Mitch went to the desk and sat upon the edge of it. "Clint," he said, "you know these men. Will more come tonight?"

Whitney lifted his hat to scratch as he answered. "Bailey. Those three outfits border one another. They're like ticks on a dog. They usually hold their roundups together and all. If anyone else comes, Mitch, it'll be Bailey's crew."

"How many?"

"I don't rightly know. He usually hires on about the same as Mister Luckner. Their outfits are about the same size. Maybe five or six of 'em, I'd guess."

Walt Landon grabbed his shotgun and walked to the door. "I'll listen for 'em," he announced, and went out closing the door after himself.

Clint gazed at the door for a moment then lifted his eyes. "He *likes* doin' this, Mitch. Did you see . . . he was grinnin' all the time that feller was beatin' on him."

Mitch drank a dipper full of water from the corner bucket kept filled for that purpose, and afterward walked to a front window as he said:

"I'll tell you something, Clint. You couldn't stop Landon with a club. That man he beat was big and strong and good with his hands. Hell, he might just as well been banging away at a rock wall."

"You reckon Landon hurt him?"

Mitch turned. "He sure as hell didn't improve him any. No, I don't think he's hurt bad. But he's not going to dance a jig for a few days." Mitch went to the desk and picked up his shotgun. "He's right. The others saw that beating. None of them will forget it, when they think of hoorawing Dunnigan again."

Clint arose and also went to lean down and look out a window. As he did so, the bear-like silhouette of Landon loomed outside. The large man was striding briskly toward the jailhouse door. He entered with the grace of an elephant and said "Coming from the north this time, right down the damned stage road, and they're riding fast."

"Many?"

"Maybe a half dozen."

Mitch started forward out of the lighted office, and Landon stood aside until both Mitch and Clint were out, then closed the door and held up a hand for silence. The sound of oncoming horses was very clear. As the three of them listened, the horsemen slackened down to a walk. Mitch said—"Just like the Luckner bunch."—and his

70

cousin cut in quickly to say: "Bailey don't hire 'em just for ridin' and ropin', Mitch. He hires 'em for fightin', too. Bailey's a mean old bastard and he likes his range men to be the same."

When they got up by the saloon, Frank was out there, also listening, and now he had a six-gun belted around his middle. He did not have it thonged down, and in fact the gun did not look right on Frank. It probably did not feel right, either. If Charley Bennett or Ray Teller or any of the other people around Dunnigan who had known Frank down the years had seen him like that, it would have been for the first time.

Frank said: "I've got enough horses tied around back to start a trading barn, Mitch. That feller who got shot last . . . the red-headed feller who rode for Luckner . . . he got his head blown punky by a rifle bullet as big as a cigar."

The men stood looking at Frank. None of them had used anything but shotguns. Frank said: "Bailer, that old gaffer who lives in a shack below town. I swear I saw him duck down the dogtrot north of Bennett's store with a rifle damn' near as tall as he is . . . Buffalo rifle."

Walt Landon was not interested in an old man with a buffalo gun; he was interested in the sound of oncoming horsemen and stepped to the edge of the plank walk to try and gauge the distance the new arrivals had to cover before they entered town. While he was doing that, a bony-tailed, slab-sided, tall mongrel dog sauntered from between two buildings and stood with his head raised, sniffing. Landon growled at the dog. Instead of retreating, the dog wagged its tail. Walt leaned, picked up a handful of grit and dirt, and flung it. That did the job; the dog ducked back between the buildings and disappeared.

The riders were entering town now, at a walk, and this time they did not hesitate even though the town was dark and silent, with an unmistakable air of trouble. They came steadily in the direction of Sabin's saloon without a word passing among them. This time, the man Mitchell watched closest was gray and grizzled, rumpled and rugged-looking. He seemed to be the oldest man among the riders around him, and he, too, had a booted carbine with the butt thrust forward and upward for quick reach.

Landon and Clint were in position, invisible as before when the horsemen approached the saloon. The only difference this time was that Frank Sabin did not retreat past the saloon doors but stood to one side of Marshal Mitchell with that ugly, murderous sawed-off scatter-gun lying lightly across one bent arm, low, while his other hand was back at the triggers and hammers. If the new arrivals got as close as the tie rack, Frank's gun would be as lethal as anything the oncoming horsemen possessed.

VII

A rider said: "Hey, Clyde . . . there's them windows." Another horseman started to speak. "Wait a minute. Where's . . . ?"

A gunshot erupted, an orange-white muzzle blast made a momentary, blinding light, and across the echoes of that shot came the sound of shattered glass. Mitch had no chance to call on this band of range men; things happened too fast after that gunshot. Frank Sabin stepped to the edge of the plank walk, leveled his shotgun, and tugged one trigger. Horses went wild and two gunshots flashed in Frank's direction. One slug struck the spindle doors behind Frank and shattered the wood, broke one spindle-hinge, and Frank went down.

Mitch saw this in the seconds while it happened, and swung his shotgun to fire, but Walt Landon, bawling like a bear, blew off a shotgun blast first. Clint fired, too. He was across the road, and the effect was sufficient. Even if the horses had not been terrified and were not fighting their bits and riders to break away, the range men would have left them in a leap to safety. As it happened one man got bucked off, went sailing over the horse's bogged head like a huge and ungainly bird, landed flat on his stomach, and got most of the wind knocked out of him.

Mitch dropped the shotgun and sprang at the stalwart form of a man who had his back to the tie rack; Mitch cleared the rack, reached for the range man's throat, felt the rugged strength of his opponent as the man staggered ahead under the weight of the man on his back, and they went down.

The riderless horses fled northward all in a terrified rush. Walt Landon was still roaring, which Mitch heard, but the man he had closed with was as strong as a bull. Not until Mitch broke free and rolled up to his feet to face the range man did he recognize him as the gray, grizzled, rugged older man who had been in the van of the riders, and after his adversary sprang upright to begin circling, Mitch had no time to worry about Landon or Clint, or anything else.

The older man had lost his hat; hair stood out in spiky disarray. The man's face was contorted. He had his arms wide and curving inward; like many brawlers of great physical strength, he relied upon a strangling bear hug to beat an adversary. Mitch tried to stay clear, but the older man circled until he had Mitch's back to the plank walk; then he rushed. Mitch stepped away, not backward, but sideward, and fired a blasting fist cocked from the shoulder. It passed between the other man's wide-open arms and struck solidly over his heart. The shock of impact rocked Mitch back on his heels. The bear-like man's arms dropped. For several seconds he hung there, then he turned and brought his arms up again ready to charge in a new direction. Mitch got away from the plank walk, aware of angry men out closer to the middle of the road but without letting any of that distract him as the gray bear of a man started in again.

This time his fingers got cloth in them. Mitch had not moved clear fast enough. The older man strained, pulled Mitch in, was closing his other arm around Mitch's back when his younger adversary got his palm under the older man's chin while twisting sideways. He put all his strength into bending the older man's head back. When it would go no farther back, Mitch hurled himself backward against the closing arms, pushed hard with his other hand against the older man's chest, and broke free. He then did not move back, but aimed and fired with his right fist as the older man's head was coming forward. The blow was bone over bone, Mitch's big knuckles against the older man's square jaw. There was a flash of intense pain all the way up Mitch's arm as the older man staggered, let his arms fall, then toppled like a felled tree. He was unconscious before he landed in roadway dirt, on his face.

Mitch's lungs burned as he turned toward the middle of the road, sucking down great gulps of night air. There had been five of them, but the man who had had the wind knocked out of him never really got his legs pulled up to arise; he tried several times, then fell back gasping for breath. Another man was down in a curled, broken position. By weak moonlight he resembled a lumpy collection of discarded clothing. Clint and a man as large and powerful were standing toe-to-toe. The difference was that Clint was a blacksmith; he did hard physical work every day, his range riding adversary was just as powerfully muscled but lacked the little edge of endurance he required. Clint was beating him back a little at a time. The man was doggedly stubborn; he would yield a step only when Clint battered him into making a move backward.

Walt Landon's shirt was pulled out of his trousers and torn. He was wading into a slighter but taller man, and as Mitch watched, the leggy cowboy began to wilt. He had been striking Landon with everything he had without effect; he could not hit hard, just fast and often, which was nowhere nearly enough against a man like Landon.

Mitch sucked air until his heart was no longer pounding, then looked over where Frank Sabin had gone down. Frank was sitting there oblivious to everything else, pulling his trouser belt tightly around his thick upper leg.

Walt Landon's adversary went down and Walt turned, looking for someone else, caught sight of

Clint and his foe fighting for each yard of ground, and started over there. The battered cowboy saw Landon coming, a fearful sight to see, and yielded by moving more swiftly away from Clint and calling out: "I've had enough!" Walt hadn't. He charged the retreating range rider, who turned to run. Clint snarled at Landon, and the big man halted, shook his head, and turned away.

Frank Sabin let Mitch help him tie off the bleeding leg, gritted his teeth against the spiraling pain, and said: "I don't think the bone's busted . . . is it?"

It wasn't. The bullet had torn through muscles, had made a bloody, ragged wound, but had been far to the left of the bone, on the inside of Frank's leg.

Clint and Landon walked over. Clint leaned against the tie rack and Walt Landon looked down at his torn shirt and began methodically to stuff it back inside the waistband of his trousers, then he went over to watch Mitch. When Frank's bleeding had stopped, Landon shouldered Mitch aside, leaned and lifted Frank as though he were a child, and carried him past the smashed doors of the saloon to a table and eased him down there, then went rummaging behind the bar for a bottle and glass, left them with Frank, and returned to the roadway where Mitch was helping a dazed and battered range man to his feet. Landon was less compassionate; he went to a fire barrel at the corner of the saloon, filled two leather buckets hanging there for emergency use, returned, and upended one bucket over the graying man Mitch had whipped who was already beginning to stir, and who coughed, gasped, and flopped in the dirt when that cold water hit him. Then Walt went over to the lanky, thin rider he had knocked senseless and did the same thing.

Not a person appeared on the plank walks. Except for the beaten, dazed men Mitch and his companions got back upright. The roadway was empty, but as the victors began driving their unsteady victims in the direction of the jailhouse, a man appeared in front of the harness shop, and from that dogtrot down by the general store another, wispier shape emerged, went scuttling out where the fight had occurred and began gathering up weapons. There were other spectators behind darkened windows; they would tell the tale of this night over the years ahead, but the men down at the lighted jailhouse were not conscious of having made local history nor, had they been conscious of it, would it have meant anything to them.

Clint leaned as his cousin was having the latest prisoners empty their pockets, murmured softly, then went over to sit down. When the beaten men were ready to be locked up, Mitch arose, gazed steadily at the graying older man, and said: "Mister Bailey, we're going out into the alley."

Even Walt Landon turned to stare. John Bailey glowered and stood dripping water on the floor, one side of his jaw beginning to turn blue under the swelling. He said: "This time with guns."

Mitch looked at the empty holster. Somewhere during the movement up in front of Sabin's place Bailey had lost his six-gun. He picked up a weapon from the ones atop his desk, which had been taken from Luckner's riders, and tossed it over. "Make sure it's loaded," he told the cowman. Bailey opened the gate, spun the cylinder, closed the gate, and sank the Colt in his holster. When he raised his eyes, Mitch said—"You're a dead son-of-a-bitch."—and walked to the storeroom door, waiting for Bailey to pass through first on their way to the alley.

Landon came alive; he grabbed keys from the desk, roughly punched the prisoners down into the cell room, shoved them into cells that were already full of men, slammed and locked the doors, then hurried back to the office where Clint was standing near the storeroom door. Landon started to push past. He was not going to miss this for anything. Clint caught his arm and said: "Bailey can't beat Mitch."

Landon pulled free, grinning. "Good," he said. "Then the troublemaking old son-of-a-bitch'll get murdered. Come along."

In the alley Mitch was pacing off the fighting distance and John Bailey was glowering at him, standing loosely up the alley a few yards. When Clint and Landon came out, Bailey turned a brief gaze in their direction, then, as Mitch faced around, Bailey said—"Sure, I didn't figure you had the guts to try it man to man."—and jerked his head to indicate the pair of armed men standing by the ajar door.

Clint, who had known John Bailey a number of years, spoke up. "Don't try it, Mister Bailey. He'll kill you."

Bailey's baleful eye shifted slightly toward Whitney. "How the hell would you know . . . blacksmith?"

Walt Landon was no longer grinning; he was looking with an expression of intense speculation at the cowman. Before Clint could answer Bailey, Walt Landon started toward him. Mitch spoke sharply: "Landon! Don't get between us!"

The bearded man paused and turned. "Aw, hell," he said, "let's do it different. No sense in someone getting killed." He moved in front of the cowman and held out a big hand, palm up. "Give me your gun, mister."

Bailey started to snarl and step back. Landon lunged, caught his shirt front, and pulled him forward with powerful roughness, reached with his free hand to freeze the cowman's wrist in a crushing grip as Bailey went for his hip holster. Then Landon explained. "All's I'm going to do, cowman, is empty your gun. The marshal'll

80

empty his gun. Then you fellers can draw against each other. No one'll get killed, and if you lose, mister, you better get some sense."

He used both hands to pry Bailey's hand away from the Colt, lifted it out, silently shoved out all the cartridges, then, grinning again, shoved it back into Bailey's holster. Fifty feet away Mitch was also shucking out gun loads. When he looked up, the grinning big cowboy stepped back by Clint Whitney.

Mitch said: "Any time, Bailey."

The cowman seemed to take forever to make up his mind. Obviously, despite the fact that he was now in no danger at all, John Bailey was an individual who never faced a challenge, even a harmless one, without fully intending to triumph. Perhaps that was why he was one of the largest cowmen in Thunder Valley. Then he moved—and Mitch was cocking his six-gun just as Bailey's front sight cleared leather.

No one spoke.

Bailey stood a moment, then rammed the gun back into its holster and moved his right arm a little, glaring straight at Mitch. He was going to try again.

Mitch eased his weapon back into leather and waited, as motionless as stone, watching the older man without blinking.

Bailey tried it differently this time. He eased his body slightly to the right to obscure his draw, not much, just enough to allow him perhaps a second head start. But it was an old trick, and the moment his right shoulder sagged just a little, Mitch outdrew him again, cocked the gun, waited for Bailey to acknowledge defeat, and when the cowman still gripped his weapon, which was clear of leather this time but not quite tipped up, Mitch said: "Pick up those loads and fill your gun. We'll try it one more time."

Clint and Walt Landon watched Bailey kneel to retrieve his slugs and methodically load the gun, then the cowman stood loosely, watching Mitch reload. As they squared around to face each other, Bailey slowly, very grudgingly, shook his head.

Mitch walked up closer and said: "There's not going to be any more hoorawing the town. Luckner had three men killed tonight. You would have been number four. You understand me, Mister Bailey? You stockmen are going to agree to fire any rider who comes to Dunnigan to make trouble . . . if the son-of-a-bitch lives to get back to you. You're going to set the rules of conduct at your ranch. You're going to be responsible for your men."

Bailey's eyes slid to the watching men over by the jailhouse door, then slid back to Mitchell's face. He did not speak; he turned away from Mitch and walked flat-footedly back into the jailhouse, stood looking at the front wall until Mitch came in, then he turned and with a visible effort nodded his head, and spoke: "All right."

Mitch pointed. "Put that gun on the desk." As Bailey was obeying, Mitch faced his cousin. "Clint, rout out someone down at the livery barn and have three horses saddled."

Neither Whitney nor Landon understood the order, but Clint left the office by the roadway door as Mitch jerked his head for John Bailey to walk ahead down into the cell room. As he shoved Bailey into a cell that had four other men in it, Luckner's top hand stood tugging absently at his droopy mustache, looking impassively out at the town marshal. Not a man said a word as Mitch locked the door and returned to the office.

He went to the wall rack to take down a carbine as he said: "We probably won't need 'em."

Landon was watching. "Need 'em for what?"

"We're going to look up Mister Luckner and Mister Kershaw, and talk to 'em," replied Mitch, turning with a Winchester in his fist. "It's not your headache."

Landon cast a critical eye at the remaining Winchesters and answered as he approached the wall rack: "You know a damned sight better. I punched the lights out of a couple of fellers tonight." He took down a saddle gun and faced Mitch. "You know where those fellers live?"

Mitch had no idea where the Kershaw or Luckner ranches were, but as he headed for the door he said: "Clint ought to know."

VIII

Clint took them out of town in a rush, and a mile up the stage road they branched off eastward, while behind them several hesitant townsmen peeked into Sabin's saloon, saw Frank sitting there, saw the covered bodies just inside the door, and finally entered to see what they could do for Sabin.

Elsewhere, here and there a light appeared, and very gradually strongly curious but very wary townsmen appeared. Ray Teller was the only one who entered the jailhouse, and although he heard men in the cells, he did not go down there, but stood gazing at the guns atop the desk, at the depleted wall rack, then went back out into the night to watch men moving toward the saloon, and walked up to join them.

Charley Bennett made a belated appearance. As he was approaching the saloon, the only lit building on the main roadway, old Bailer greeted him with a great, gaping grin. Bailer had two carbines leaning at his side against the saloon wall and three six-guns shoved into the front of his britches.

It was late, later than Mitch or his companions knew; at no time tonight had they thought about the time, nor were they thinking about it now as they loped along in silence until they encountered two huge cedar posts athwart a rutted roadway leading crookedly northward, and Clint drew down to a halt. "Two miles," he said, nodding to the roadway. "He's got a ranch cook and maybe a wrangler, but otherwise I think he'll be alone."

Mitch said: "Let's go."

They walked their horses a mile, then loped again, slackening only when they topped out along a land swell where it was possible to see darkened buildings down the far side in a vast, grassy vale. There were big trees around the yard and a number of log buildings including two barns, one very large, the other one, obviously a horse barn, with a lower roof and different dimensions. The network of peeled-pole corrals were behind the big barn, and as Mitch rode slowly into the yard where he could see the size of the corrals, he guessed that George Luckner ran a lot of livestock on his range.

The bunkhouse was dark, as was the cook house. Dead ahead at the south end of the yard was the rambling, low main house with a broad verandah along the entire front. Everything about Rafter Ranch looked substantial, prosperous, and efficient. It was one of those places that, as a stranger rode in, left him with an impression of a large, thriving, efficiently operated cow outfit.

As they were tying up, an old dog, stiff in the shoulders, too fat, and with watery eyes, came down off the porch to sniff and wag his tail. Walt Landon leaned, briefly scratched the old dog's back, then turned to follow his companions to the front door, with the old dog at his heels.

Mitch rattled the door with a balled fist three times before a wavering light appeared somewhere deep within the house, and moments later came along toward the parlor. When the door opened, Mitch recognized the handsome, graying man, raised a hand to Luckner's chest, and gave a rough push. Luckner's eyes widened as he stumbled, caught himself, and watched the three armed men enter his parlor. Luckner was dressed in trousers, shirt, and boots, but he had obviously been in bed when the knocking had awakened him.

Mitch took the lamp from him, set it atop a small, elegant table with a marble top, shoved back his hat, and turned to face the cowman.

Luckner looked from the badge Mitch was wearing to the other two men, looked longest at rumpled, torn, and disreputable big, bearded Walt Landon, then he said: "Have a seat, Marshal."

Mitch remained standing, facing the rancher. "You lost three men tonight, Mister Luckner. What's left is locked in the jailhouse. Maybe you're the one had better sit down."

Luckner stood like stone. "What are you talking about?"

"A red-headed man, a dog-faced feller, and

another man," stated Mitch. "And now I'm going to tell you something, the same thing I told a man named Bailey. Every damned cowman in Thunder Valley is going to be held responsible for how his riders act when they ride into Dunnigan. And you damned stockmen are going to agree to fire any man who works for you and comes to town and makes trouble . . . if the son-of-a-bitch lives to get back to the ranch. You're going to pay damages, and you're going to jail right along with any man who works for you and makes trouble in town."

If Luckner had been hazy from sleep before, by now he was wide-awake. He looked Mitch up and down, then did the same to Clint Whitney, and Walt Landon. Then he spoke in a ringing voice: "Who the hell do you think you're talking to? No one comes out here from the damned town and tells any rancher . . ."

Mitch lunged, caught hold of Luckner's shirt front, and held him close. "*I'm* telling you!" he exclaimed, and roughly released Luckner with a shove toward a large chair. The rancher stumbled backward and sank down. When he would have arisen, Walt Landon moved toward him with a snarl, and Luckner sat back.

Mitch considered the handsome man a moment before speaking again. "You think you run Thunder Valley? Mister Luckner, I have your riders and I'm going to hold them."

"Under the law . . . ," stated the cowman, and got no further.

"Under the damned law, Mister Luckner, you can't send your men into a town to make trouble, scare hell out of folks, and destroy property, but you did it. Under the damned law I can't hold your men for more'n twenty-four hours, but I'm going to do it. And I'm going to do something else. When I release them, it's only going to be providing they give me their word they will pick up their bedrolls from your bunkhouse and leave the country. If any of them try to back out, I'm coming out here with a posse, and the next time, when I lock them up, I'll throw the damned key away. Or I'll bury them. That goes for Bailey and Kershaw, too. One more thing. Dunnigan will be closed to all range riders unless you and the others agree to be responsible for everything they do in town. And if you think hoorawing the town is your right, from now on the town law is going to make damned certain no one who passes through Dunnigan looking for directions to your ranch will ever get here. Try running your outfit with a cook, a kid wrangler, and no one else."

George Luckner sat looking up at Mitch, speechless for a long time, then he said—"You won't last a month."—and leaned to arise.

Walt Landon caught the cowman's shoulder in a steel grip and swung him half around as though, large as Luckner was, he had no more weight than a child. "That's bad talk," the big bearded cowboy said, looking blackly at the cowman. "Mister, if one hired gunman shows up anywhere in this valley, I'm coming for you and I'll break half the bones in your carcass."

Luckner flinched under the painful grip on his shoulder, and Landon released him with a contemptuous snort, then stalked to the big stone fireplace and stood with his back to the dead coals as he said: "Mitch, we're wasting time on this son-of-a-bitch. I'll kill him."

No one spoke for a time. Mitch did not take his eyes off George Luckner. Clint, who had scarcely moved since entering the house, now went over by the elegant little table with the lamp on it and thoughtfully gazed at an oil portrait of a handsome woman in a gilt frame above the mantel. He said: "She was very beautiful, Mister Luckner."

It was such an unusual thing to say that even Mitch turned. Luckner swung a glance from the portrait of his dead wife to Clint, then he seemed to sag slightly. He remained silent a while longer. Finally he faced Mitch again. "My range boss was with the men tonight. His name's Bill Foster."

Mitch did not know which man had been the Rafter range boss but his cousin knew. As Clint turned away from the portrait, he said: "He's dead. So is Oliver, the red-headed feller who used to come in now and then for supplies, and a younger man I've seen around town but I never knew his name."

"The others?"

Clint replied quietly. "Like the Marshal told you, Mister Luckner, they're locked up, along with Mister Bailey and his riders, and Mister Kershaw's men. Some are hurt."

Luckner stared straight at Clint. "Who helped you three?"

Clint shook his head. "It doesn't matter."

"Yes it does!"

"Why, so you can write down their names and send someone after them?"

"It would take every man in Dunnigan to do what you say was done."

"No, Mister Luckner. There was one other man, Frank Sabin who owns the saloon your men busted up a week ago and came to town to bust up again tonight. And maybe another feller . . . an old man with a big-bored rifle. Mostly, it was us three." Clint quietly gazed at the cowman. "Mister Luckner, you know as well as I do what'll happen if you and the other ranchers keep this thing alive. Maybe we won't survive it, but you won't, either . . . nor will a lot of other men. You started it, you cowmen, not us folks in town."

Walt Landon spoke for the first time since his anger had made him threaten Luckner. Walt demonstrated again that peculiar quirk to his tough nature that, back in town, had made him look forward to seeing John Bailey killed, and moments later had devised a way to keep Bailey alive. Now, as he stood, big-legged, before the fireplace, he said: "Maybe you've been through a range war. I have. Seems to me cowmen fighting a town can't be much different. If you've ever been through one, mister, then you ought to know what this feller just said is the gospel truth. You'll lose. I don't care how many graves you fill in town, you'll lose. The marshal isn't asking anything more'n you cowmen ought to have done a long time ago. The difference is that now you're going to do it anyway, but if you make a war out of it, you're still going to do it in the end, but you're going to be under the ground along with some fellers, and still having to do it."

Mitch gazed at the bearded range man, not exactly surprised, although he had not expected Landon to be a man of hard logic, and a feeling of respect stirred for Walt Landon.

Luckner went to a carved sideboard and half-filled a glass with blood-red wine, drank part of it with his back to the rough, soiled man in the center of the room, and turned finally toward Mitch. "I'll be in tomorrow with a wagon for the men that have to be buried."

Mitch nodded. The mood in the big room was different now. "You can have the others. I just want your word about the things I've said to you."

Luckner continued to stand, holding his glass of red wine. "I don't believe this will end it," he said quietly.

Mitch was ready to concede this. "Maybe not. I think it will, but you might be right. Anyway, I want your word."

Luckner drained his glass and put it gently aside, then turned with a shake of his head. Before he could speak this time, Mitch had one thing to add to what he had already said. "If the cowmen bring in gunfighters, the townsmen have enough money to do the same. Will you tell me how the hell either side can come out of something like that without more bitterness than anyone can have after what happened tonight? It'll turn this valley into a graveyard. It may ruin the town, and it sure as hell will ruin the cattlemen. Over what? Some broken windows in a saloon and some men who've been riding into Dunnigan like spoiled little kids, badgering folks for no reason except that they like to bully people?"

Luckner glanced again at Clint, who was impassively gazing back. Then he said—"Marshal, I'll be in with a wagon tomorrow."—and strode across to the door and held it open. Walt Landon passed out first, then Clint Whitney, and finally as Marshal Mitchell passed through, Luckner said: "I'll take my riders back with me." He nodded and closed the door.

They went down to the tie rack where Walt Landon lifted his old hat, vigorously scratched, and said: "Does that mean he's willing?"

Mitch was snugging up his cinch and did not reply, but his cousin did. "Yeah, I think that's exactly what it means."

"Then why in hell didn't he just up and say so?" asked Landon as they all swung across leather to leave the yard.

Clint's answer was right to the center of the target. "Because a man like George Luckner with all his cattle and land and riders and money just can't do like you and me, Walt. He can't just cave in and say he's been wrong. You and me . . . someone might whip us, we'd get up out of the dirt, pick up our hats, and admit we got licked, then go wash and head for the saloon. Luckner's type can't do that. When they get whipped, they lose a lot more than the hide off their knuckles."

The night was turning cold as Clint led them due westward from the Rafter Ranch yard. Mitch had very little to say while they alternately loped and walked their horses back in the direction of the stage road, crossed it, and continued westward, dropped to a walk when their horses evinced nervousness, and watched ahead until they saw the band of big gray wolves that the horses had scented. One wolf stood his ground while the others fled. He was large enough to be a buffalo wolf. They watched him, and Walt Landon finally whistled. The wolf turned and trotted away, looked back once, then resumed his dignified withdrawal. Landon shook his head. "He's not going to live long hanging back to cover the retreat of the others."

It was true. Range stockmen killed cougars and bears on sight, any meat-eater who came out of the mountains to raid their grasslands, but they were particularly merciless toward wolves.

An hour later, buttoned to their throats, they heard the wolves sounding behind them and northward. It was a sound that made hair stand up on the back of even armed men's necks.

Clint loped another mile, hauled down, and as Mitch came up to ride stirrup, Clint mentioned the man they were riding to meet, Will Kershaw: "He's as hard as iron and as rough as a rock. I don't know him very well. I've spoken to him a few times in town but can't really say I know him. Around town they say he's as honest as the day is long, and a fair man. The only thing I can tell you from experience is that one time a few years back I saw him tie into a big freighter with his fists and beat that freighter to a fare-thee-well. He's more like old Bailey than Mister Luckner."

Mitch nodded, eyeing the slightly rolling country ahead. He was tired. The excitement back in town had taken a lot out of him. Also, he was hungry and the cold was filtering through his coat. "How much farther?" he asked.

Clint raised a thick arm to point in a slightly southerly direction. "Four, maybe five miles."

They booted their horses into another lope and held them at it.

IX

Where the trail turned southward stood a huge sawed-off dead tree from which a large part of the bark had been cut off and someone who was very experienced with a running iron had burned a large circle with an arrowhead inside it. Clint pointed. "Kershaw's brand. That post is also one of his boundary lines. But I got no idea which one. He owns land all the way to the mountains to the north, and west for more miles than a man can cover on a good horse in several days."

The buildings were log, as were all ranch buildings in Thunder Valley, but unlike the Rafter outfit, these were older structures. It showed even by starlight that the yard they were entering had been organized and established many years before. Like most of the very old ranches, Kershaw's place had had its buildings spaced for defense, and that was still apparent long after the last hostile Indian had been driven out of the country.

Clint led them from the branded tree down into the big yard, and as they reached the upper end of the yard, dogs began to bark. There were four of them, and as long as the riders rode ahead toward the main house, the dogs maintained a decent distance—they had all probably been kicked and rolled before.

Where the horsemen halted, ready to dismount, the dogs edged closer, snarling and showing fangs. Walt Landon remained on his horse after Mitch and Clint had swung off. He was the last man to touch the ground, and as he looped his reins, he did not once take his eyes off the dogs.

Two of the animals had pale blue eyes. One had a brown eye and a blue eye, and the fourth dog was obviously part wolf; he had the broad head, tapered muzzle, and tawny eyes. It was this latter dog that had singled out Landon. He stopped snarling but kept up a deep growl as he circled far around Landon's horse to approach from the bearded man's opposite side. Walt turned very slowly and ignored both his companions and the other dogs until Mitch stooped to find a rock. He did not find one; the ground was gritty and whatever stones had once been there had over the decades been broken to chat by shod hoofs. But just the bending down was all it took. The four dogs tucked tail and fled at high speed.

Walt looked up at the big old dark house, then after the dogs, and plaintively said: "Why the hell does anyone need four dogs?"

He got a bone-dry answer from the dark front of the house where a man was standing in an open doorway with a shotgun in both hands.

"Just in case some damned fools come riding into this yard in the middle of the night, when decent folks should be abed!"

Mitch started toward the porch steps, but the old man stopped him. "That's plenty close. Right where you are! Who are you and what d'you want?"

"My name is Mitchell, I'm town marshal at Dunnigan, and I came out here to talk to you, if your name is Kershaw."

For a moment the shotgun did not change direction, then it drooped slightly, and the gruff voice said: "Come up onto the porch. Where's your badge?"

Mitch opened his coat, and while the older man was peering, Mitch got his first impression of William Kershaw. He was older than John Bailey, less than average in height with a mop of snow-white hair, had a deeply lined and permanently weather-reddened face, and had a wide, lipless mouth above a granite chin. Physically he was thick and like solid oak.

Mitch let the coat drop back into place. "You want to talk out here?" he asked mildly, and the cowman cleared his throat, kicked the door wider, and entered first with his shotgun as he said: "Come on in. I'll light a lamp."

The old house had a smell of cooking. When the lamp was alight, Mitch, Clint and Walt saw a large room with a huge old smoke-blackened stone fireplace along the back wall, rough, much used chairs and sofas, and Indian trophies hanging forlornly from the wall near the fireplace. There was none of the luxury they had encountered at the Luckner place, but Kershaw's parlor looked more as though people had lived in it under both good and bad conditions.

The old cowman had dressed hurriedly, his trouser legs were partially inside his boot tops, his shirt was outside his trousers, and, although there was no mistaking Will Kershaw's age, he was a powerfully built man with a neck as thick as the neck of a rutting bull and arms like oak limbs. He leaned the shotgun aside and went to poke in the fireplace to stir coals before pitching in several pieces of kindling. When he was finished, he straightened around, looking steadily at his visitors. He nodded curtly at Clint, who he seemed to recognize, then made no offer of hospitality as he said: "Spit it out, Marshal . . . just remember, my men work hard all week and they got a right to relax in town."

Mitch returned the granite-jawed old cowman's stare. "They won't work hard next week, Mister

Kershaw. In fact, they won't be back to work for you again."

Kershaw did not move. He kept staring at the lawman as though waiting.

Mitch did not make him wait long. "They got larruped in town and locked up . . . along with Luckner's crew . . . except that three of Luckner's men are dead. And Bailey's locked up, too, with his riders."

Kershaw still did not move or say a word. After a long time he went to a chair and sat down, and finally offered hospitality by waving his visitors to chairs. None of them accepted. Kershaw faced Clint Whitney. "Blacksmith, where's Jess?"

"Locked up just like the marshal said, Mister Kershaw."

As though he would accept what Mitch had said now, because it had been corroborated, Kershaw turned back to gaze at the lawman. "What's the fine, Marshal?"

"You know damned well there's no judge in Dunnigan," stated Mitch. "I can't levy a fine. I think you know that, too."

Kershaw answered curtly. "You're damned right I know it. Turn 'em out!"

"I guess you weren't listening when I told you they're not coming back to work for you." Mitch watched dark color come into the older man's face. "From here on every damned cowman in Thunder Valley will be responsible for his riders.

That means, if you don't want me to come get you and lock you up, too, you'll fire any man who rides into Dunnigan and makes trouble. And you'll foot the bill for the damages done by your riders."

Kershaw sat with both scarred big hands resting upon the arms of his chair, staring directly at Hugh Mitchell. Then he shoved up out of the chair and walked to the door, hauled it open, and jerked his head. "Out!" he exclaimed.

None of the younger men moved. Kershaw waited, studied each face, then slammed the door closed, and strode to the wall where he had propped the shotgun. Walt Landon let him almost get there, then walked up and caught the older man around the gullet with one massive arm.

Kershaw kicked backward. Walt took the blow and tightened his grip across Kershaw's windpipe. The older man was like a desperate bull; he lashed backward, arched and strained and tried another vicious kick. Walt closed down until his muscles bulged, Kershaw's eyes bulged, his color heightened; he made one final great effort, lifted Walt completely off his feet and staggered six or seven feet, and when he lost consciousness, they both crashed to the floor, breaking a small table to splinters under them.

Landon freed himself and was halfway up off the floor when a raw-boned woman wearing a heavy robe and nightcap over a great mane of iron-gray hair appeared in a doorway and leveled a cocked Colt at Landon.

The bearded large man froze in position, and Mitch used a quiet tone to explain who he was, why he had come to the ranch, what had happened to the Arrow Circle men in town, then explained what his demands were to the cattlemen, and along toward the end of his talk, Will Kershaw was breathing deeply as he rolled up onto his knees, then arose a trifle unsteadily, looking murderously at Walt Landon, who also arose.

The gray-haired woman had a strong chin and a firm mouth. She watched Mitch, watched her husband, and when he moved toward the leaning shotgun, she said: "Will!"

Kershaw stopped.

The woman faintly scowled at Mitch. "What about our men in your jailhouse, Marshal?"

"They stay there until they agree to pick up their gatherings and leave the country."

"Have you ever been a range man, Marshal?"

"Yes'm."

"Do you know any way to work a cow outfit during the riding season without hired men?"

"No, ma'am. I don't know how to keep the peace in a town, either, with range men coming in every Saturday night and breaking windows, shooting dogs, scaring the whey out of folks, but I think this might work."

The woman allowed the heavy old Dragoon pistol to sag, then let her arm hang at her side as she eyed Mitch over an interval of stillness. Finally she said: "Have you other range men locked up?"

Mitch nodded. "Luckner's men and Bailey's men, and John Bailey, and three of Luckner's men got killed out front of the saloon."

The woman moved her eyes slowly to her husband's face, moved them back, and said: "We need those riders, Marshal."

Mitch knew that. "If I have Mister Kershaw's word he'll agree to be responsible for anything his men do in town, and he'll fire any man who hooraws the town, ma'am, you can come get them in the morning."

Kershaw growled in his throat. His wife ignored that and said: "Would you boys like a cup of coffee?"

Mitch smiled straight into her eyes. "No thanks. We've got to get back . . . but you're the first person I've met tonight I'd like to sit down and drink a cup with."

The older woman smiled back, a tough, frank, understanding smile. "We'll be in for the men in the morning, Marshal."

Kershaw would not go to the door with them, nor did his wife see them out, but when they were off the porch down by the horses, Clint turned to Walt Landon. "I wish there'd been a woman like that at the other places we've been tonight."

Walt was watching for dogs and wasted no time in answering as he swung across the saddle without even testing the cinch.

They rode out of the yard by the same route they had used to ride in. It was much colder now, horse breath turned to steam, and a great distance eastward there was a rind of dead gray spreading slowly along the curve of the earth.

They loped steadily, which kept the horses warm but which did not do much for the cold riders. Once, when they hauled back to a fast walk, Walt Landon said: "How old was that gaffer?"

Clint made a guess. "Sixties, I'd guess, but maybe older."

"That's what I was thinking," murmured Landon. "I've never run across an old man as stout as he was before. I think if I'd grabbed him from in front, by golly he might have been hard to handle."

Mitch reached under his coat to scratch, then yawned mightily, and watched the fading stars for a while. They were within a few miles of Dunnigan when he asked his cousin if the Thunder Valley stockmen had an organization.

"Yeah, they got one, but not many of the little foothills cattlemen belong. It's mostly men like Bailey, Kershaw, and Luckner. Why?"

"Sure as hell they'll hold a meeting in the next day or two," explained Mitch. "Kershaw won't give in easy, and I don't see Bailey or Luckner doing it. Well, maybe Luckner might . . . if his word's any good, but those other two . . ." Mitch shook his head.

They reached the outskirts of town as the sky was steadily brightening and saw the rising ropes of smoke from the wood stoves around town where people were preparing breakfast and heating their homes.

At the livery barn the day man was just coming to work and the night man was heading out. Mitch, Walt, and Clint left the horses and went stiffly to the jailhouse where Mitch got a fire going. When men got cold all the way through, it took a lot of warming to get the stiffness out. He also shoved the coffee pot atop the stove, then he went to the desk and dropped down, looking at his companions as he said: "I'm worn down to a nubbin."

Walt and Clint nodded, sitting in chairs, waiting for the heat to increase sufficiently for them to shed coats. Clint said: "If you're right about Kershaw and Bailey, then what?"

Mitch replied thoughtfully. "I've got to find out where they hold their stockmen's meeting, and when."

"They usually hold 'em at Sabin's saloon. The times I've seen 'em arrive in town for that has been in the morning, but exactly *when* I've got no idea."

Landon, though, had an idea. "It'll be damned soon, you can bet on that. Like the lady said, you can't run a cow outfit unless you've got riders. Anyway, Sabin could let us know when they show up . . . unless they decide not to meet in Dunnigan. If I was in their boots I sure wouldn't, not after what happened here last night."

Mitch agreed with that. "Maybe they'll meet at one of the ranches."

Landon pursed his lips and furrowed his brow in thought, then offered a suggestion. "Bailey won't be out of jail. That leaves Luckner's place or old Kershaw's place. One man can handle that. Either way, one or the other of them, Luckner or Kershaw, will head for his friend's ranch. All a man's got to do is set out there and watch, and wait." Landon scratched his face under the beard. "I can go out there today, get some sleep, and watch at the same time." He grinned. "Most of my life I've been sleeping with one eye open."

Mitch considered the powerful range man. "That's asking an awful lot," he said.

Landon laughed. "Like hell it is," he said, and stood up. "I'll get a bait of food across the road, tank up on coffee, hire me a fresh horse, and head out. My guess is that they've got to meet damned soon, maybe today, no later'n tomorrow. And if I was marshal here, I'd turn that old bastard Bailey

105

out so's he could be there, too." Landon stood, gazing down at Mitch. "You're figuring on riding in on them at their meeting, aren't you?"

Mitch nodded.

"Then when we ride in, wouldn't it be better to lay down the law with all three of them setting there, once and for all?"

Mitch slowly smiled and arose to remove his coat. "Walt, are you ready to reconsider and take the job as deputy marshal?"

Landon's intense very dark eyes glowed. "Naw. I don't like living in towns, and I've got other reasons, too. I've got to keep moving around. I get stove-up and barn sour if I stay in one place too long. If I see those fellers riding across country, I'll spy them out, then get back here and let you know."

Landon went out into the chilly new daylight, walking directly toward the café. Clint also arose. He was not especially hungry but he was tired and drained. As he stood in the doorway, he said: "Are you going to turn John Bailey loose?"

Mitch nodded. He had intended to anyway, before Walt had suggested it.

Clint started through the opening. "I think it's a good idea," he said, leaving his cousin standing over by the desk looking slightly skeptical.

Mitch draped his coat from a peg, got some hot, black coffee, then brought in the wash rack basin, filled it with water, and put the basin where the coffee pot had been so he could shave. After that, he intended to feed his prisoners, then head for his quarters at the rooming house and sleep—if he could.

X

Frank Sabin had a good bandage on his wounded leg, and although the pain was considerably less toward morning, that was in part because Frank had gone to his back room behind the bar and bedded down. As soon as he arose in the morning, the pain started up again. He used an old cane to hobble out back to wash and shave, and also to hobble into the barroom for his first cup of coffee for the day, and lean on his uninjured leg with the cup in his fist, gazing stolidly at the shot-out window on the south side of his roadway entrance.

Last night Ray Teller had supervised the removal of the defunct range men. Under Charley Bennett's pained protest Ray led the way down to Charley's icehouse across the alley behind the general store and left the bodies there in the cold until arrangements could be made to bury them. Other townsmen had taken the horses Frank had tied out behind the saloon down to the public corrals and left the saddles, blankets, and bridles atop a corral stringer there.

Frank knew Mitch, Clint, and that big, bearded range man had returned to town. The livery barn night hawk stopped by the saloon with dependable regularity every morning after he got off work for one jolt of malt whiskey before heading home. He had told Frank the marshal was back.

Normally, Frank built a fire in his wood stove on cold mornings. This morning he did not move from behind the bar to do this. When Ray Teller walked in on his way down to the smithy, Teller offered to lay the fire and Frank in turn offered Ray a shot of whiskey. Teller made the fire but declined the whiskey; he hadn't had breakfast yet. They discussed the events over the past ten or fifteen hours. Frank told Ray that Hugh Mitchell was back in town, and Ray told Frank that he was going to begin organizing a town protective committee this very day. Frank agreed to join, which was all Ray had really stopped by for, and after the blacksmith departed, Frank hitched over in order to back up to the stove.

He was standing like that, absorbing blessed heat, thinking unpleasant thoughts while the sun was steadily rising, when a small, pale-eyed man with red hair walked in tugging off a pair of doeskin gloves. The stranger wore a tied-down Colt with ivory grips. He greeted Frank with a quick, wide smile and asked for a jolt of whiskey.

Sabin made the trip back behind the bar,

wordlessly got a bottle and glass, set them before the smaller man, then would have returned to the stove but the stranger was in a talkative mood.

"What happened to your window?" he asked.

Frank sighed. "Got shot out last night."

The red-headed man turned, considered the damage, then said: "I'll be damned. You must have a pretty wild town here, barman."

"No," stated Frank, "it's not the town, it's the damned range men."

The stranger downed his whiskey and placed a silver coin beside the sticky little glass. "I've heard they hooraw the town. In fact, that's why I'm here. My name is Burt Jennings. I've been a lawman. I heard a feller named Bennett headed up your town council. You know him?"

"Charley Bennett? Yeah, I know him. He runs the general store down the road. But if you figure to apply for the marshal's job, we already hired a man."

The stranger considered this for a moment, then spoke again. "Local feller?"

"No. He's related to the man who works for the town blacksmith. His name is Hugh Mitchell."

"You think he'll work out, barman?"

Frank put a steady look upon the red-headed man. "Yeah, I think so. Last night he cleaned up the town, filled the jailhouse, and about tomorrow we got to hold three funerals."

The small man's eyes widened. "By himself?"

"Well, no. There were two other fellers . . . and me, only I just got in the way, and some son-of-a-bitch shot me in the leg. I guess a man could say Mister Mitchell did it by himself."

The stranger drew the gloves from beneath his shell belt, carefully pulled them on, smiled at Frank and said—"I guess Dunnigan don't need me."—and departed.

Frank hitched over to stand with his back to the stove again. The stove was a large, potbellied, cast-iron cannon heater, but even if the room had not been large, that broken window would have made it impossible to get the place warm very fast, and when Charley Bennett walked in looking quizzically over where Frank was standing, there was less cold, but not a whole lot less of it.

Charley was brisk. "How do you feel?" he asked, and barely allowed Frank to reply dryly before he also said: "We've got to organize a town protective committee, Frank. The way I see it if the local merchants . . ."

"Ray's already organizing one," Frank stated, leaning on the cane. "I joined. He was in here a while back."

"You joined?" stated the storekeeper, looking slightly skeptical. "You can't ride, Frank. You can't even walk very good."

Sabin's eyes flashed. "Well, god damn it, I'm not going to be like this all my life, Charley."

"Yes, but, Frank, Luckner and the others aren't

going to just sit down and take what the marshal did last night. They'll come to town. Especially Mister Luckner. I've seen him mad before at something or other here in town. It looks to me like we got to organize something right now, today maybe or tomorrow."

Frank shifted his weight slightly. He was a stocky man and perching all that weight on one ankle was tiresome. "Didn't anyone tell you last night," he said, "that Mitchell jugged every damned troublemaking bastard who came to town . . . except for Luckner's range boss and two of his riders?"

Bennett knew this. "Frank, that was last night. We're talking about today and tomorrow and the future. They'll hire more men."

From the doorway a quiet voice said: "I doubt that they will." Mitch walked in, freshly scrubbed and shaved. He still looked tired, and he certainly could have used another few hours' sleep, but it was difficult to sleep when a man's mind was busy. Nonetheless, he had got three hours' sleep, which left him feeling much better than he had felt in the cold pre-dawn when he and his companions had returned to town.

Charley Bennett did not pursue the topic he and Sabin had been discussing. He waited until Mitch arrived at the bar, then said: "What happened after you left town last night, Marshal?"

Mitch declined Frank's offer of a bottle and

111

glass before answering. "We rode out and talked to Luckner and Kershaw."

"And Bailey?"

Mitch's comment about that was dry. "We had a sort of an agreement at the jailhouse last night, Mister Bennett." He then related the terms he had set down for the cattlemen to live up to. When he was finished speaking, Charley Bennett got that pained look on his face that he showed when something did not seem logical to him.

"Marshal, those are big cowmen you're talking about. They've got money and they're used to hiring rough men. I just don't believe you can gun-whip a few of their riders and have them toe the line at some rules you made up on the spur of the . . ."

"Mister Bennett," interrupted Mitch, looking directly at the older man, "what I had in mind was for the Dunnigan town council to approve those terms I gave the ranchers. If you don't want to do that, why then I guess you'll need another town marshal . . . and if you *don't* do it, you can bet your butt next Saturday night will be like every other Saturday night around here for the past year or two, only this time it'll be worse."

Frank Sabin shifted weight again, clasped both hands atop the cane, and ignored Bennett to say: "We're organizing a town protective committee. We're starting to get it organized today. The town council can go suck eggs. They can approve or not. The rest of us are going to organize, and the first son-of-a-bitch who rides into Dunnigan now is going to learn a whole lot of respect in a damned short space of time. You care for a cup of coffee, Marshal?"

Mitch had already had breakfast and coffee down at the café, but he nodded his head, and, as Frank went hobbling for the cup, Mitch smiled at Charley Bennett. "If the town council approves of my terms, and folks around here get organized to protect the town, you're not going to have any real trouble. Mister Bennett, maybe Luckner and the others had to eat crow . . . and they're not through eating it yet, either . . . but they're cattlemen. This is the riding and working season. They aren't going to have the time to keep this thing alive. By the end of summer a lot of tempers will have cooled. But your town council had better back me up, and the folks here in town who are organizing, otherwise you fellers might be on the outside looking in."

Frank brought the coffee. Mitch thanked him for it and asked about his injured leg. While Frank was replying, Charley interrupted to say he had to get down to the store, and briskly departed.

Sabin wagged his head but did not mouth the derogatory things he was thinking, instead, he asked about the prisoners.

"They've been fed," said Mitch. "A couple of

them have had some rags tied around a hurt."
He tasted the coffee and put the cup down again.
"Bailey is a tough old bastard."

Frank could agree with that. "Yeah, and so is
Will Kershaw. But the one to watch is Luckner.
Bailey and Kershaw'll meet you head-on in a
butting contest but George Luckner'll outthink
you."

Mitch smiled; that was the same judgment he
had made last night. He twisted to gaze at the
broken window. "It was a Bailey rider who did
that."

Frank nodded his head. "Yeah. Curly-headed
feller named Clyde. He's been right where you're
standing fifty times."

Mitch reached in a shirt pocket, extracted some
crumpled old greenbacks, and counted out nine
of them. Frank watched, then reddened. "I don't
want your damned money, Mitch."

"It's not my money. It's Bailey's money. I took
it out of his hat."

"His hat?"

"Yeah. I always have prisoners empty their
pockets into their hats."

Frank counted the money. "Hell, that's what it
cost to have both windows fixed last time." He
started to peel away some of the notes, and Mitch
stopped him.

"Keep it. If that old bastard thinks windows are
that expensive, maybe he will think twice before

sending his riders to town to raise hell. Where are those dead fellers?"

"In the icehouse out behind Bennett's store."

Mitch reached, gave Frank a rough slap on the shoulder, and said: "Thanks for standing with me last night." Then he walked out of the saloon and nearly collided with a man he had seen around town and thought worked in one of the stores, but whose name he did not know. The man pulled back. "Excuse me, Marshal, but I'm organizing for the Dunnigan Protective Association. Mister Bennett at the store is getting it going. Him and another feller who is on the town council. Mister Bennett's especially working for it. You've got to hand it to Mister Bennett, Marshal. Most towns don't have councilmen as willing to work for the people as Mister Bennett. Good old Charley Bennett."

The man hurried along. Mitch turned to gaze after him, and, as he stepped down into the roadway on his way over to the jailhouse, he repeated what the man had said, but without quite the same inflection: "Good old Charley Bennett."

He was name-tagging guns when old Bailer walked in resembling an ambulatory arsenal, and widely grinning. Wordlessly he placed two carbines and three six-shooters on the desk, then stepped back. "Picked 'em up in the road out front of the saloon last night after everything was over. Kept 'em for you, Marshal."

Mitch sat down and gazed at the wizened, wiry old man. "Thanks," he said, "I'm right obliged. How is Mister Harriman?"

"By golly, you know, Marshal, for the first time since his dog got killed he come alive last night. Kept me over there giving him the details until dawn this morning."

Mitch continued to gaze at the old man. "Bailer, do you own a big-bored old buffalo rifle?"

The old man's bright little eyes subtly changed expression before he replied. "Well, as a matter of fact I do own such a gun . . . but it ain't been fired in, hell, must be twenty, thirty years."

"You sure of that, Bailer?"

The old man's entire expression changed. He looked surprised and even a little hurt. "Plumb certain, Marshal. You can come look at it yourself. It's standing in a corner. The barrel's chock full of dust and all."

Mitch smiled. "I was just interested is all," he said quietly. "Someday I will come down and look at it. I remember when I was a kid men talking about those buffalo rifles. It's close to dinnertime, Bailer, care to come over to the café with me . . . on me?"

Instantly the old man's eyes were bright again. "I'd admire to," he replied, and went gallantly to the door to hold it for Marshal Mitchell to walk out first.

XI

The marshal was not quite allowed to finish his meal. Charley Bennett's clerk, Sam, came into the café to tell Mitch the Kershaw ranch wagon had just pulled up over in front of the jailhouse. Mitch paid for the two meals, winked at old Bailer, and left him still eating at the counter.

It was not Will Kershaw; it was his wife. She was standing in the office when Mitch walked in. She was wearing a man's old hat, high-topped boots below her skirt, and had a man's old blanket coat around her. She was one of the least feminine women he had ever seen, but she was past the age of caring about anything like that.

Her dead-level gray eyes met Mitch's smile. "My husband didn't come," she stated, then abruptly said: "I'm here for our riders."

Mitch offered her a chair, which she ignored as she watched him walk to the desk and sit down. He looked up at her, at the honest, level gray eyes, at the lines, the uncompromising mouth and chin, and said: "Missus Kershaw, I need your husband's word."

She finally accepted the chair, sat down, and said: "My word is enough, Marshal."

Mitch fidgeted a little. "I'd take your word any day of the week, ma'am, but, you see, my quarrel is with your husband, and the others. Missus Kershaw, I'm not trying to bully anyone. I'm just trying to stop the hoorawing, to get the range men to ride in and play poker or have drinks or whatever they want to do . . . but not chouse the town nor fire guns within the town limits, nor wreck things."

She continued to look at Mitch. After a moment she leaned back to get comfortable in the chair, then she used blunt words. "I understand what you're trying to do, Marshal. I believe in it. Marshal, I pay the men, my husband don't. He can't add two plus two. I pay all the bills, keep the books, and figure out at the end of each year how much we've made . . . or lost. I don't care what Will says. No one who rides for Kershaw will hooraw the town again, but if any of them try it, they won't get paid until you've told me they didn't bust things, then they'll get fired."

Having said all that the gray-headed woman sat perfectly still, looking directly back at Marshal Mitchell—until he smiled and arose. "They're your men," he told her, and picked up the key to the cells. At the door he halted to look back at her. "Last night one of the fellers who was out at your place with me said he wished someone like you had been at the other places we had trouble. Missus Kershaw, I wish that, too."

He growled at the Kershaw riders, herded them to the office where the gray-eyed woman stared steadily at them, while Mitch got their hats from the back room, put them on the desk, and growled for each man to pick up his own property. He did not say a word as he got the guns with the little name tags on them, handed them around, and stood back.

Mrs. Kershaw arose, said—"Jess, open the door."—and took them outside. Mitch heard her ordering them to go find their horses and meet her over in front of the general store.

He closed the roadway door, then went down for John Bailey and also brought him to the office, alone. When the cell-room door was closed, he got Bailey's gun and put it on the desk. "Go on home," he said, "and take that gun with you."

Bailey did not ask the obvious question—why was he being released?—instead he said: "What about my riders?"

Mitch stood by the desk. "They stay."

"For how long?"

"Maybe they'll never come back to work for you."

Bailey rubbed an unshaven jaw and glanced around the room, then back again at Hugh Mitchell. In a tone lacking the gruffness Mitch expected, the cowman said: "Did Will Kershaw come for his men? Was he here in the office when you taken them up here from the cells?"

Mitch went to the door and opened it. He had

119

rather thought Bailey might have profited from his night in the jailhouse, might have something else to discuss. Since he did not, and stood there looking as craggily unrelenting as ever, Mitch jerked his head. "Get out of here."

Bailey went; he stopped outside to look up and down the roadway, then he struck out southward, and Mitch closed the door with a mild curse.

Last night Bailey had seemed ready to concede, or at least to talk. Ordinarily a night in an uncomfortable, confining jail cell made a change in men; if it had in Bailey, he had shown no indication of it this morning. He had not seemed as hostile as he had last night, but he had not given any signs of yielding, either.

Clint came over shortly after noon and shared a cup of coffee with Mitch. Something was amusing him. "Ray and Charley Bennett are both organizin' the men. Charley seems to be doin' it because maybe someone told him if he didn't he might not get re-elected to the town council next time, and Ray's doin' it for better reasons, but it's got to where they're competing, and that's funny. I've listened to them both. They sound like a pair of real politicians."

Mitch smiled. He liked Teller, but he did not particularly care for Charley Bennett.

They discussed last night. They also discussed the probable reaction of the cowmen, and Clint asked if Mitch had turned Bailey loose. Mitch nodded. "Yeah. He's a hard old nut to figure out."

Clint did not think so. "Maybe, but not this time. None of them's goin' to be hard to predict this time."

Clint probably would have explained what he meant, but the roadway door opened. Walt Landon walked in more than ever in need of some personal changes, went to shake the coffee pot as he said: "They're meeting at Luckner's place. I saw Kershaw riding east and he came onto Bailey. They sat a while talking, then both of them turned eastward." Landon turned, holding a cup. "Something else. That lady who threw down on me last night, Kershaw's wife . . . she was driving an old wagon and had men with her, but they weren't coming toward town. They were too far away for me to make them out very well. I recognized her, but that was all."

Mitch explained what he had done, how he had released the Arrow Circle range men to Mrs. Kershaw. He also told Walt about freeing John Bailey, but Landon had already known this. He tasted the coffee and looked thoughtfully from Clint to Mitch. "It's not going to be the same this time. We arrived out there in the dark. This time they'll be able to see us coming for miles. If they're hostile, it'll be like shooting ducks in a rain barrel."

Mitch arose from the desk chair. "If we wait and waylay each man after he leaves, it won't be the same, Walt. This meeting has got to be the one where we're all face to face." Mitch took down a Winchester, and turned as the other two men watched. "But maybe, if I rode out there alone, they wouldn't feel threatened."

Walt Landon snorted. "That's silly," he said, and put the cup aside. "Meet you out front of the livery barn in a few minutes." He winked at Clint and stalked out of the office.

Clint, too, arose. "I'll tell Ray I won't be around this afternoon."

When he was alone again in the jailhouse office, Mitch inspected the saddle gun, shoved it in a boot by the door, and stood a while gazing out the front wall window, thinking. He did not believe there would be trouble at the Luckner place. As far as Arrow Circle was concerned, he felt that between himself and Will Kershaw's wife they had driven a very effective wedge where Will Kershaw would be unable to dislodge it. That left Luckner and Bailey. He felt that they, too, were teetering. Whether they liked the idea of co-operation or not, they were in the midst of the working season. Without riders they would be unable to work their ranges. Even if they brought in new riders, it would take time to get them organized to work the unfamiliar ranges correctly.

Mitch left the office and walked southward with the Winchester in its boot hooked in the bend of one arm. He saw people turn to look. At the livery barn Clint and Walt were waiting out front with saddled horses. The day man hostler brought forth Mitch's animal, then hovered discreetly to see in which direction the marshal took his men. When he saw them leave town by the north stage road, the hostler scuttled across the road to pass the word. He did not quite make it; a pair of lanky men rode in, saw him leaving, and called after him. The hostler dutifully turned back. One of the strangers loosened his own saddle and let the hostler take charge of the animal while the stranger packed his own outfit into the harness room. The other tall man tugged loose the latigo to let the cinch hang, but let the hostler do the actual unsaddling, and while he was doing it, the man asked him where the marshal was.

"Gone," stated the day man. "Left out of town with a couple other fellows not fifteen minutes ago. I don't know where he was going."

The strangers were interested. They followed the day man down into the barn and watched him care for their animals. For the hostler it was a fine opportunity; he was rarely the center of attention. He told them of the fight in town, about the jailhouse being full of range men, and how the town was forming a protection committee, and tapped his own chest about that. "I joined, too. No one's goin' to ride into Dunnigan no more and badger folks."

The pair of strangers returned to the sun-bright roadway and stood privately talking while they studied the town, then they walked off in the direction of the café. They seemed to be calm, unhurried individuals, and while they were dressed as range men, neither one of them actually quite got that impression across. The café man, for example, thought they might be cattle buyers. He had been studying men all his life and was not often wrong.

Later, when they strolled up to the saloon where Frank was sitting with his sore leg raised to the seat of another chair, and arose without smiling to hobble behind the bar and serve them, the carpenter who was installing a new window in the front wall thought they were either gun-fighters or outlaws, and Frank categorized them as cardsharps, or perhaps lawmen. He talked to them longer than anyone else, but they said nothing about themselves; instead, they asked a lot of questions about Dunnigan, about Thunder Valley, and about the troubles that were still current. Frank leaned heavily atop his bar while he talked with the strangers. When they were ready to leave, he gave them directions to the rooming house at the north end of town, then went back to place his throbbing leg gingerly in a position where it bothered him the least, and argued with the carpenter about the strangers, not because Frank cared who they were but because he was feeling cranky today, and being disagreeable without having a way to express it was much worse than just being disagreeable.

Charley Bennett came up to the saloon after the carpenter had got his money and had departed with a malicious remark to the effect that his rates would be going up on installing windows in saloons; Frank was evidently not the only one feeling cranky.

Bennett complained that Ray Teller had organized the most townsmen. The reason Charley did not approve of this was because Ray had not done it with the sanction of the town council. Frank sat there, looking morosely at the storekeeper. But there was no point in saying what he thought, since nothing as bland as common sense had ever seemed to affect Charley. He asked how many townsmen had joined, and Charley said: "*My* group . . . we got six. Ray's got nine, but his group don't have official . . ."

"That's plenty," stated Frank, looking steadily at the larger man. "Charley, go tell Ray the town council wants 'em all in one committee."

"The council hasn't discussed that, Frank."

"Then go around and discuss it . . . *then* go tell Ray. He doesn't care about what's official, and neither do the rest of us . . . just so's we got a protective committee. I'll bet you a bottle of whiskey Ray'll hand the whole darned thing over to you. You can be head Indian of the Dunnigan Protective Committee."

Charley fidgeted. "I don't have the time. I've got to run the store and I've got other . . ."

"Then ask Ray if he'll be head Indian. He'll do it."

Bennett glanced around, patently seeking an object upon which to base a fresh conversation. He said: "How's the leg?"

Frank answered truthfully. "It'd have to feel better just to die."

"You likely need a doctor. Can you stand a stage ride down to . . . ?"

"It'll mend, Charley. Given enough time it'll mend. But I wish to hell I knew which one of those sons-of-bitches shot it."

"Maybe it's infected, Frank."

"If it is, there's no sign yet. It's just swollen like a flour sack, and hurts like hell," said Sabin. "Now, I don't think it's infected, Charley. Last night when I washed it out I used some of my best bonded whiskey, none of that other stuff."

Charley departed, leaving Frank to wonder whether the pain was worth it—to get to the drawer behind the bar, get a cigar from the box there, light it, and return to the chair. He decided there might be another way, so he sat for almost a solid hour before one of the yardmen from over at the stage company's corrals walked in for some beer. He got the yardman to fetch him the stogie—but he had to also give one to the yardman, and also allow the yardman to draw off his own beer, free of charge. He savored the cigar while unhappily reflecting upon what it had cost him.

Later in the afternoon he saw those two strangers walking southward upon the far plank walk and speculated about them again. If they had been cardsharps, since Frank had the only saloon in town, and there were tables scattered throughout the big room, they surely would have made him the customary proposition— twenty percent to the house, eighty percent to the gamblers. They had not made the proposition, therefore Frank discarded that judgment of the strangers and reverted to his second judgment of them. They were lawmen.

XII

When Mitch and his riding companions turned eastward off the stage road, the same country they had passed through in darkness after the fight in town looked generally unfamiliar by daylight, but in each man the sense of direction left them feeling satisfied they were riding the right way. Clint, who knew the countryside, pointed out something that had been invisible on the previous ride: a tamarack windbreak someone had planted many years earlier. It was unkempt, unlovely, and although it ran eastward for a solid mile, it did not add a single thing to the beauty of the countryside. Tamaracks were probably the only trees that did not have a saving grace, unless it was their ability when planted close enough together to break the fierce, biting-cold winds of early springtime.

It was good cattle country on both sides of the roadway. Walt Landon voiced strong approval of it. "Plenty of late feed, if they manage it right, and good protection up northward toward the mountains." He rode beside Mitch for a while, then said: "If a man had a mind to settle down, this would be the country to do it in."

Clint offered a dry observation. "Yeah, except that every yard of it we're passin' over belongs to either Luckner or Bailey, and up north in the foothills it belongs to some stump ranchers."

They stopped conversing once they had the roof tops of Rafter Ranch in sight. The day was glass-clear and pleasant, visibility was excellent, but they could not make out objects in the yard until they were less than a mile out, and by then, as Landon reminded them, anyone in the yard, if he happened to be looking westward, could see them coming. "And," he added with a sense of conviction, "they just damned well might be watching."

But they weren't watching or, if someone was, not a sound or a sign of movement broke the hush and stillness as Mitch led off up around the big barn and down into the yard on a direct course toward the house. There were no tied horses in sight, but all that probably meant was that Kershaw and Bailey had stalled their animals in the barn. Neither were there dogs, which seemed unusual. The last time they had ridden in an old dog had walked down to meet them. They tied up out front of the house, and Clint gestured toward a lazy-rising spindrift of smoke from the parlor chimney.

Clint stood gazing around as he said: "He's got a cook and a kid wrangler. There'd ought to be someone . . ."

Finally the old dog came around the far side of the house, stiff, with watery eyes and matted hair, but evidently not yet senile enough to forget; he walked past Mitch and Clint, his tail wagging, and sat down directly in front of Walt Landon, brushing dust with his tail and looking up with a smile. Walt leaned, scratched for a moment, then gave the old dog a gentle pat, and turned toward the house as he arose.

As before, when they walked to the porch, the old dog remained directly behind Walt. Whatever Mitch had expected, and he had rather suspected there would be no trouble at the ranch, when the door opened and he was facing George Luckner for the second time, Luckner was wearing an ivory-handled Colt, low and tied down, and his gaze at Mitch was direct, unreadable, and cold. He said: "You're not welcome. There's a meeting in progress in which you have no part."

Mitch's answer was direct. "Mister Luckner, I didn't expect to be welcome, but I'm going to have my say."

The handsome, graying man's eyes slid past to Clint and to Landon. It was up to him; he could admit them or he could refuse to admit them, and have trouble erupt in his doorway. Old Kershaw appeared at Luckner's shoulder, his perpetually ruddy, weathered, and lined face showing very little, but what *did* show was antagonism. But Kershaw did not speak, and Luckner finally made his decision. "We'll finish the meeting, then call you in." As he said this, George Luckner stepped back to close the door.

As he did this, Mitch shoved his foot forward and spoke. "I'd like to have my say before you gents finish the meeting." And now Mitch was prepared for the trouble he had not expected; he reached to push Luckner back inside the parlor. Luckner moved first, eluded the rising left hand, and let his right shoulder drop. Mitch's right hand and arm seemed scarcely to move, but the gun was out, tipped, and being cocked before George Luckner had his gun barrel clear of

130

leather. Without raising his voice Mitch spoke again. "Back up, and take that hand away from the gun."

Luckner did not obey, not until Will Kershaw growled. "Let 'em in. Let him have his say, Walt."

Luckner stepped clear, so did Kershaw, and as Mitch shouldered past into the room, he saw John Bailey over by the fireplace. Clint closed the door and stood in front of it. Walt Landon stepped sideways where he had a good view of the room and everyone in it. Walt always seemed to know the correct thing to do under these kinds of circumstances.

Mitch kept Luckner in front of him as he reached the center of the room. He said: "You don't need that gun, Mister Luckner. When I've had my say, we'll leave. I'm not here to fight anyone . . . unless I have to." He pointed. "Put the gun on the table, Mister Luckner."

Again the handsome, graying man did not obey until Will Kershaw intervened. "Do it, George. What the hell, he wants to sound off, we'll let him."

Luckner placed the handsome weapon atop a table, and turned as he seemed to loosen, to lose most of his stiffness. "Say it," he rasped, and went over to take a stance before the fireplace where dying coals were giving off a trickle of gray smoke.

"I've already said it to each one of you. You'll be responsible for your men, you'll fire the ones who make trouble in town, or I'll keep you from hiring new hands this season, and I'll keep your regular hands locked up until they agree not to go back to work for you. That's all . . . well, not quite all." Mitch looked at them each in his turn. "Mister Kershaw, you might as well go home. I turned your riders loose this morning . . . in your wife's custody. I hope you listen to her. I think she's got better common sense than you have. Mister Bailey . . . I didn't kill you, but I could have. I may still do it, if I have to. That's not going to do me any good, and it sure as hell won't do you any good. Mister Luckner, last night I was beginning to respect you as a man of decent judgment."

They waited for more, but Mitch had said all he intended to say. He went to Luckner's sideboard where the carafe of red wine stood and, with all of them watching, filled six glasses, lined them up, and let them stand there while he turned to face the cowmen. "That's all, gents, we'll leave now . . . unless you will drink with me to an end to this feuding." Not a cowman moved, so Mitch went to the door and opened it to allow his companions to precede him to the porch, closed the door after himself, and went down where the horses were tied.

Clint spoke for the first time since they had

met the stockmen. "You put on a hell of a show, Mitch."

Clint's cousin unlooped his reins, ran a thumb under the cinch, then turned the horse to him as he mounted, and when he was settled in the saddle, he replied: "Yeah, well, I saw that done one time at a playhouse in Cheyenne. It worked that time, but it sure as hell didn't work this time."

They rode slowly from the yard, kept riding until they were far enough westward to start angling toward town, and after a while Walt Landon spat, swore a little, then said: "Those pig-headed fools." He thought a moment, then added something to that. "I should have let you shoot old Bailey."

When they eventually reached town, it was getting dark. There were lights at the saloon, as there were every night when all other business establishments on both sides of the road were dark, and, down at the livery barn where they left the horses, Mitch dragooned his companions into helping him lug buckets of stew and coffee from the café to the jailhouse for the prisoners.

They did this chore in unsmiling silence; the prisoners took their cue from the mood of the three armed men and did not say a word although several of them clearly wanted to.

Later, Clint departed, and Walt stifled a mighty yawn as he sank into an office chair, disconsolately gazing at the cold stove. "I thought they might give in," he mused aloud. "I figured they'd be willing to talk sense. What in hell does a man have to do to people like that, short of blowing off their heads?"

Mitch had considered that all the way back to town. "Do like I said, Walt, keep their riders locked up unless they'll agree to leave the country . . . and every range man who comes to town to hire out around here, run him off, too. But that won't work for long."

Landon agreed. "It won't for a fact. They'll get more riders."

"I guess I could swear out warrants for Luckner, Bailey, and Kershaw, and lock *them* up."

Walt roused himself slightly after considering this idea. "By golly, *that* ought to do it," he said, and yawned mightily again, arose from the chair, and added: "I've got to get a bath tonight, and get some sleep up off the ground."

He left the office, and Mitch pitched his hat upon the desk top, propped up his feet, and leaned back with both arms behind his head. He was sitting like that when he heard horses out front at the hitch rack, but he did not stir. Very often if the other racks up and down the road were full, horsemen used the jailhouse rack.

Luckner, Kershaw, and John Bailey walked in out of the lowering night. Mitch continued to sit back, gazing at the cowmen. He did not say a word, and for a moment or two neither did they, then Luckner, who had evidently been chosen to do the talking, said: "All right, Marshal, you win. We'll agree to your terms."

Mitch hauled down his legs and removed the clasped hands from behind his head, leaned forward on the desk, and spoke directly to George Luckner. "I'm not winning anything. I never had winning in mind. Hell, this never should have happened like it did, and if the townsmen had bunched up against your riders a long time ago, I doubt like hell that anything like last Saturday night ever would have happened. Gents, I appreciate your being willing to lend a hand, and I apologize for busting in on your meeting." He looked around. "Wish I had some wine and glasses."

Luckner stood gazing steadily at Hugh Mitchell. Eventually he said: "Marshal, you're a hard man to hate. None of us is sure why that is, but it is." Luckner offered a hand. Mitch arose and shook with all three of them, then Will Kershaw let go a big rattling sigh, as though he were gratified it was all over. But Bailey did as he had done before when he was in the jailhouse office with Mitch, he said: "Kershaw's riders are out. Now you can turn mine out, too."

Mitch picked up the cell keys. "I'll fetch them," he said, and left the three stockmen standing there while he herded the full complement of his prisoners to the office, and got their hats and weapons. The awkward moment for them all was when they nodded before filing out into the night. Only George Luckner handled that with gallantry, all the others did it quickly, in an embarrassed manner, and trooped outside.

Mitch went out, too—and halted in astonishment. The range men were completely motionless. Twenty-five feet away in the center of the road there were not less than twelve men, all with belt guns and carbines. Ray Teller was to one side and slightly ahead. He very briskly addressed Hugh Mitchell.

"We saw Luckner, Bailey, and Kershaw ride in, Mitch. If there's anything wrong here . . . them three forcing you to turn out their riders. . . ."

Mitch saw his cousin out there with the others. It was the Dunnigan Protective Committee on its first alarm. When the surprise passed, he almost wanted to laugh. Instead he thanked them, assured them there was nothing wrong, told them, too, that the ranchers had agreed to the town's terms, and smiled at Ray Teller. "It's a darned good committee, Mister Teller, but at least this time I don't need the help."

As the men began leaving the roadway George Luckner turned. Mitch was sure he could detect an ironic twinkle in the cowman's eyes, but it was too dark to be sure.

As the range men went after their horses

down at the public corrals, Mitch remained out front in the pleasant night. He was still leaning there a while later when a pair of tall strangers approached and one of them pushed out a mechanical smile as he said: "Marshal Mitchell, my name is Jim Wheaton. This here is Homer Watson. We'd like a few words with you."

Mitch straightened up off the rack and studied the pair of strangers, then he said: "Not tonight, gents. I'm tired plumb to the bone. In the morning." He then nodded and turned to padlock the jailhouse and walk past the pair of strangers with another nod, heading up in the direction of the rooming house.

One tall man turned to the other one. "That's the man who tamed Thunder Valley's cowmen? He don't look like Wyatt Earp to me."

The other tall man was watching Mitch in the distance when he answered: "The only thing you can tell about a man by looking at him is that he has two legs, two arms, and a head. All the rest of it you can only figure out by being around him. Let's go back to the saloon. What the hell, we been five days getting here, one more day isn't likely to make any difference."

It was a pleasant night for either bedding down or bellying up to a bar, even though the barman was as green as grass at his trade and the swarthy, cranky man sitting at one of the poker tables with a cane, smoking a big cigar, looking malevolently at his new employee seemed best left entirely alone. It was very difficult for Frank to sit there and watch another man working his bar, especially since the man he had talked into helping out was a corral-yard hostler from over at the stage company's corrals and had never tended bar before in his life. Every blunder he made caused Frank to bite harder upon the cigar and strangle a desire to curse.

XIII

For the first time since arriving in Dunnigan, Mitch had a good night's rest. He was in excellent spirits when he went down to the café for a late breakfast, and the mood held as he went over to unlock the jailhouse. It only began to diminish when he entered the cell room and saw the mess the range men had left behind.

Later, when Charley Bennett arrived in response to a rumor he had heard that morning about the town marshal's having released his prisoners, Mitch told Charley why he had turned out the range men, then asked if Charley and the town council had decided to enact an ordinance in support of what Mitch had accomplished. The council had, Charley said, by meeting in extraordinary session. They had also agreed to budget funds for the township marshal to hire a full-time deputy. Then Charley said: "Now will you get those dead men out of my icehouse? Every time a customer goes back there for ice, they come out white as a sheet."

Mitch was willing. "Is there someone around Dunnigan who makes pines boxes and head-boards?"

"Yes, there's a local carpenter."

"Then, if you'll send him to see me, we can plant those gents this afternoon. Care for some coffee?"

Bennett declined. "I never touch the stuff before noon. It's bad for the kidneys."

Mitch sat gazing at the storekeeper, thinking of a caustic retort, but he did not offer it; he simply arose to go to the door with Charley and see him out. Then he went back to the desk, wagging his head.

He had scarcely got planted at the desk before those two strangers he had encountered at the hitch rack last night walked in. He remembered their names—Jim Wheaton and Homer Watson— but as he nodded, he could not remember which was which. Jim Wheaton was the elder of the two. He was a smiling man with deep-set eyes and a wide, lipless mouth. He gave Mitch the impression that the smile was a façade, that behind it was a man who did not really smile at all. His eyes remained fixed on Mitch as he sought a chair and sank into it. The younger man,

Homer Watson, had a long nose, a prominent Adam's apple, and a pair of dry-looking pale eyes. Mitch made no assessment of Watson. He was clearly the shadow of Jim Wheaton.

"We've got a problem," said Wheaton, speaking slowly and smiling. "We've got a warrant for a man we think is in Thunder Valley, and around town last night we picked up what seems like the description of our man . . . only it doesn't exactly fit." Wheaton's smile deepened. "This feller is called Dill Turner. *Dill* not Bill. He's wanted for horse stealing in southern Colorado. They've got a fair reward out for him. The last information we have on Turner is that he was riding north."

Mitch waited for more, but evidently Jim Wheaton had said all he had to say, so Mitch leaned back at the desk. "Why Thunder Valley?" he asked. "A man riding north could veer off east or west."

"Thunder Valley," said Jim Wheaton, speaking slowly again, "is on the way north to Deer Lodge up in Montana. That's where Dill Turner's got kinfolk. We've got two men up at Deer Lodge waiting for him to ride in."

Mitch was beginning to understand. Wheaton and Watson were on this horse thief's trail from the south. North were two more men waiting up ahead while Wheaton and Watson drove Turner toward Deer Lodge. Mitch said: "Are you a law officer, Mister Wheaton?"

The smiling man fished inside his coat, produced a worn envelope, and tossed it down upon the desk in front of Mitch. "That there is a governor's warrant, Marshal. You know what a governor's warrant is? Well, it's given to a man authorizing him to act in the capacity of a lawman in the pursuit and capture of a fugitive."

Mitch did not open the envelope. He did not even pick it up.

Wheaton kept smiling. "Of course, that warrant's only really good in Colorado, where it was issued, but mostly lawman in other territories honor them like they'd honor a badge."

Mitch sighed. Warrants of that kind were issued to professional manhunters. Lawmen did not need them. He said: "There must be a pretty fair reward, Mister Wheaton."

The smiling man's little sunk-set eyes shone. "Three thousand dollars, Marshal."

Mitch blinked. "For a horse thief? What did he steal?"

"Just some using stock horses. But what else he done was larrup hell out of the man's two sons who owned those horses, and the man's right fond of his two sons, and he's got the money to put up for Turner."

Mitch said: "Dead or alive?"

Wheaton crossed one long thin leg over the other leg before replying, and then his drawl dropped a notch or two. "Well, now, Marshal

141

Mitchell, in this business you sure enough know they don't all throw down their guns when a man calls 'em."

Mitch shifted his attention to Homer Watson. The younger man was staring steadily at Mitch without blinking, his face devoid of expression. He had a weak mouth and a long, angular jaw that ended in a thrusting, pointed chin.

Jim Wheaton spoke again. "I've got an extra dodger along. I'll leave it with you while Homer and me do some scouting around over the valley. Turner's a top hand cowboy. That's about all he knows to do for a living. If he's here, he's maybe working."

Mitch watched the tall man arise and fish in a pocket for the dodger. "Didn't you say he was passing through, Mister Wheaton?" he asked.

"No, sir, Marshal. What I said was that this here town is on his route northward." As he finished speaking, Jim Wheaton dropped a large folded paper on the desk in front of Mitch, then went on speaking. "We've been on his trail better'n two months. Up north, they haven't seen hide nor hair of him, but he's had time to get up there. That's why Homer and me are now asking around, because we figure Turner isn't going straight on through to Deer Lodge. Maybe he ran out of money, or maybe his horse gave out and he's got to work a month or two in order to get cash to buy another horse. All I can tell you, Marshal, is that he ain't at Deer Lodge, and he ain't back down the trail, and that leaves the country between, and Thunder Valley is a very likely place."

Wheaton went to the office door and smiled back at Mitch. He allowed Homer Watson to precede him out on the plank walk before he made a final remark. "Marshal, we do a little work on percentages. If you can lay this son-of-a-bitch in our sights or in our hands, you'll earn ten percent of the bounty money. Can't beat that, can you?"

Wheaton continued to smile back at Mitch as he eased the door closed.

There were any number of names for men like those two, and manhunter was the most flattering. Mitch arose to close the cell-room door because there was a draft, and before he got back to the desk old Bailer came in, looking worried.

Mitch pointed to a chair, but Bailer shook his head. "Marshal, I think Josh Harriman's sick. He's lying on the floor of his shack and I can't get no whiskey down him, but he's breathing."

They left the office together, Mitch walking with long strides, Bailer almost skipping to keep up. They passed the livery barn, and one of those tall strangers was in conversation with the day man. Both he and the hostler turned to watch Mitch hasten past.

The door of the elderly blind man's tar-paper shack was ajar. As Mitch shouldered inside, he noticed that someone had closed the window Mitch had opened, and drawn the gunny-sack curtain closed again. He told Bailer to let some light in, and kneeled where old Harriman was lying on his side, breathing but not very well. Bailer's bottle of dreg whiskey was on its side nearby. Mitch lifted Harriman and was surprised at how light he was for his big-boned size, carried him to the littered wall bunk, and placed him down with his head toward the light that Bailer had let in by opening all the windows and pulling aside the gunny sacks.

For five seconds old Harriman looked directly at Hugh Mitchell. He said: "Marshal, you look just like I figured you'd look. I need a favor from you . . . look after Alfred for me." Then his whole body flattened in a manner that had no likeness in life. Old Harriman was dead.

Mitch leaned a moment longer, then pulled a soiled old ragged Army blanket up over Josh Harriman, and straightened around with a question. "Who is Alfred?"

Bailer looked embarrassed. "His dog. The one that got shot in the roadway two Saturdays back. I guess Josh's mind was going. I been sort of suspicioning that for a while now, only I kept it to myself. Marshal?"

"Yeah."

"He couldn't see you, could he?"

Mitch turned toward the door. "Let no one

come in here, Bailer. I'll be down later and we can make arrangements to bury him."

Outside in the fresh, clean summer air Mitch stopped at the broken gate and gazed back, then did as any man would have done—had a fleeting moment of pure wonder tinged with uneasiness, then put the little mystery to which there would never be an answer out of his mind, and started back up toward the jailhouse.

He was not in a smiling frame of mind an hour later when that pale-eyed man with the pointed chin, Homer Watson, strolled in out of the sunshine and said: "Some old guy died, eh, Marshal?"

Mitch's answer was curt. "Yeah, an old feller died. What can I do for you, Mister Watson?"

The pale eyes dropped to Mitch's untidy desk. "You ain't looked at the Wanted dodger yet?"

Mitch hadn't. It was still lying where he had last seen it. He had been on the verge of unfolding it when Bailer had come in. Now, something in the pale-eyed man's voice made him look from the folded poster to Homer Watson. "No, but I will."

Watson's lips pulled back in a mock smile. "I can wait, Marshal."

Mitch's temper slipped a notch. "You don't have to wait. When I get damned good and ready, I'll read the thing."

They exchanged a long look before Homer Watson nodded and walked back out into the sunshine, and Mitch dropped his hat atop the desk, sat down, unfolded the dodger, and did not stir for ten seconds. Except for the beard he was staring at the likeness of Walt Landon. The description also fitted perfectly. Even the beard, clearly grown after the picture from which the likeness had been made, did not conceal the look around the eyes, the facial structure, the hairline, or the expression. Mitch shoved the dodger into a drawer, fished for that bottle of whiskey his predecessor had left, took a long pull of it, returned it to the drawer, and leaned back, staring out the window at the beautiful day.

Clint came by later, and Mitch asked his cousin if he had seen Walt. Clint had not. Mitch said: "Go find him. He might be at the rooming house, or maybe at Frank's place, but find him and tell him to get his damned horse, keep to the back alley, and go north up the stage road into the foothills, not to make a fire tonight, and watch for me. I'll be along as soon as I can."

Clint very slowly inclined his head, both eyes fixed on his cousin. "All right, but what's wrong?"

"When you get off work this evening, I'll tell you. In fact, you can ride up there with me, if you're of a mind to. Go find him, and remember . . . the back alley out of town."

After Clint had departed, Mitch put the folded dodger in a pocket and walked up to the saloon.

146

Frank was near the stove, a fire was burning in it despite the warmth outside, and when Mitch walked in, Frank's sour expression brightened slightly. "People," he told Mitch, "have given me a pain right where I sit the last day or two, but you're the exception. Pull up a chair. And what's wrong now?"

Mitch handed Frank the dodger to unfold while he brought up a chair, but farther from the stove than Sabin was. When Frank finished looking, he handed back the dodger and said: "I knew it. I smelled it."

"That he's a fugitive?"

"Naw. There's two strung-out strangers in town asking around. I figured they were lawmen."

Mitch made the correction quietly. "They're not lawmen, Frank, they're professional manhunters. One is named Wheaton and the younger, rat-faced one is called Homer Watson. There's three thousand dollars on Walt's head."

Frank blinked. "For stealing horses?"

"Well, they told me he stole them from some cowman, and beat up the cowman's sons in the mess, and now the cowman wants Walt's blood more for whipping his sons than for stealing his horses. It's a sort of grudge."

Frank was still very impressed. "By God, Mitch, I hold grudges, but never three thousand dollars' worth. Well, now what?"

"Frank, he sure as hell did more than Charley

147

or almost anyone else around town, except you. He's ridden with me each time I went out to brace Luckner and the others, and he . . ."

"All right, all right. I know. But I can't help, Mitch, not with one leg."

The marshal sat back, looking steadily at Frank Sabin. "You're about the only one who *can* do something."

"What?"

Mitch cleared his throat. "They come in for a drink, don't they?"

"Yeah, when they first got to town and again last night."

"You've been at your trade a long time, haven't you? Frank, I'm going to a rendezvous with Walt tonight after dark. One or the other of those sons-of-bitches is going to be watching me like a hawk. They know Dill Turner is Walt Landon. I could tell the way that ugly one acted this afternoon when he came by about the poster. They've sure as hell been around town, giving descriptions. You can't miss a man who is built and who looks like Landon even with that beard. They've got it figured out. Men like that are like buzzards. They can scent up a body ten miles away. And they'll know how to shag me without me knowing they're back there."

Frank frowned slightly. "What is it you want . . . ?" He stopped speaking, and stared. For a moment he was silent, then he said: "All right, but they've got to come in here, they've got to come to the bar and ask for a drink."

"You can do it?"

Frank's glance turned saturnine. "Like you said, I've been at this business a long time. Yeah, I can do it. I can put them to sleep for ten hours. They'll wake up feeling like the wrath of God."

Mitch smiled slightly, leaned and slapped Frank's good knee, and arose. "I'll see to it they come in tonight," he said, and went back out into the roadway.

Across, upon the far plank walk and southward, leaning patiently upon an overhang upright out front of the jailhouse, Clint was gazing toward where a peddler's sided-up and roofed-over wagon was coming up from the south roadway. Mitch went down there, took his cousin into the office, and raised a quizzical eyebrow. Clint said: "I found him. He was sleepin' in his room. I told him what you said and he didn't even wait, but grabbed his gun belt, his hat and saddlebags, and left. Mitch, is he an outlaw? What is this all about?"

"He's wanted for stealing horses, Clint. There's something else you can do. There are two strangers in town, one is named Wheaton, the other one is named Watson . . . they're staying at the rooming house, too. Get talking to them about suppertime. Offer to tell them about the fight, and

149

invite them to buy you a drink for what you can tell them. Mention Walt a little, too. Then take them to Frank's bar and order three rounds from Frank."

"That's all, just bait them down there and get them a round of . . . Mitch, have you talked to Frank in the last hour or so?"

"Just came from there."

Clint sighed. "I know what Frank's goin' to do to those fellers. But hell, if they're lawmen . . ."

"They've got a governor's warrant from Colorado, Clint. They not law officers, they're professional bounty hunters."

Clint thought that over, then shrugged, and went to the door before saying: "Don't worry. I'll see to it. But I was sort of hopin' to ride with you to the foothills tonight. Well, tell Walt . . . aw hell, tell him anything you want. I just think he's one hell of a partner."

Mitch went for a drink of water. Sitting next to that hot stove in the saloon had got him to sweating like a stud horse. Then he glanced out the front window to gauge how much sunlight was left in the day.

XIV

Dusk settled before Mitch left Dunnigan. By the time he was well up the north road and had stopped three times to ascertain whether or not he was being followed, darkness was on its way. He did not see or hear anyone back down the road, but as he'd told Frank Sabin, professionals like Wheaton and Watson knew their trade; he would probably have been unable to detect them anyway.

He made one final halt before entering the foothills. For a long while he stood beside his horse, gauging the night down the back trail. No matter how accomplished manhunters were, there was one thing they could not avoid doing, and that was to keep riding; sooner or later, if they were back there, they would have to approach, and they never did, so Mitch swung up and let his horse walk for a mile before the animal put up its ears and shifted because ahead in the darkness something had caught its attention, but without really frightening it.

Walt was leaning against a spindly jack pine and allowed Mitch to come within a few yards before straightening and strolling to the edge of the roadway. He smiled and said: "Nice warm night, Mitch."

Instead of replying immediately, Mitch swung off and led his horse away from the road. Where he halted to face Landon, he said: "It's two fellers. One is named Wheaton, the other one Watson. You know them?"

Landon shook his head. "No."

Mitch dug out the dodger and passed it across as he said: "There are two more waiting for you to show up at Deer Lodge. The reward is three thousand dollars. Walt, Wheaton and Watson aren't just scalp hunters. Wheaton is a man I wouldn't want on my trail. Watson . . . well, Watson looks to me like the one who does the gun work, if there's any to be done."

Landon returned the dodger and squatted on his heels. He waited until Mitch was also hunkering, then he said: "You want to know about it?"

"Sure I want to know about it."

"Yeah, I stole the horses. I've got no excuse for that. And I was taking them out of the country. I didn't even know the name of the outfit I stole them from. If I had, it would have helped. The owner's name was Blodgett. He had two sons who thought they owned the world. I didn't know that, either, until one morning when I was breaking camp, maybe seventy, eighty miles westward, and saw two riders on my trail. I headed up into the trees to hide the horses and keep from making dust. But there was eighteen barefoot horses and me on a shod horse, and you can't hide tracks like that in broad daylight. They came right on up to where I'd camped. I had 'em covered with my Winchester. Hell, I was even beginning to regret turning into a horse thief by then, but I sure as hell didn't want to kill anyone." Walt's face split into a rueful smile. "They were going to split up, were going to be real clever. They were moving off when I figured the hell with it . . . I wasn't a very good horse thief, after all . . . and called down to them to stand still. They obeyed me. I told them to hobble their horses and toss down their belt guns. They did those things, too. Then I walked down there . . . and that was my mistake. Anyway, when they saw me, they said a big posse was on the way." Walt ruefully grinned again. "That was a damned lie. I'd been able to see a hundred miles before they showed up. There wasn't any posse. I told 'em they could have their horses back. They said they wanted the hide of a horse thief, too, and I laughed at 'em. They were husky fellers, in their twenties, sort of obnoxious and overbearing. Their paw was a rich rancher . . . but I didn't know that until later. Anyway, when I laughed at 'em, the oldest one did a damn' fool thing, he rushed me. Hell, he wasn't even armed, and I was still holding my Winchester. I just upended it and caught the fool on the jaw with the steel butt plate. He went down like a stone, but the other one was ten feet away and I didn't have a chance to use the gun again. He came in swinging like a windmill. I'll say one thing for the damned fool, he wasn't scared of me."

"And you whipped him," said Mitch.

Walt nodded his head. "Yeah, but I'll hand it to him, he took a lot of beating before he went down and couldn't get up off his knee. The other one never moved. I heard later that when I hit him with the gun butt, it cracked his jaw. The younger one . . . he had the spirit to fight on, but he just couldn't get back onto his feet."

"And?"

Walt shrugged mighty shoulders. "I told him . . . take your damned horses back. I'll help you get your brother on his animal. Leave the guns here."

"That's what they did?"

"Yeah. I think the younger one would have stayed after me except that his brother wasn't up to it. That's all there was to it . . . until later, when I saw one of these dodgers. That's when I figured anyone as mean and vindictive as the father of those fellers would be a good man to get clear away from."

"You were heading for Montana?"

"Yeah. Deer Lodge. I got family up there. But I guess that old son-of-a-bitch's not going to give up, is he?"

"No, not for a while anyway," replied Mitch, and stood up. "You got grub in the saddlebags, Walt?"

The burly cowboy also stood up. "Yeah," he replied, gazing steadily at Mitch. "And a few cartwheels in my pocket, and a good horse." He smiled and gestured. "And ten million acres to get lost in. You know something, Mitch? If I hadn't got tied up with you and Clint, I'd have ridden right on up to Deer Lodge. I guess things sometimes work out for the best. Where are those sons-of-bitches now?"

"Frank doctored their whiskey so they'll sleep for ten hours or so."

That tickled Landon. He laughed and reached to slap Mitch on the shoulder. "You're a hell of a bunch of fellers," he said.

Mitch smiled. "Clint said for me to tell you that you make a hell of a partner."

Landon stood briefly, gazing at Hugh Mitchell, then shoved out a mighty paw. As they shook, he said: "Well, if I got ten hours' head start, I better get to using it, hadn't I?"

Mitch nodded. "Good luck, Walt."

"Same to you . . . and thanks."

For a while Mitch stood beside his horse. When he heard shod hoofs among the broken country out a ways, he mounted and turned back toward Dunnigan.

It was longer going back than it had been going up, probably because he was lost in thought nearly all the way, and probably, too, because since he allowed the horse to walk along on loose

155

reins, the beast did not extend himself any, even though he was heading home.

Dunnigan's roadway was two-thirds dark when Mitch rode down it to the livery barn and left his horse. He went up as far as the jailhouse but did not enter. Up in front of Frank's saloon there were a number of cow horses at the rack. That interested him; he had not expected the ranchers to allow their riders to return so soon.

He considered a nightcap, decided against it, and went to his room up the road, and for the second night in a row slept like a log. In the morning he had barely left the rooming-house porch when a rather raffish older man approached, smiling to announce that Mr. Bennett at the store had asked him to see Mitch yesterday, but he'd had no luck finding the marshal; he was the town carpenter. He and Mitch strolled southward while they discussed coffins for the dead range men in Charley's icehouse, and for some macabre reason the carpenter was amused. Mitch left him to hike on over to the café for breakfast. Several townsmen nodded amiably when he reached the counter. Afterward, while he was standing outside, he remembered seeing a couple of them among Ray Teller's committee men out front of the jailhouse when the range men had walked out. He grinned about that; neither the range men nor the armed committee men had acted as though they had really expected that confrontation.

Over at the jailhouse he fired up the wood stove, set the pot atop it, and decided that today he would clean up the mess in the cell room left behind by his recent prisoners. He did not get a chance to do it. Charley Bennett arrived, looking solemn. He knew about old Harriman's passing and surprised Mitch by offering to pay for the pine box, and for the preacher's services. Mitch almost liked Charley at that moment. They discussed the arrangements, then Charley said: "And the carpenter was over to take measurements for those men in the icehouse. Maybe the town could shave a little off the cost by burying them and old Josh Harriman at the same time."

Mitch sighed. "Maybe. Who makes those arrangements?"

"I'll do it. I've done it lots of times before. By the way, about that deputy marshal the council set aside money for . . . do you think you'll really need him, now that we've got the cattlemen straightened out?"

Mitch went to lean on the desk, regarding Bennett. "No, I guess not," he replied, thinking privately that the only man he would had liked to have fill that position was somewhere in the mountains, heading west.

Charley beamed. "Good. There's no substitute for money saved." He went to the door and nodded, then departed, and after he was gone Mitch muttered sourly—"Now that *we* got the cattlemen straightened out."—and went to check the coffee pot.

An hour later Wheaton and Watson walked in. Watson looked pale and Wheaton's sunk-set eyes were not only not smiling, they showed pure malevolence. Mitch accepted this; in fact, he felt more comfortable with Wheaton looking like that, because he felt it was the man's genuine disposition showing. He could react better when he knew someone was being natural with him.

He said—"Coffee's hot, gents."—in a genial tone of voice.

The older man stared icily back. "You know the penalty under the law for aiding and abetting a fugitive from the law, Marshal?"

Mitch leaned on the desk, both arms crossed. "Yeah, I guess the town council will fire me."

Watson sat down, but the older man remained standing. "You think we won't get him?"

"Who are you talking about, Mister Wheaton?"

The tall man flushed red. "You know damned well who I'm talking about! You and that barman . . . and that big feller who works for the blacksmith, and anyone else around this stinking cow town who . . ."

"Wait a minute," interjected Hugh Mitchell. "The man down south got his horses back, didn't he?"

"A damned horse thief is still a horse thief," insisted Jim Wheaton.

Mitch did not deny this. He said: "Yeah, I reckon that's right, but a horse thief down south isn't necessarily a horse thief up here in Thunder Valley. Up here, he was about half again as much of a man as I figure you ever were." Mitch unfolded both arms and let them hang while he and Jim Wheaton exchanged a long, cold look. Then Mitch also said: "Mister, I'll take a horse thief any day of the year as opposed to a man packing one of those governor's warrants. Now you gents do whatever you think you've got to do . . . then get the hell out of Dunnigan."

"I'll send for a federal marshal, that's what I'll do, Marshal. You can get five years for what you've done."

Mitch replied softly. "What did I do? Did you see me do it? Did your friend there see me do anything?"

Homer Watson spoke for the first time. "That feller at the saloon put something in the whiskey. He sure as hell didn't do that just for the hell of it. I got the damnedest headache I ever had."

Mitch turned slightly to gaze at the narrow-faced younger man. "If I were you, I wouldn't go around town saying that. We've got a lot of roiled-up people in Dunnigan right now. We've got three dead men to bury today who thought they could buffalo the town and be troublesome, too." He faced Wheaton again. "Go on up to Deer Lodge, Mister Wheaton, and when you see the man who lost those horses, tell him for me he's damned lucky his sons didn't get killed. A lot of men, if they were jumped by two fools when he was armed . . . well, that cowman wouldn't have any sons now." Mitch strode to the door, opened it, and waited. Jim Wheaton did not seem ready to depart just yet, but the younger man arose and plodded outside without even glancing back, so Wheaton went, too, but when he was on the plank walk, he turned another venomous look toward Hugh Mitchell before they both went up in the direction of the rooming house.

Mitch watched them, then walked down to Teller's shop. Clint was out back, working on another wagon. Ray was washing in the clinker bucket and eyeing a freshly shod handsome big thoroughbred-type bay horse. He turned and nodded. "Did you see some range men come to town last night?" he asked, and when Mitch nodded and looked for a clean place to sit down, the blacksmith also said: "Kershaw's bunch. I was up there having a jolt with Frank. There were a couple of strangers . . . they had a drink at the bar, walked out, and didn't get more'n two-thirds of the way across the road in the direction of your office, and down they went. A feller came into the saloon and we all went out to see." Ray finished rinsing, reached for a foul old towel to wipe off with, and shook his head. "Men who can't handle whiskey any better'n that hadn't ought never touch a drop of the stuff. We hauled them up and dumped them at the rooming house. When I went back, Frank was smiling. That's the first time I've seen him do that since he got it in the leg. It must be bothering him less now."

The liveryman came over for the handsome big bay horse, and Ray untied him, led him outside to make him track so that the liveryman could watch with a critical eye. Mitch went out back where Clint was cursing over a tire he was having a difficult time fitting to the wheel. Clint looked around, shook off sweat, and waited until Mitch was perched on an old anvil.

"He's gone," stated the marshal. "Thanks for getting the strangers to Frank's place."

"Frank told me who they were, and the rest of it." Clint shook off more sweat. "I've been thinkin' about Walt. I could see where he might steal horses, but hell. . . ."

Mitch understood his cousin's dilemma. "I guess maybe it's the disposition," he said. "Some men are more forceful and direct than other men. What I *do* know is that a man who might preach here in Dunnigan on a Sunday could be a hell of a poker player thirty miles away in some other town the next Saturday night, along with the cussing and whiskey-drinking that goes with a lively card session."

"Will they catch him?"

"I doubt it. But if they do, at least he knows now they're looking for him."

Clint considered the tire he had been struggling with as he said: "I don't think I'd want to be in anyone's boots who got on the wrong side of Walt." Then he turned and winked at Mitch. "Goin' back to everyday work is going to be tiresome." He reached for the steel tire. "But I've had all the excitement I reckon I'm goin' to need for a long time. Hold that damned wheel up for me, will you? I made this tire to the exact measurements a few days back, and some idiot let it get wet out here, and now the wood's swollen and I can't get the tire on it." They worked for a half hour before the tire was finally forced onto the wheel. Mitch left his cousin to do the rest of the fitting and walked up to the saloon.

Frank was finishing some fried meat and cornbread with a glass of beer when Mitch entered. He shoved the plate out of sight below the bar, offered to stand Mitch to a drink, and when the lawman declined, Frank sucked his teeth for a moment, gazing at his front window, then said: "I'll tell you something. I figured those two sons-of-bitches would buy two drinks so I only put a little stuff in their first drink. Then, by golly, they walked out of here, and I was sweating bullets. I figured it hadn't worked and they'd be looking for you."

Mitch was thinking of Watson's face when he dryly said: "It worked. They were in the jailhouse about an hour ago. The younger one looked green to the gills and the other feller was mad as a wet hen."

"Where are they now?"

"Gone I guess. At least I told them to leave town."

"How about Landon?"

Mitch changed his mind. "One glass of beer," he said, and watched Frank hobble after it. "I told him they were looking for him. He left the country."

Frank hobbled back and placed the glass in a sticky ring. "I hope he makes it. For a fact I do. Kershaw's riders were in last night." Mitch nodded and tasted the beer. "I'll tell you one thing. Between you and old Kershaw's wife, they got a lot of respect. Mostly you. They talked about last Saturday night. One feller quit when he got back to the ranch. They need a replacement. Too bad Landon's gone, eh?"

Mitch finished the beer before replying. "Yeah, but if he'd been out there, those bastards would most likely have got him. Frank, that's awful beer."

Sabin's dark eyes rested steadily upon Mitch for a moment. "Someone told me before you came up here you were managing a freight outfit."

"That's right."

"Mitch, I've been at this trade about half my life. Of all the fellers a man serves from behind a bar, the ones who know the least about good beer from bad are freighters. Then comes lawmen. Then comes cowboys. That's *good* beer."

Mitch considered the swarthy man a moment, then laughed. After a moment Frank joined in. Then he said: "It's maybe a little green. Every batch I make doesn't turn out the same. It's got to do with the amount of dust in the air."

The room was empty, the stove was lighted even though it was warm out, and Frank was feeling for his cigar box under the counter when old Bailer came in, smiling toothlessly from ear to ear. Frank took his hand out of the cigar box and straightened back up, then turned to get a bottle and glass. As he set them before the wizened old man, he said: "I was right sorry to hear about your old partner dying."

Bailer filled his glass. He was in a philosophical mood this morning. "Yeah, he's the only feller I ever knew who could play checkers by feel. And them cards you fixed for him, Frank. Maybe he never told you, but he told *me,* and that meant a lot to him, too. He was real fond of you." Bailer drank his shot of whiskey and set down the glass gently. "I think we really ought to have one to send old Harriman on his way, don't you, Marshal? He thought an awful lot of Frank. Used to say old Frank had a heart of gold."

164

Mitch turned and saw the look Frank was putting upon Bailer. He laughed in spite of himself, and Frank picked up the bottle to refill Bailer's glass, wagging his head disgustedly all the while.

Later, over at the jailhouse, Mitch was closing the stove damper when George Luckner walked in. Mitch was surprised, but not very greatly. He offered the handsome, graying man a cup of coffee that Luckner declined. He was wearing his gun belt with the sterling silver big filigreed buckle. "I brought the crew in for the funerals," he said, not sounding unfriendly but not sounding particularly friendly, either. He looked at Mitch for a few moments, then went to a chair, and sat down. "I heard in town a while back that cowboy with the whiskers who rode with you was in trouble with the law."

Mitch nodded as he went to the desk chair.

"What did he do?"

"Stole some horses and larruped a couple of fellers who ran him down."

"And now he's gone?"

"Yes. Why?"

Luckner crossed his legs. "I'm short three men. I could have used one like him." Luckner's eyes swept upward to Mitch's face. "Mostly, I need a range boss. It pays better than being a town marshal."

Mitch smiled at the cowman. "I'm obliged for

the offer . . . if it is one . . . but I've done my share of that kind of work, Mister Luckner."

The cowman looked around the dingy little room, nodding his head. "I didn't think you'd accept," he mused, and dropped his gaze back to Mitch's face. "I'll tell you something. You were right all along. We all knew it. I suppose you could call it pride, but you were a stranger, a fella who rode into town with nothing, and started laying down the law to those of us who could . . ."

"Buy and sell me any day of the week?"

"Something like that, yes," Luckner replied, and arose with his hand outstretched. "There are all kinds of fools, aren't there . . . but the biggest ones are the prideful ones."

Mitch arose to shake. "After the burials, if you're of a mind, Mister Luckner, I'd like to buy you a drink." The cowman accepted without smiling but with a look of respect in his eyes, then he went out into the warm sunshine leaving Mitch feeling satisfied, finally.

THE STORY OF BUCKHORN

I

Gard sat relaxed behind the cigar smoke and looked at Elisa Benton. She was good to look at. His gray eyes were thoughtful as the stream of her talk engulfed the supper table in the low-ceilinged room, where generations of Gard's people, the Ashleys, had eaten and talked. He shifted his glance a little and saw his older brother beside Elisa. Court was drinking in each word, every little gesture that accompanied Elisa's conversation, with a relaxed, fixed smile. Gard kept his own face impassive in spite of the dislike he felt, and looked at the girl again.

Elisa Benton was more than a singer at Russell's Varieties in Yankton. She was the undisputed queen of the frontier professionals. This included everything from dancers to variety girls, singers, actresses, players—the lot. She had startling amber eyes, creamy flesh, and a handsome, even beautiful, face. The rest of her was just as good to look at. The waist was small, flat and supple below a breath-taking bosom of grand proportions that stood out proudly, rising and falling with each breath, and the rest of her was similarly striking and symmetrical. But Gard still didn't like her. It wasn't the woman's looks. It was a number of small things, the things she talked of, the way she talked of them, and the hard, slumbering fire that moved far back in the depths of her eyes every now and then.

He arose slowly, nodding gently with an effort to keep irony from showing in his face or actions, and smiled at them both. "Excuse me, will you? There's some paperwork that has to be done tonight. I'm sorry. . . ." He was moving away toward the office across the large living room when Court called after him.

"Gard, it'll keep, won't it? I told Elisa you'd play the banjo for her." There was irritation in the deep voice.

He turned, saw the annoyance in his brother's undisciplined face, and looked beyond it to the girl. She was looking straight at him, saying nothing. He smiled back and shrugged.

Court Ashley was his brother. His older brother at that, and yet he was a problem to Gard. A profligate with his share of the estate, Court spent lavishly, lived riotously, fought at the drop of a hat, and was notorious for a short temper and a shorter tolerance. Gard mused in the soft light. This Elisa Benton had Court in the palm of her hand. He had actually given her $3,000. For what, Gard neither knew nor cared. It was the fact that Court refused to return any of his profits from the ranch that rankled Gard most. He had to make it up out of his share. When their parents had died in a runaway, Buckhorn had been the mightiest ranch in Cortez Valley. It still was, but Gard's acumen alone kept it that way. Buckhorn was more than a ranch and home to Gard Ashley; it was his life and love as well.

The night was quiet. Just the usual sounds of a large cow-calf operation. Horses squealing across corral bars at one another. A cow bellowing for her calf that she couldn't find in the dark, getting no answer because the calf was full anyway and trying to sleep. Infrequent howls of laughter from the log bunkhouse where the nightly ritual of poker was in session. These, and the vague fragrance of a summer night with its perfume of bleached-out, cured grass, oily junipers, and brittle brush, sumac, sage, manzanita, and the huge old cottonwoods that had been planted decades ago around the ranch buildings, all conspired to gentle Gard's thoughts of his brother and this woman with the spirit of steel—and fire.

He fished around for a cigar, found one in a desk drawer, licked it, bit, and lit up. He was drawing in some of the smoke when someone rapped lightly on the great oaken door. Without moving, Gard called out: "Come in."

It was Elisa Benton. Gard was surprised. The stunning amber eyes flicked over him as she closed the door, went over the bare desk top, and back to his face with a wry little smile. "All this work that had to be done . . . it wasn't so, was it?"

Gard arose easily, and held out the chair his feet had been athwart of. She sat down like the lady most men considered her to be. Gard returned to his own chair, regarding her levelly, not answering.

"Gard . . . why?"

"Why, what?"

"Why don't you like me?"

He sucked on the cigar, wondering at her candor. "Odd you should ask that."

"Oh?"

"Yes, because I don't like you and you know it. Generally that's sufficient."

Elisa shook her head. The black hair absorbed the lamplight. "I don't agree. When folks are disliked, they want to know why. Don't you?"

He shook his head at her. She noticed how the light reflected a dull, metallic rust color from his hair. "No. I don't care. Usually I can guess the reason, anyway."

"Well . . . what about me? What have I done?"

Gard shifted a little in the chair. "Hadn't you better go back to Court? He'll be wondering where you are."

"No, he had to go talk to your foreman about something. All right, you evaded it nicely. Will you tell me now?"

Gard wagged his head again without a sound, exhaled a gust of bluish smoke, and smiled thinly at her. "No. 'Fraid not. Court's bad enough as he is. If I told you anything that would antagonize him, you'd tell him the first time you wanted to strike at me."

"Why would I want to . . . strike at you, as you put it?"

"Ma'am, I don't know, and, like I said, I don't care."

Elisa stood up, looking down at him thoughtfully. "You're quite a man at that. Maybe I snared the wrong one of the Ashley brothers."

It was her tone that stung. Gard put down the cigar. "Lady, you haven't got either, yet. But this one wouldn't touch you with a prod pole. Another thing, too, the next time you lift three thousand dollars from an Ashley, have your things packed. You won't stay in Cortez Valley ten hours afterward." He saw the fire spring up in her light golden eyes. "Now you can see why I wouldn't tell you anything you could use to drive a wedge between my brother and me, can't you?"

The savage flames were licking far in the background of the amber eyes. "You . . . think everyone fights like you do, don't you?"

"I fight fair, Elisa. When I'm pushed, I fight, but I don't stoop to win."

"You must," she said, "otherwise you wouldn't think others do. If you think I'd fight you by driving a wedge between you and Court, you're mistaken. I have standards, if you haven't."

Gard arose and smiled coldly at her. "Let's leave it like that, ma'am."

"No. Not yet. You mentioned the three thousand dollars."

"I'm not interested in what it was for, Elisa. Just remember what I said, the next time you're tempted. Good night."

Elisa stood without moving, looking up at him, seeing the thin nose with the flaring nostrils, the wide, steely gray eyes, scornful-looking now, and the proud set of his head above the column of his neck and shoulders. Then she turned gracefully and left the office.

Gard sat down again, picked up the cigar, sucked on it, found it out, and sat still, holding it between his teeth, mixing saliva and juice together and swallowing them both. His mind went to many things, but always the thoughts came back to Buckhorn Ranch, the great herds, the far boundary lines, the oceans of grass, and the purple mountains to the west that were the bulwarks of his domain. He made a wry face at the wall, below the oval pictures of his parents who looked down austerely at him. There was just one thing in life for Gard Ashley. Buckhorn, the Ashley empire in Cortez Valley.

Gard guessed it was late when the light in the bunkhouse went out, and shortly after he heard Court's gig wheel lightly out of the yard, heading for Yankton. He turned slightly, looked out the window, and saw the girl sitting beside the hulk of his brother. He got up, stretched mightily, tossed the cigar away, and shrugged, watching the moving shadow of the buggy and team, rolling against the lighter background of darkness.

Court would probably marry this one. That made him smile wryly. There would have to be another house built at Buckhorn, because he couldn't imagine Elisa Benton and himself living under the same roof. He went out of the office, across the empty living room to his own room, and went to bed. The last thought he had was of the strange, vital fire that showed in Elisa's eyes when she was angry. He smiled sardonically and went to sleep.

Buckhorn came to life ponderously and reluctantly when the cook beat the triangle. Gard lay there, listening, mentally taking the pulse of the big ranch. He knew, for instance, if the cook hit the triangle more than four stunning, reverberating blows, he would harvest an immediate crop of profane abuse from the men in the bunkhouse. Four blows came and went, then the racket stopped as abruptly as it had begun. He arose, cleansed himself, dressed, and went through the house. A faint odor of whiskey and tobacco clung there, like it does in the womanless household of all cattlemen.

They ate mostly in silence, and Gard listened as Buck Gault, the foreman, gave out orders and positions to the riders. He saw Court come in late, grab a dish full of hoecakes, eat standing, and head for the door with the rest of the men.

"Court . . . see you a minute?"

The older brother turned, his jumper dangling from one arm, and came back where Gard had several papers in his hands, standing beside the long table.

"Here, this one goes to Johnson of the railroad office at Hurd's Crossing. It's a copy of our tally sheet. This one here, in the envelope, you're to mail at the Crossing. It's for Kansas City, so they'll know the beef is on the road, and this one here is for old Clarendon. It's the usual power-of-attorney thing for the draft."

Court took the papers and tucked them away in his wallet. "Did they deposit cash or vouchers this time?"

"They said cash. Clarendon'll know. It doesn't make much difference, though. They're reliable."

"I reckon. Well, you'll see Martin at Yankton, so I'll have a clear run when I bring the money back?"

Gard nodded. "Yeah. I'll ride into town in another hour or so and tell him you're bringing the money back for our account." Gard looked at his massive brother with a wistfulness that went back to boyhood. He smiled and stuck out his hand. It was an Ashley ritual. Court had taken every annual Buckhorn drive for the last seven years. Gard was the brains, Court the brawn. They shook, embarrassedly as always, every year it was the same, then Court raised his head and looked at Gard.

"Do you like her?"

It was totally unexpected. Gard was already smiling so he let it stay there when he inclined his head. "Prettiest woman I ever saw, Court. You're lucky."

The big features relaxed a little. "I'm glad," he said simply. "I asked her to marry me, last night."

Gard was numb all over but he had sense enough to let the smile that had become a grimace slide off his face. "What'd she say?"

Court swore feelingly. "Wouldn't come right out and answer. Women're funny that way."

"But you're confident?"

Court smiled. It changed his face entirely. Made him look almost shy, which he certainly wasn't. "I reckon," he said. "But I got to work on her a little more. It takes time."

"Good luck," Gard said.

Court was self-conscious. He pulled on his gloves and smiled again without looking up. "Thanks, Gard. *Adiós*."

"*Adiós*."

The sound of Court's spurs sounded like distant cowbells in the empty, sepulcher silence of the big dining room. Gard listened to them fade away without moving. It wasn't that he didn't want

Court to get married; it was just that Buckhorn was a man's empire. He couldn't visualize a woman there at all, least of all a woman like Elisa Benton. He went through the kitchen from habit, took down his jumper from the rack near the back door, and stomped out into the pre-dawn chill, listening. The seven-hundred head of grassed-out steers, as uniform and slick as moles with lots of tallow under them, were being roused from the bedding grounds. Gard could hear the distant cries of the riders encouraging them to move out. The animals were lowing protestingly, grumpily, like they did every year, and had since he could remember, which was over thirty years, then the sounds lessened as the animals were lined out over the trail.

Gard went down to the barn, roped a horse from the leftovers in the corral, saddled up, and rode east toward Yankton. He would arrive too early for business, but he had never gone to bed after a drive had started in his life. Now, there was the unpleasantness of his thoughts about his brother and Elisa Benton to occupy him as he rode.

Coffee at the Burch House, which was open, although empty, because it was the stage stop, warmed Gard a little. In spite of the scorching summer heat of daylight, the pre-dawn was always cold, summer or winter, in Cortez Valley. Johnny Curtain, the sheriff, brought his coffee over and sat down beside Gard. Johnny was a likeable, lazy man, an ex-rider who had traded his saddle for a chair and drew sly satisfaction from the fact that he rarely had to ride in bad weather any more and, when he did, got better pay for doing it. He was a little shorter than Gard, and maybe five years older, with an infectious, raffish smile and ready laugh. Still, he was a man thoroughly versed and willing with the gun he wore thonged to his right leg.

"Once a year you show up like this, Gard. Cattle drive?"

Gard smiled a greeting and nodded. "Yeah. Court's taking them to Hurd's Crossing."

"How many head this year?"

"A little under last year, Johnny. Seven hundred."

"Rough spring?"

"No, about like always. Just can't get 'em even enough."

Johnny grunted. "Well, when I was making up herds for XIH, they used to send what was fat. Nowadays they all got to be uniform."

"They don't have to be. Bring a better price if they are, is all." Gard looked over at the sheriff. "What's got you hanging around in here, this time of morning?"

Curtain shrugged. "Oh, I had to take over tonight . . . last night, rather. My deputy got sick on me." He smiled broadly. "Don't care much, though. There's some more girls coming in for the Varieties on the six o'clock stage. I'll get first look anyway."

Gard's mind snapped immediately to Elisa Benton. He downed the last of his coffee and fished for a tobacco sack. "Johnny, you know Elisa Benton very well?"

"Not as well as I'd like to. Why?"

"Just curious. She hits me as being sort of . . . well . . . cold."

Sheriff Curtain looked up, astonished, then his raffish smile came up slowly. "She sure as hell don't hit me that way at all. No siree. Prettier'n a Christmas tree to me."

"I don't mean looks."

"Listen, you're always thinking of cattle. Of Buckhorn. Why don't you get a woman, a wife? They're handy things to have around."

Gard grinned slyly. "When did you get married?"

Curtain laughed. "I'm still looking, pardner, still looking. Don't think I won't, when the right one comes along." The laugh died out but the twinkle remained. "Y'know what the boys say around the livery barn?" Gard shook his head. "They say Gard Ashley's married to the biggest, fattest, calviest female in the world."

"Who do they mean?"

"The Buckhorn."

They both laughed, Johnny Curtain uproariously, Gard wryly, shaking his head.

"Well, they got something there at that, Johnny. *One* of us has to stick to business."

That sobered the sheriff but he didn't take it up. He knew the Ashley stock. They might growl at one another, but Lord help the outsider who jumped in. He looked over Gard's head, listening. "She's coming, cowman." He got up, taking the coffee mugs. "I'll draw us two more cups so we can relax and look 'em over. Besides," he threw over his shoulder, "after they're through, there might not be any left."

Gard was still smoking his cigarette, letting it dangle thoughtlessly from his lips, the smoke curling up so that his eyes were narrowed under the chocolate-colored Stetson tilted forward on his head, when the stage rattled to a stop and people disgorged, tumbling inside the restaurant, beating their hands against the chill. He could feel Johnny's interest as the three pretty girls came, threw a rapid, appraising glance over the place, and went up to the counter and sat down.

"Easy, Johnny, easy." It was said in a low, mocking voice that made the sheriff smile in spite of his preoccupation. Gard was turned, looking at the newcomers, when he saw something move at the corner of his vision. He turned and found himself looking up into the amber gold eyes of Elisa Benton. Their glances held; the girl nodded slightly, saw Johnny's eyes glued to the new arrivals, and showed an ironic humor that Gard hadn't seen in her before. He could feel the antagonism before she spoke.

"I thought you were cattle driving this morning."

"No. Court does that." He was immediately conscious of a feeling of inferiority, the way it sounded.

"Oh?" It had daggers of ice in it. "Court, the work horse." The amber eyes went back to the pretty girls at the counter, then dropped to Gard's face again. "This is a better pastime for the *brains* of Buckhorn, isn't it?"

Gard flushed without answering, then he arose, still looking down into her face, and smiled. "I thought that's about the way you were built. Saying things like that in public." He turned away from the abrupt sheathing of flame that lashed out at him from the amber eyes, and walked outside, angry with her—and with himself as well.

Yankton was stirring and awake. Stores were open now and people were hustling to beat the heat with their chores and shopping. Gard saw the bank's shade was up and crossed the manure-littered road, rattled the door, and was admitted by George Martin himself.

Martin's smile flickered briefly. "In my office, Gard. I've got a second's more work out here, then I'll be right in."

Gard went to the office, took a chair, and sat down, looking moodily out at the cow town.

His thoughts went back to the latest exchange between himself and Elisa Benton. It confirmed his dislike of the woman more than ever.

George Martin hurried in, leaned over his desk, and arranged some loose papers with tireless fingers before he sat down. "What'll you have, Gard?"

"Court's taken the drive to rail's end. He'll be back with the money tomorrow. You know how Court is about paperwork. Thought you'd take care of it while I'm in town."

"Sure, of course. You'll sign 'em and all Court'll have to do is leave the money. Like last year, right?"

Gard nodded. "Right."

The banker arose again, fished around for some paper, and headed for the door. "I'll have Maudlin fill 'em out. Be right back."

Gard waited until Martin returned, signed the papers, filled in the amounts with a preoccupied air, took up his hat and nodded thanks, then went back outside. The sun was working itself up to its usual summer fury. He drifted down to the livery barn, got his horse, and rode slowly back toward Buckhorn.

He was still two miles from the ranch buildings when he saw a top buggy whirling toward him in the shimmering heat waves. He reined up, slackened the reins and waited.

Elisa Benton pulled up the livery team, eased

off the lines, and looked up at Gard. "I've been to the ranch. You weren't there . . . hadn't gotten back yet."

"Naturally," he said dryly, slouching forward, hands clasped easily over the horn. "Anyone in Yankton could've told you that."

The amber eyes flashed sparks but her beautiful features were pulled off center a little, the way she bit her under lip to force back the angry retort that was dammed up behind her teeth. "Please, Gard. Isn't there some way we can be friends?"

It startled him, but he recovered quickly. "I don't know of any." It was tartly spoken. "Why should we be?"

"Because Court asked me to marry him."

"I know. You wouldn't accept him, though, and that's to your credit."

"I didn't say yes because of you."

"That's not the only reason."

"What other one is there?"

"You'd have to earn your money, then. Besides, you don't love Court."

Elisa's restraint was fast failing. Her eyes were narrowing, and the sunlight wasn't responsible, either. "Gard, aside from being despicable, you're ignorant . . . and blind."

He lifted the reins, preparatory to riding on. She held him with her glance, determined to hurt him like he had hurt her. "I don't think you want Court to marry. I think you're in love yourself, with Buckhorn. If that's so, I pity any woman that ever goes there to live. It's warped you . . . your precious Buckhorn, but it hasn't warped Court yet . . . and I hope it never does. You know why? Because, as long as he stays himself, he'll be a thorn in your flesh, and I can always look back on *that* with no regrets."

Gard regarded her somberly. She *was* handsome, no doubt about it. He wondered if Court had ever seen her angry, and doubted it. His brother was the type that an intelligent woman could mold like clay. He would be a Sampson for one smart woman, and Gard had no doubt he was looking at the one woman on earth who could reduce proud, truculent, boyish Court Ashley to clay, and, ironically, Court would be robbing himself of something fascinating, too. He'd never see the magnificent tigress in Elisa Benton, either. The best of her would wither and die, with Court. It made a sardonic smile tug at the corners of his mouth.

"What are you smiling about, you . . . ?"

"Elisa, if I had your disposition, I'd cull wildcats for a living. Let me tell you something. You're not the woman for Court Ashley, and he's not the man for you. Court's rough and naive, but somebody like you would take all the fire out of him. Without his temper, Court wouldn't be anything more than a four-bit-a-day cowboy."

"And you! A bloodless block of ice!" She was

185

on the defensive and it angered her to think he had outmaneuvered her, as much as his words did.

Gard laughed outright, and saw the rust stain her throat and face. "No, I don't think so. Tell me . . . what made you change your mind so quickly? This morning you were a real rattlesnake at the Burch House. What happened?"

"I've already told you. Court asked me to marry him. I wanted to see if you wouldn't change your opinion of me."

He began shaking his head before she finished. There was scorn in his look. "That's not the truth, either, ma'am."

"What do you mean?"

"Elisa, why do you care whether I'm your friend or not, when you don't intend to marry Court?" He raised his head a little to forestall the answer she was framing. "No you don't. There are only two ways you would marry him. For spite . . . and for money. You had some other reason for riding to Buckhorn. What was it, a hope I'd buy you off?"

Elisa's knuckles were white where she gripped the lines. Very deliberately and slowly she leaned forward, took the whip from its socket, raised it, and lashed out. The little braided tip went flashing through the air. Gard saw it coming and braced against the blow without taking his eyes off her face. Just the bulge of jaw muscles showed when the lash cut him across the right cheek under the eye and let a heavy drop of scarlet gather at the base of the cut for a moment, before it fell on to his knee. He saw the sudden shock and horror spread out like a film of light oil, in her eyes. The wound stung enough to make him conscious of it and no more.

"That's my answer, isn't it?" he said contemptuously. "Like the answer I got this morning at the Burch House. And you're the one that fights fair. That's you through and through, Elisa. I reckon you know now why we'll never be friends." The gray eyes were flails. They scourged her soul if not her body. He straightened in the saddle, still looking at her without moving an eyelash. "Now, I'm going to tell you this. If you marry Court, Elisa, I'll break you like I would a rustler who steals Buckhorn beef. Remember that. You're evidently after money. Don't go near Court again, or Buckhorn, to get it, or you'll beg me to use a buggy whip on you before I'm through."

Elisa's emotions were a roll of confusion. She hated the lean, harsh man with the swelling, bleeding cheek like she had never hated anyone in her life before, but she couldn't strike him again, although her anger was overwhelming. There was nothing she could say, either. He had deliberately let her do it. Faced her anger with the hope of an open cause for a personal war between them, and had looked at his hate and contempt unflinchingly when she had lashed him. Actually she felt ill. She sat there, looking up at him, feeling sick to her stomach and shaken.

"Well," her voice was flat and dead sounding, "I guess I shouldn't have . . . come out." The amber eyes were dull. It didn't look natural to Gard. "It was a mistake from start to finish."

He nodded slightly. "I reckon. But you got one thing you wanted. A good wedge to pry Court away from his brother with. A means to stir up trouble."

"No," she said slowly. "I told you I didn't fight that way and I meant it. I'm handing your precious brother back to you right here. Now, your mighty Buckhorn is intact again, like you want it, at no cost to you."

"Well," Gard said dryly, lifting his reins and turning his horse a little as he spoke, "at very small cost, anyway. Just a cheap cut from a buggy whip, and Court's three thousand dollars."

Elisa saw the horse flick its tail once, as he nudged it with the heavily silver-overlaid spurs, and loped away. She slapped the team. A shudder shook her, then the sobs welled up and overflowed in spite of her, and it made her furious. Swearing blisteringly, she tooled the buggy over the Buckhorn range toward town, half sick and completely miserable—and angrier than she had ever been in her life.

Gard didn't raise his hand to his cheek until he knew she was out of sight, then he reined up, felt the sullen, angry flesh gingerly, dabbed at the drying blood as he loped out again toward Buckhorn.

When he got home, he turned the horse out, hung his saddle, and flung the bridle over the horn with short, savage movements, and went into the house to the office. There was a half empty bottle of rye whiskey on top of the desk. He drank two shots, fast, fished for a cigar, cursed because he couldn't find one, and made a cigarette, inhaled deeply, and turned toward the window. The surprise of seeing his own hands shake calmed him a little. He frowned down at them, letting the smoke drift upward. He had never seen his hands shake from anger before. It puzzled him vastly, then he had an uneasy thought that there might be something else inside of him at work, as well as his violent hatred of Elisa Benton. He tried to analyze his feelings but gave it up with a disgusted grunt and went over to the desk. There wasn't much to do, really, but there were always a hundred small, insignificant tasks, like tag ends, that he could do, so he did them.

The heat gradually stole into the house and routed him from the office. He ate moodily and went back outside. Afternoon was descending. He sat on the verandah and drew a measure of inner peace from the panorama of breath-taking beauty that spread out in all directions from the old house. He was still sitting there after dusk, the dead fires of his anger banked and cold, when he heard the hard-riding horseman thundering down the land. The sound was far off, but it had an insistence that made Gard get up, peer intently over the shadowy, ghostly range, listening. He went down off the verandah, out into the yard, and made another cigarette, lit it, and waited. The rider was getting closer. He scowled uneasily, in spite of a vague premonition that was stirring within him. He was first a stockman. There could be few reasons for riding a horse like that in the middle of summer.

The silhouette rocketed toward him. He recognized Buck Gault and fear clutched his heart because the foreman was too old a hand to kill a horse for something trivial. Perhaps it was the raw aura of disaster that emanated from Gault as he slid the horse and swung down, white-faced and shocked-looking, but Gard knew, before the words were spoken, in some mysterious way what the message was Buck had brought.

"Gard! Court's dead. Shot down and robbed by four men west of Hurd's Crossing."

II

Hurd's Crossing was an ugly town with just one reason for existence—the end of the railroad tracks that came across the giant land like parallel steel snakes, and followed each curve and rise of the turbulent belly of Cortez Valley. It was a slatternly town, too, where cattlemen, section hands, freighters, gamblers, and dozens of other varieties of frontier life met, and jockeyed for supremacy, each a clique of virile, hardened men with the law of the States behind them in the turbulence of the Dakota Territory. There was none of the staid, calm temperament that Yankton had. Hurd's Crossing wasn't a cow town anyway; it was a melting pot of men, ideals, and cross-purposes. Like any boom town, Hurd's Crossing was a madhouse of noises, smells, faces, and pitfalls.

Gard absorbed all this with a sense of repugnance. He rode in, saw the harassed sheriff, and rode out once more. There was nothing more known than what he had already heard from Buck Gault and others. Court had left the Crossing, riding toward Yankton, that's all anyone knew. Later, some freighters had found his riderless horse, then the dead rider. Shot in the back, his clothes torn, and the money belt gone, Court

Ashley had been brought back to Hurd's Crossing lashed indifferently inside a stinking freight wagon, and Gard knew the rest. Buck had sent the Buckhorn riders through town to see what they could pick up, which was nothing, and he had ridden for Buckhorn as fast as he could.

The daylight waned slowly, lean shadows flattening out over the cured grass and rocky stretches of earth, making a somber, sullen land as far as he could see, sowed and beaten by the flagellation of blasting sunlight. He rode with bitterness for a companion, a solitary man, like steel in spit and features, saddened by the sense of loss that robbed something from his world—though something that hadn't fully belonged. Conscious, too, of something within himself that hadn't been there before, something that shouldn't have been there, either, because it was new and beyond description, too vague and nebulous for a name. He shrugged out of the twisted corridors of his mind, remotely aware of an inner need that was being starved into great proportions, confused by it, and goaded, too, lashing out in blind and furious resentment against it, using the murder of Court as the outlet for this undefined feeling.

Yankton was rowdy with night life when Gard rode into town, swung off the main thoroughfare, and tied up at the iron post before a blistered, sagging picket fence, and walked to the house beyond, where merry squares of golden lamplight threw distorted shadows over his gaunt, tired, slack-muscled face.

The doctor was a wiry, bird-like man with a deep, calm look. He motioned toward the small private office off the living room with its closed inner doors with a hand that flicked into the warm atmosphere like a conqueror's fist waving a flag of triumph.

"Gard Ashley. Glad to see you, son. You don't get sick often enough to drop in any more." The intent blue eyes studied the weary sag of Gard's face, the delicate, wonderful hands sought out pockets and hid themselves, and the doctor closed the office door and pushed forward a straight-backed chair. "Sit down. We'll visit a spell."

"Doc, Court's dead. Ambushed by four men this side of Hurd's Crossing. I came here because you're the undertaker. They're bringing him over in a buggy. I rode ahead to tell you."

The doctor's eyes stopped moving in his face and grew round. He had known both the Ashley boys since childhood, and their parents before them. "Court," he said, stunned. There was a silence while the doctor remembered what he had heard shortly before Gard had ridden up. That Court had taken the Buckhorn beef to rail's end. He had heard it from their supper guest who was beyond the doors of the living room, visiting with his wife. "Good Lord. I saw Court yesterday."

"I reckon," Gard said. "Will you take care of the burial end of things for me . . . let me know what you work out and send word when the funeral'll be?"

"Of course, Gard. Naturally." The intent blue eyes came up. "Have the killers been found. Did you talk to the law over at the Crossing?"

"They don't know any more than I do. Than you will, by tomorrow night, when the boys get back."

"Was it robbery, Gard?"

He nodded. "Yes." A thought crept into his mind. Court had been riding back toward Yankton, ahead of the Buckhorn riders. There had been a reason, of course. The odds were very good that his brother was hurrying back like that, recklessly, disdainfully, like he did a lot of things, in order to press his suit with Elisa Benton. Court had said he had to "work on her a little more." What else could have made him ride out alone like that, with $70,000 in his money belt?

The doctor turned abruptly and went to the door, flung it open, and bobbed his head. "Come on."

Wondering, Gard followed. They went to the kitchen in the back of the house by devious ways that avoided the living room. The doctor poured two large mugs of coffee, gave Gard one and kept one for himself. The remains of a roast duck dinner lay in fragrant disarray. Gard pushed some of the plates aside, sat down at the kitchen table, and dumped his hat on the floor beside his chair. The coffee was hot and bracing. The doctor wandered out of the room, still holding his coffee cup, and Gard scarcely noticed. He didn't know he was conscious of the low murmur of voices in some other part of the house, either, until the noise stopped, then he drained off the last of his coffee, and raised his head, looking across the room. The surprise froze him to the chair, disbelieving. Elisa Benton was looking at him from the doorway. Her face was ashen, even the usually full lips were pale, looking washed-out and unattractive.

He made a small noise of surprise and indignation in his throat and started to get up, wiping his sweaty fingers on a soiled napkin close at hand.

"Gard. I'm awfully, awfully sorry." She was holding one hand a little in front of her. It reminded him of a gut-shot bird, the way it seemed to hang there, fighting for life.

"I can imagine," he said coldly.

"I am, Gard." She half turned away, made a fast, graceful movement toward the bountiful front of her dress, and came back holding out a slip of paper. "I've been carrying this since this morning. I . . . want you to see it."

Gard watched her cross the room and lay the paper on the table in front of him. Just one thing caught his eye a second before he stooped for his hat. Court's signature. He straightened slowly, reading. The paper was a signed note of thanks for a loan of $3,000. He thought instantly of the things he had said to her about the money. The worse things he had thought and hadn't said, and was ashamed of. Perspiration oozed out a little on his upper lip.

"I didn't *take* any money from Court. I loaned him some and he repaid me. That's all."

"What made him go to you, for money?"

"I didn't ask. He was in town here, one night, and wanted it. Maybe you were too far away . . . at Buckhorn. Perhaps he didn't want to ride out and back again. I don't know, Gard."

"Gambling?" The gray eyes raised sardonically to her face, saw the sadness there, and dredged up immediate defenses against it.

"I said I didn't ask. I'm sorry."

The hat brim was sticky in his fingers. "Well . . ."—it was gall and torture, what came next—"I made a mistake. I apologize."

Elisa shook her head at him. "I don't care about that. The way you think, Gard, you're justified. It's just that I don't want you to remember me that way, is all."

"You're leaving?"

She nodded. He could feel her eyes go to the welt on his cheek, which he had all but forgotten. The fingers on the hat brim tightened. "Court was riding toward Yankton, alone, when he was killed. Do you suppose he was heading for Buckhorn? I don't. My guess is that he took that crazy risk to get a straight answer out of you about this marriage business."

Elisa looked like he had struck her. "You're saying . . . thinking . . . that I'm the cause of his murder. Gard. Lord. How *can* you be this way? You're even less human now, than you were this morning. If I could have kept Court from this, don't you think I would have?" She looked up at him. "Of course I would have . . . whether I loved him or not, whether I intended to marry him or not."

"Elisa," he said slowly, "you're trouble. I'm not saying you caused Court's death, but you sure as the devil couldn't have helped it more, if you'd been working with the four men who shot him. That doesn't matter. He's dead and that's the end of his life, but you've been nothing but trouble since I first saw you . . . since that dinner he had for you at Buckhorn. Well, I'll take care of the killers, but the best news I've had lately is that you're leaving Cortez Valley."

He walked past her, fighting back the impulse to look down into her face as he went. Outside in the backyard, he donned his hat and swung around to the front of the house to his horse, mounted with a tired grunt, reined around, and rode back through Yankton again, seeing puddles of orange light where they fell against the building fronts, ran down the sides, and spilled out across the scuffed sidewalks into the dirty, dusty roadway.

Buckhorn's lights winked at their owner from a vast, flat world of monotonous gloom, as he rode toward them, into the yard, and over to the barns. With savage, brusque movements, Gard turned his horse out, hung up his gear, and went through the house to the office. Inside, he took down a bottle of rye whiskey from above the roll-top desk, had two quick pulls of the stuff, rummaged for a cigar he didn't find, made a cigarette, and went over to the window, noticing for the second time in his life that his hands were shaking. Irritated, he turned abruptly and went to his own room, dropped on the bed fully clothed, and fell asleep almost instantly.

The cook's triangle had a harsh, exacting sound to it when Gard awakened. He got up, and cleaned himself. There was a new grimness to the face he shaved; he noticed it without approval.

Buck Gault was waiting for him in the big dining room. "Gard, the boys are back." There was a hesitant inflection in the foreman's tone that meant he was stumped, at wits' end for a course of action, waiting to be set on the right trail by his employer.

"All right," Gard said, "there's plenty for them to do. You're the boss for a few days, Buck. I've got some other things to do."

"Sure," Gault said quietly, indicating he thought gun justice should be meted out to the killers of Court Ashley. "I understand."

"Good. Then I'll be moving. Have to see Johnny Curtain in Yankton before he lopes off somewhere." He turned without waiting to eat and strode out of the house, across the big yard to the barns, caught a horse, saddled up, and rode easily eastward, blind to the prismatic glisten of new light on dew, or the turquoise sky, as yet unbleached by the heat.

The news of Court Ashley's killing had come with the first stage from Hurd's Crossing. The town buzzed with it, but no one approached Gard, and with good reason; the harshness of the rancher's face, the unpleasant coldness that lay like a chip of ice in his eyes, turned acquaintances away. All except Johnny Curtain, who received his caller at the little cubbyhole office and jail combination.

"Gard, I'd give a little to know 'em, too."

"Yeah, that's what I'm here about. Isn't there some way you could at least find out their names?"

Curtain lowered his head frowningly. "Hurd's Crossing has a boom-town law set-up, Gard."

"I saw that yesterday. You could buy the

199

sheriff's soul, but you couldn't get anything out of him he didn't want to part with."

Curtain's eyes came up. "Did you try it?"

Gard nodded. "Sure, but there's seventy thousand dollars involved, Johnny. If he's got any idea about that, my offer of five thousand wouldn't interest him."

The sheriff made a dry whistle. "You offered him five thousand? For what?"

"Any information he had about the killers. Names, descriptions, where they're from. Like that."

Curtain's eyes were flinty sharp. "And he couldn't give you anything at all?"

"Nothing," Gard said dryly. "Now you know what I mean."

"I reckon. I'd also come close to guessing he either don't know anything . . . or he knows more than five thousand dollars' worth. His name's Rupert, isn't it? Clyde Rupert?" The sheriff didn't say anything for a while, then he began to shake his head in exaggerated wags, back and forth. "Seventy thousand dollars. Gard, that's more'n most men make in a lifetime."

"I know," the rancher agreed. "It's a lot of money. Buckhorn won't suffer much without it, Johnny. We've been in the cow business a long time, but the thing that worries me is that these gunmen can make big tracks and hide out for a long time with that kind of *dinero* in their hands.

In other words, it'll be twice as hard now to find Court's killers, and I want them bad."

Curtain made a cigarette and tossed the little sack on the table in front of him. "That works two ways, Gard. If you didn't have any money, I'd say you'd more'n likely never find 'em, but you can buy your way to these *hombres* just like they're trying to buy their way clear of you. In a pinch, you'll have more money than they will. You'll win, I reckon, but she's going to cost like hell."

"That's how the law works?"

Johnny Curtain shrugged with a tight smile. "Not always. You know that, Gard. Not in Yankton, but Hurd's Crossing is different."

Gard got up, stretched, and pulled his hat forward, low over the gray eyes. "I reckon I'll ride back over to the Crossing again. Spend a few days over there, if necessary. There's bound to be something a man can pick up."

"Yeah. If nothing else, maybe a bullet in the back." Johnny got up, too, regarding the cowman speculatively. "You're no gunman, Gard. The Ashleys are cattlemen, not gunfighters."

"They have been gunmen, Johnny," Gard said dryly, "when they had to be."

Curtain shrugged. "You'll probably see Elisa over there."

Gard stood stock still, looking at the shorter man without blinking. "Why her?"

201

"Oh, she pulled out early this morning on the first stage. I was down at the hotel when she came along. Said she was going to sing over there for a while, then maybe work her way East again."

Gard didn't answer. There was a feeling of miserable triumph in him that was slightly bitter and altogether unpleasant. He nodded and went out of the office, over to the stocky bay horse with the prominent Buckhorn brand on the left shoulder, swung up, and reined around, heading south out of town until he was clear, then rode eastward once more, and leisurely went over the flat land, still cool before the daily siege of sunlight.

It was late when he arrived at the Crossing. He got a tiny room in a flea-bug, shanty hotel, and slept once more fully clothed. At the break of day he was stirring, going among the newly opened establishments making small, useless purchases and asking questions.

He saw many men and met with no success whatsoever until he stopped at the blacksmith's shop across from the Bird Cage Theater, where a sign painter was laboriously working over a by-line, announcing Miss Elisa Benton as Hurd's Crossing's newest theatrical attraction. The blacksmith was a burly squatty man with a dented, ferocious face. He was sweating already from the perpetually opened pores of his trade, and welcomed Gard's questions as a legitimate means for stalling.

"Well, sir, it's funny you come in like this." The blue eyes under the scarred brows of a fighting man searched Gard's face. "It ain't been an hour since Hooker Emmons was picked up, right here in this shop. You know Hooker?"

"No, 'fraid not. Who's he?"

The mighty shoulders moved disdainfully. "Oh, a sort of two-bit badman. Never done anything really bad, just sort of tags along with them that do."

"Why was he picked up?"

"Don't exactly know. He came in here about daylight. Just when I was opening up. Had to have his horse shod all around right away. Said he was getting to hell out of the Crossing. Acted a little scairt. Well, sir, I had the front end finished and was moving around to get the rear, when this deputy sheriff comes in, disarms old Hooker, and walks him away as neat as you please." The man turned his face and nodded toward a drowsing horse tied back in a corner. "That's his horse," he said simply. "Nice sorrel, sound feet."

"You know this deputy's name?"

"Naw. They come and go too fast for me, around here. Young buck, though. About your size, I'd say. Wore two guns. Hadn't ought to be hard to find a two-gun deputy, though."

Gard nodded. "Thanks, I'll go look for him.

Why should Hooker Emmons be in trouble? You got any idea?"

"Like I said before, I don't, but you asked if I'd heard anything about that rancher that was dry-gulched outside of town the other night, and I was still thinking of Hooker. He's as near to an outlaw as I know, then he got tagged right here, in this shop, so naturally I figured he's mixed up in something. Might be this killing, might not."

"Yeah . . . well, thanks again." Gard moved back out into the increasing bustle of Hurd's Crossing, looking up toward the sheriff's office. The plank walks were alive with people, some solidly shod in the cumbersome footwear of freighters and laborers, some less hardily shod in the boots of riders, with musical spurs, out a notch for town wear, adding to the general clamor of the town. He went to the office and got a blank-eyed reception from Sheriff Rupert.

"You again, Ashley. What's it now?"

"A man named Emmons."

"What about him?"

Gard's temper was bubbling just under the surface. It showed in his face, but Sheriff Rupert had dealt with angry men most of his life. He wasn't impressed, only warned.

"He the only prisoner you got?"

A look of scorn flitted over the sweaty, square face. "Hurd's Crossing's got more damned trouble per square inch than any other town in the territory, and you want to know if . . ." He stopped there, finishing with an exasperated shrug and shake of his head. "We've got at least fifteen, maybe more, counting drunks. Why?"

"I'd like to talk to him."

"Not a chance."

"Why'd you pick him up, then?"

"On a lady's complaint."

Gard shifted his weight uneasily. The premonition he had felt once before, the night Buck Gault had ridden back with the news of Court's killing, was coming slowly to life inside of him. "What lady?"

"Singer at the theater. Miz Benton. She wanted to talk to him."

Gard's suspicions crystallized. "You mean you jailed him just so's a woman could ask him some questions?"

Rupert's face was reddening. "Listen, cowboy, maybe you don't like our brand of law. I got that impression when we talked before. That's tough. We got a job to do and we do it. Don't keep horsing around like you're doing now, or you might get a taste of it yourself." His face was settling into tight, savage lines. "This lady wanted to question Hooker. That's all right with us. He's no damned good anyway and we'll get him one of these days. In the meantime anyone wants him jailed, we'll do it. Maybe it won't do no more'n scare hell out of him. That's fine with us. If they want him sent away, we like that, too. Just one less renegade to sweat over. This lady helped us. All right, now you know as much about him as I do. I got work to do."

Gard left without another word. He wandered through the Crossing, wondering why Elisa had interested herself in this small-time outlaw. It disturbed him to think she was achieving what he hadn't even started to do yet, getting somewhere in her own affairs. Crossing through the ankle-deep pulverized manure and dust of the roadway, he made his way to the Bird Cage Theater, and in as far as the manager's cubicle.

"Where can I find Miss Benton?"

The manager, a short, fat man addicted to atrocious sleeve-garters set with fabulous rosettes of pearls and precious stones, made a wry face. "Don't believe you can, mister. You're not the first that's tried, though."

"Listen." Gard's anger was just behind his teeth by now. "I've got business with her, and I reckon I'll see her, too."

"Yeah, you probably will. Tonight, when the show opens."

Gard moved forward menacingly. "All right, *hombre*. We'll let her judge for us. You know where she is?" The man's head bobbed once, stolidly, but slightly uneasily, too. "Then go tell her Gard Ashley wants to talk to her. Understand? Gard Ashley."

The manager got off his chair and looked up into the unpleasant face. "All right If she says no, you leave. Agreed?"

Gard regarded him solemnly, then inclined his head curtly, saying nothing. The man went down the dark, musty coolness of the theater, up on to the stage, and disappeared behind a wing. Gard looked idly at the place, saw the prodigious litter of cigar butts and unclean table tops, and turned impatiently away as the little fat man returned with a baffled look of irritation on his face.

"She'll see you." He turned to hide further annoyance, and pointed. "Down through there, up on the stage to your left, and the door with the gold star painted on it." He looked up again, frowned and pursed his lips. "Don't be long. This ain't a hotel." Gard did an unexpected thing then. He fished out a gold double-eagle from his pants' pocket and handed it to the manager, who looked down, astonished, then let his eyebrows straighten out suddenly and smiled with a slight nod. "Take your time, cowboy, take your time."

Gard knocked on the door and entered at the sound of Elisa's voice. She was sitting on a small sofa dressed in a filmy thing of some light, soft material that made a startling, awesome contrast to the golden amber eyes that were looking up at him. Gard darted her a startled look. In his hatred of her he never remembered her as she was, then, when he saw her, especially sitting there, calm and poised and beautiful; it shocked him.

"Mister Ashley, of the overbearing Ashleys. Sit down." The words were designed to cut, but the eyes didn't back them up.

"Why did you have this man Emmons jailed?"

"Because I wanted to talk to him."

"I know all that," Gard said acidly. "But what about?"

"Does it concern you?"

"It might. You can guess why I'm in Hurd's Crossing."

"Of course," she said, motioning toward the chair across from her. "Please." Gard made no move toward the chair and she looked up at him again, smiling slightly. "No, on second thought I prefer you standing." She didn't speak for a moment, then shrugged. "Anyway, what I do doesn't concern you. In fact, I had the definite impression you never wanted to see me again."

"You're very right, lady. I don't. But it looks to me like wherever I go, you're already there."

"Ahead of you, in fact, Gard Ashley."

"You're meddling, aren't you?"

Elisa closed her eyes briefly, then opened them again, and leaned forward just a trifle, amber eyes fixed steadily on his face. They were eyes that had just accepted a challenge, unwillingly, no doubt, but accepted it nevertheless. Not luster-less, either, like they had been before. "Gard . . .

you have this coming. I've thought about it a lot, and I mean what I say."

"I hope it concerns Emmons," he said dryly.

"No, it doesn't. It concerns you alone. You and Buckhorn. Gard, Buckhorn isn't your empire, it's your master. You've made it that way. You're dedicated to it, even to the exclusion of your own emotions. You don't think like other men or live like them. You've let Buckhorn become so overpowering that it's taken the normal juices in you and turned them to water." Her face was pale and alive with intense feeling. Gard couldn't look at her without seeing the earnestness in every expression, and the fire that moved across the background of her eyes. "Buckhorn has warped you so much, Gard, that you won't let anything come between it and you. Not even Court. You blame me for his death. Hasn't it occurred to you that, if you'd been with him . . . at least at the Crossing with him . . . that he'd never have ridden off with that money alone? You wouldn't have let him. Court was just the opposite of you. Reckless, loud, and troublesome. You had only two things in common. A common name and . . . unhappiness. Do you know why he was so different? Because of the things he saw in you that he didn't like, and tried to make himself as different from you as he could."

She saw the ashen coloring fill in slowly behind his ruddy cheeks, the smooth, indrawn look to his mouth, and the mounting fury in his gray eyes. It made her want to cry out to him, beg him to understand so she wouldn't have to go on, but she knew it would take something at least as explosive and naked as this to force him back to normality again—and even then, it might be too late. "Gard. Why do I have to tell you these things? Haven't you noticed this change yourself?" She caught herself pleading and stopped, shook her head openly, and went on. "You hate me. All right, I can stand it. But you're doing something worse to yourself. Listen, you've become a machine. You operate by instinct. When you find your brother's killers, you won't give them a chance. I know it, whether you do or not. It's part of the way you've become. Opposition should be crushed without a hearing, a chance. Well . . . you wanted to fight me and now I've accepted. I'll fight you, and you'll be the judge of whether I'm fighting fair or not. You won't, but you'll find that I do. Emmons? Sure, I'll tell you the whole story. I bribed half of Hurd's Crossing until a man told me Hooker Emmons had been out the night of your brother's murder. He told me other things about Emmons. I bribed a deputy sheriff to lock him up, then I questioned him." She hesitated, seeing the glitter in his eyes, leaned back, and bit her lips. "Emmons was one of them, Gard, and I have the names of the other three. It almost made me sick the way that deputy beat it out of Emmons, but I stood it . . . and you're too blind to know why. Well, it doesn't matter. You want a fight, so I'll give you one."

Gard's voice came back slowly, raspingly. Every word she had said was burned into his brain. He nodded at her without being aware of it. "Why? You didn't love Court."

"Oh, you damned fool!" She spat it out, then there was almost a full minute of silence before she went on. "I told you. Because you dared me twice to cross you . . . now I'm taking up your challenge."

"Is that the reason?" he asked quietly.

Elisa shook her head. "No, it isn't. But it'll do . . . for now."

"All right, what do I have to do to get those other names? How much do you want?"

Her palms were damp and she longed for the buggy whip again. It took another full minute to get the wildness quelled. He didn't help any, either, standing there as cold and emotionless as a rock. "There's nothing you can do, Gard Ashley. I have those names and I intend to use them my own way."

"And just what is that way?"

"I'm going to have these men hunted down, one by one, and turned over to the law."

He laughed bitterly. "You *are* a fool, aren't you? Do you think for a moment that'll recover the seventy thousand dollars? Are you such a dude you think territorial law won't let them loose, even if these crooked sheriffs like Rupert won't?" He shook his head. "Elisa, for seventy thousand dollars, these four men can buy their way clean across the frontier and back to the States."

"Then let them go."

"Not while I'm alive!"

"If you found them, you'd kill them, wouldn't you? Sure you would. You know what that'd make you? Well, it would, Gard, because you've become a machine. You'd shoot them down like dogs."

"Shouldn't I?" he asked coldly.

Elisa shook her head vehemently at him. "No, of course not. It'd ruin you. You're close enough to the brink as it is. Your sense of justice and mercy have dried up. If you kill these four men, there'll be others, their friends, maybe, I don't know, but there will. That means killings right on down the line until you're killed. To see you killed wouldn't be so bad, Gard. In fact, right now, this minute, I'd enjoy it. Not quite . . . but almost I think. Anyway, you'd lose Buckhorn, you'd become an outlaw, a killer, a . . ." She stopped in mid-sentence, tense as a coiled spring. It angered her that this man could arouse her so. She leaned back again and tried to control her breathing.

"Can I *buy* those names, Elisa?"

She shook her head adamantly. "No, I told you, you wouldn't ever get them, and you won't!"

He still held the sweaty doorknob behind himself. Now he began to twist it slowly, looking down at her with a saturnine, grim smile. "Well . . . if you bought what you know from the law, so can I. Buckhorn's got money, too, Elisa."

Her laugh startled him. The doorknob was forgotten and twisted back into position again.

"Gard, you're so . . . so masculine. You have a brain, but you don't use it. Do you think for a moment I didn't know you'd find out about Emmons? Do I look stupid enough to leave him where you can lay hands on him?"

His eyes became as cold and menacing as the stare of a rattlesnake, unblinking, fixed, and venomous. "Isn't he in jail . . . here?"

"Of course not." It rang with contempt. "He's not in Hurd's Crossing at all. He's gone."

"You had him freed." It wasn't a question. There was a subtle threat in each word. Elisa heard it and raised her eyes with complete confidence, defiant, not defensive. "I didn't have him freed. He's a murderer, whether he fired the shots that killed Court or not. I had him escorted to a place where he'll be safe from anything . . . you included . . . until he's brought up for trial."

"Lady, I've half a . . ."

"Stop calling me lady! I don't like it and never

213

did. Any man, even a man like you, should have enough courtesy to use a woman's name."

He didn't answer right away. The remark was so irrelevant, seemingly trivial, that it stopped him cold. His mind grasped at it, though, as a possible concession that might help him in the quest. There had to be a way. "Miss Benton, I reckon I've sold you short. You've got more sense than I figured you had. All right, state your terms. I want those four men, and, by God, I intend to get them."

"You won't, Gard Ashley."

He nodded still looking into the amber eyes. "Yes, I will. I will . . . if it costs me everything I have in the world."

She was staring at him, startled, seeing the look in his eyes. She started to rise, held herself, then sank back, bewildered and saying nothing at all. There *was* something above his love of Buckhorn, then. He wasn't as abandoned as she had thought. This loyalty to Court was definite and blind, then, after all. She had made a mistake in her analysis of this man, a serious mistake.

"Miss Benton," the not unpleasant, cold voice went on evenly, "I've offered you money. You don't want it. I'll give you whatever I have that you want, for those names. You can show your . . . affection . . . for Court by helping me in this. Say it's for him . . . not me, if you like, just tell what it is that you want."

The golden eyes were strangely brilliant and illuminated. There was the thinnest veil of moisture over them, like dew-dampened leaves in autumn, but when Elisa spoke, her voice again was not in accord with her eyes. "I want you to get out of here . . . now!"

Gard's wrath rioted. He spun, wrenched the door open, and slammed it behind himself. He was stalking hurriedly over the stage and couldn't see or hear the anguished sobs that shook Elisa's shoulders—her entire body in fact, tore it with a sadness and bitterness combined, that raged like an ocean tempest. He had no way of knowing that her grief racked her until exhaustion came along with a blessing and touched her with it, then she slept, still tugged by paroxysms that decreased gradually, and finally left her, spent and asleep.

The little fat man at the door looked up, smiled uncertainly, and looked hastily away. Gard's face wasn't a nice thing to look at.

He went to the livery barn, got his horse, and rode out on to the stifling range, an erect, savage shadow of a man lost in the endless shimmering wastes, until he found a juniper tree, dismounted, and sat under it, thinking.

III

When daylight waned in Hurd's Crossing, the sounds of activity didn't cease. They altered their tempo, but didn't stop. The racket of growth—hammers, saws, cursing, and shouts—changed to a subtler, but just as unrefined, clamor for amusement. Gard became absorbed in the din of the place. He allowed it to carry him into saloons and eating places and cast him out on to the duckboards again, a floating, thinking member of the general turmoil, a part and yet apart from it.

He went into the Bird Cage Theater with a sense of attraction toward the featured singer, took his place at a table and lounged there, sat back, cigarette dangling from his mouth, and eyes slitted. He saw Elisa Benton make her first appearance and, knowing nothing about music, he judged her voice correctly, the way music should be judged, simply and honestly. If the sounds pleased him, he liked it, if not, he didn't. He watched gestures and recognized their grace, along with the lithe wholesomeness of her, the abundance and health that radiated out into the smoky room. He thought of her as an opponent and spat out the cigarette. There was a way of fighting her—somehow. She couldn't be called out, beaten to a pulp or run out of town—hung or horsewhipped or shot down. The narrowed eyes fastened themselves on her, listening indifferently to the song called "Garry Owen" that she sang. He had misgivings and let his glance wander over the room. The men were charmed like savages before the judgment choir—quiet, intent, and soothed. His gaze wandered still farther over the room. Standing against one wall was a lean, two-gun man, his arm draped casually around the small waist of a very pretty blonde girl.

Gard watched the couple, seeing their profile, wondering whether they liked Elisa's singing or were bored. It was hard to tell, the way they were sideways to him. Then the girl moved, looked up into the man's face, said something, and started to walk through the room. Gard saw the man twist a little, watching her go. He got a shock then; the man was wearing a dull nickel star. He was the two-gun deputy Elisa Benton had hired to beat the names out of Hooker Emmons for her.

Gard felt the tenseness coming into him. It was an abrupt and invigorating alertness. His expression didn't change. There, across the room, was the one man in Cortez Valley who held the secret he wanted so badly. He watched the deputy turn back, regarding Elisa, and studied the man's thin lips, hard, cold, cameo-clear features, and read the slight arrogance that lay in the chin, the brow, and the cant of the man's head. He drummed on the table, thinking. The blonde girl had passed him and was fifteen feet behind his table before the idea was born. He turned slowly and watched her. She was a pretty thing, not over eighteen at the most, with nice eyes, a little sprinkling of freckles over the saddle of her nose, and a full, ripe mouth that could be destructively generous or violently savage and hateful. It was a passionate, weak mouth, unformed by character and therefore pretty.

The idea was still an embryo when Gard arose, threw a hard look at the beautiful woman on the stage, caught the quick, lingering glance of recognition she flashed at him, turned quietly, easily, and walked back toward the dingy entrance to the place. The blonde girl was several doors ahead of him, walking north. He might have missed her entirely if it hadn't been for the rocking-hipped gait she had. The night was cool and freighted with a fragrance of dried grass, sage, and curing seeds. He followed, caught up, and spoke. The sidewalk was almost deserted where she turned and faced him, a dull, unfriendly look on her face.

"Ma'am, I saw you back at the theater with a deputy sheriff. He a friend of yours?"

She nodded brusquely. "A close one, stranger."

Gard heard the threat in her voice but didn't smile. "He's the only two-gun deputy in Hurd's Crossing, isn't he?"

Another nod. "Yeah, what about it?"

Her obvious truculence made him shift his weight a little uneasily. He had been so preoccupied with his idea that he hadn't considered the likelihood of this girl's opposition to her part in it. "Well, would you ask him some questions for me, without letting him know they are for me, and bring me the answer for . . . say . . . a price?"

She was looking at him a little differently. It wasn't avarice so much as interest that showed in the blue eyes. Her pert nose, with its scattering of small freckles, crinkled adorably. "What kind of questions? Will they get him in trouble?"

"No, ma'am. He got the names of three men out of Hooker Emmons today, for that lady who's singing at the theater. I want to know those names. It doesn't mean anything to him, but it does to me. Will you ask him . . . keeping me out of it?"

She didn't answer right away. The blue eyes were ranging over him, probing, feeling, then she relaxed a little, looking up into his face again. "Well, how much?"

"Fifty dollars now . . . fifty when you return with the names."

"A hundred dollars?" Doubt rang in her voice.

Gard didn't answer; he fished in his pocket, counted out half the total amount, and handed it to her, raising his eyes as he did so.

The girl lowered her head long enough to count

219

the money, then shot him a hard glance. "You're sure this won't mean trouble for Jack?"

"You have my word on it."

She was moving past him, heading back, when she spoke again. "You wait right here, mister. This won't take long."

Gard sat down on a bench in front of a mercantile establishment and made a cigarette. The night was snuggling in around the drab fronts of the Crossing. He sat back, crossed his long legs to the accompaniment of soft music from his spur rowels, and smoked. There was a glint of hard triumph in his eyes, too.

An opportunity had presented itself, or, more correctly, it had been recognized and bent to his purpose when it was put in front of him. A sardonic little smile tugged at the outer corners of his mouth. Elisa's very presence on the stage had prompted him to act, to recognize the value of the two-gun man's girlfriend to himself. She had almost offered him this chance to best her in the challenge she said she had accepted. Then a load of guilt came out of nowhere and leaned heavily on his shoulder. Its body was formed out of Elisa's words: *You won't fight fair . . . but I will.* Gard squirmed on the bench. This wasn't fighting fair—or was it? Hadn't Elisa hired a deputy sheriff to beat the names out of a man? Then what could be wrong with using this same man's girl to milk him of the names for Gard

Ashley? He tossed the dead cigarette into the dust at the edge of the duckboards. Right or wrong, he had just one justification for what he had done—vengeance. That was all. Perhaps it was wrong to use the girl like this, but Elisa had used even more brutal methods. Their ideas for punishment of the killers differed. She was ruthless in getting the men who had shot down Court, and he was just as ruthless in demanding that they pay the full price for their killing of his brother. If there was a difference in the way they were fighting each other, it was a nebulous thing to Gard.

A distant sound of applause, stamping boots, and muted shouts indicated the men of Hurd's Crossing had just seen something they liked mightily. He turned every so often and looked up the way. Impatient, he was beginning to anger when he saw her coming back, a small, curvaceous girl, swinging through the gloom with an obvious purpose.

He arose and nodded down into her upturned face. "Did you get them?"

"Yeah, Carl Dentzel, Ed Billings, and Jack Snider, where's the other fifty?" It all came out in a rush of words with no distinguishing, separating pause.

Gard almost smiled. He handed her the balance of the $100 and watched her face relax. "One more thing. Do you know where I might find these men?"

She scowled thoughtfully, studying him. "Are you the law . . . by any chance?"

"No'm. I've got an interest in them is all."

"See that road north out of town?" Gard nodded without looking around. "Well, you follow that about twelve, fourteen miles until you come to an old tumble-down shack on the west side of the road. Right behind that old cabin there's a little trail. It goes up the mountain among the trees. Dark as the inside of a well, in there. There's a cabin on the lip of the meadow. It's Dentzel's hide-out." The blue eyes ranged over him again. "He can see the whole valley from up there. You'd be taking an awful chance, you know."

Gard shrugged. "Maybe, but it's pretty dark tonight."

"You're going up there tonight?"

"Yes, if you'll give me your word not to . . . ."

She interrupted with a contemptuous toss of one hand. "Don't worry, mister. You played fair with me. I like that. Damned few men ever have. I won't say a word to anyone."

Gard smiled down at her. "Thanks, lady. You don't happen to know anything about Billings and Snider, do you?"

"No. They pulled out of the Crossing a couple of days ago, I think. Haven't seen 'em around, anyway." The blue eyes flickered somberly, shrewdly. "If you get Dentzel . . . and he don't get you . . . there's ways of getting what you want out of him. He'd know, if anyone would."

"All right. I'm indebted to you. Thanks a lot."

She didn't answer at all, just looked a little past his shoulder until he turned and went across the road toward the livery barn, then she sank down slowly on the bench he had warmed, caught her full under lip between her teeth, and stared after him, eyes bright and dry-looking.

The road north out of the Crossing flung itself against the gentle rise of the land far ahead as though anxious to escape the squalor of the rail's end town. Gard rode over it, allowing the noise, smells, and faces of the place to rock slowly to the rear, merging into the dark like a nightmare fading before wakefulness. He checked his carbine and handgun, then made a cigarette and smoked pleasantly as he went up across the slumbering expanse of deserted range.

His mind went back to Elisa Benton. The way she had looked up there on the stage, and before—when she was firing both verbal barrels at him, tense and stunningly beautiful, with her amber eyes large and round and fixed on his face. It surprised him that he could recall her so vividly. Before, when he had thought of her at all, it was just a name in his mind with hatred smeared over the memory, obliterating whatever she looked like as a person.

The cigarette grew small. He spat into his palm

and crushed the thing before throwing it away. The sight would carry for miles, a little dazzling eye of red flame that showed where a man was. Why was she doing it? The recollection of the things she had said came back. She hadn't loved Court and didn't ever intend to marry him. Then why? Nothing distracted him for long from his thoughts of the woman. Somewhere, there was a good, plausible, concrete reason. He shifted in the saddle. At first he had thought it was money, but he knew better now. Court could be ruled out even more quickly. Then why?

The sound of coyotes broke the chain of monotony in his mind. Shrugging irritably, cold-eyed and angry-looking, he listened to their taunts. Once, a big cat screamed off to his left somewhere, making all the other noises of the night break off instantly in rigid fright. Gard's horse snorted softly and shook his head a little, wagging it so the rein chains made small, rattling sounds.

Gradually the stage road hurried itself upward, over the long, low pass that showed pale in the weak moonlight ahead, and Gard saw the grayishness of something on his left. He rode with eyes glued to the bulky ruin and smiled when it came closer and assumed perspective, became a rotting, caved-in old cabin. He threw a glance upward, into the deep purple of pine and firs where the sloping land became an abrupt hill, once a mighty bulwark that jutted up into the underbelly of some long dead sea.

He was closer now than he had been yet to unraveling the mystery of his brother's murder. Leaving the horse in a dense growth behind the cabin, Gard shucked his spurs, buckled them to the rear rigging, pulled out his carbine, and went forward afoot, head low, searching out, and finding the almost indistinguishable little trail that twisted away from the cabin and wound its way tortuously upward, throwing itself against the silent giants and falling back, chastened, skirting, trying again, until it came out on a hidden plateau where knee-deep feed was, and there it ended, exhausted and lost in the maze of rugged uplands.

Gard went slowly. He didn't know who might be up there. Dentzel might not be alone; if not—or if they had word of his presence in Hurd's Crossing—there would surely be a guard somewhere ahead. The moon was low in the ragged tapestry of sky overhead. A weak, watery light filtered eerily through the trees, giving nothing but a tantalizing opalescence that ended whenever it was wanted, obscured by the great host of fragrant trees, huge and silent and sentinel-like in their formidable impassivity. He went in closer to the shaggy trunks as he felt the ground leveling off a little. The rich meadow spread out in ghostly grandeur suddenly, and deer walked unafraid, looking up now and then through the rank grass, lifting damp, velvety muzzles to the still night air, searching for the scent of fright that didn't come.

Gard watched the meadow for a while, then looked farther into the gloom until he found what he wanted. A small, squarely built, and massive log house nestled close to the lip of the upland pasture, secreted furtively among great trees where a breathtaking view, even on this ghostly night, spread in an awesome panorama out over the tremendous sweep of land that ended in the far distance, against corduroy mountains as dark and forbidding as the ones he was crouching in. There was no sign or smell of life. Gard's heart sank a little, but he clung to his caution and went like a lobo wolf among the rank underbrush where the trees became a fringe. A saddle lay carelessly on its side close to the cabin door. He went on, heartened, descending the gentle slope toward the place, crouched and careful until he was close enough to see the small window, too high for a short man, like a sightless, dull eye, to one side of the cabin door.

The carbine was clammy in his fingers. He cocked it, stepped around the saddle, and pushed with the barrel on the door. It resisted. Gard tried again. This time the door gave way with nothing more than a sighed protest and he could smell the closeness of the place, an odor of food and humanity. He closed the door, standing to one side of it, letting his eyes become accustomed to the deeper gloom of the interior, then he went toward a lump of something that appeared to lie asleep on the bunk built into the cabin's wall.

The face was unshaven and thick with sleep. A mouth gaped, emitting long, even breaths that made a rhythmic bellows out of the thick, deep chest. Gard had never seen the man before and laid his carbine barrel across the open mouth. There was a sudden paroxysm of alert, frantic movement and Gard looked down into the open, staring eyes. He removed the barrel gently and flung back the rolled quilts, darting a quick glance along the sprawled, paunchy body's length and seeing instantly the pistol close to the right hand. The carbine barrel was very close to the man's eyes when he spoke.

"Raise your hands, *hombre*. Raise 'em and put 'em on top of your head. Don't make a mistake."

The man didn't. His eyes bulged and the hands came up very deliberately and joined fingers over the tousled hair.

Gard stepped back a little. "Sit up." Another slow, careful movement and the stranger was sitting on the edge of his bunk.

Gard had him sit close to the upright post at the foot of the bunk, retrieved the gun, quickly found the rope that lay near a littered log table, and tied the man's hands behind him to the post. There was only the rasping noises of Gard's movements and the sound of his shuffling feet in the cabin.

He leaned the carbine, uncocked, against the table, lit a candle, and made a cigarette. His upper lip was moist and shiny. "Dentzel," he said calmly, "where're the others?"

The answer was slow in coming. "What others? Who are you? What you mean, busting in on a man like this?"

"Well," Gard said softly, "I'm not Hooker Emmons. He's no longer around, is he?"

It was a shot in the dark, but an effective one. Dentzel stopped working his shoulders against the rope, craned his neck, and looked up at Gard. "Who are you?"

"Name's Ashley. That mean anything to you?"

Gard could almost see the man's mind working. Astonishment, then terror intermingled with a malignant look flitted across his little pale eyes. "What you want?"

"You for murder. You and Billings and Snider."

"Snider and Billings went west. You'll never find them, either."

"You know where they went . . . where are they?"

Dentzel's small, myopic eyes, light-colored and sly-looking, raised to Gard's face again when he nodded. "Sure, I know. Fat lot of good that'll do you."

Gard smoked his cigarette in silence, looking at

his prisoner. He had anticipated trouble in getting the man to identify himself. It had been childishly easy. The silence grew into something almost tangible with lacings of violence. Gard shrugged, regarded his cigarette end for a moment, then, without another word kneeled and gathered some scattered kindling from around the blackened stone fireplace, bunched it around cigarette papers, and blew on the end of his quirly. The little flame came eagerly to life, digested the brown papers, and licked greedily at the pitch wood. It didn't take long.

Dentzel sat transfixed, watching the yellow light flicker, feint, and dance, casting shifting patterns of shadows under his captor's hawkish, hard face, falling into the hollow spots, gouging deeply under the eyes and along the lean temples, making the hawkish nose more prominent, evil-looking. He saw no trace of mercy in the bronzed features at all.

"What are you doing there? You'll set the shack on fire!"

Gard looked down at the fire as he arose. It was six feet from the fireplace, crackling happily on the tight planking of the dry old flooring. "That's the idea," he said evenly.

The outlaw watched in dawning, stunned com-prehension, full understanding coming slowly, unbelievingly to him. He strained again against the rope although he knew it was hopeless. The little flames were eating away by then, spreading greedily among the kindling, fighting for a foothold on the tight decking of the floor. The smoke began to rise, dark gray and heavy where some pieces of damp bark hissed against the onslaught of the flames.

Gard watched the fire for a moment longer, turned, and tossed Dentzel a casual, disinterested look and walked to the door. The killer's eyes were starting from his head. This was no bluff. Ashley didn't even look back at the doorway, just passed through it, taking his carbine. The renegade heard the man's boots clump off the porch, then only the sound of his boot steps in the weeds, and he howled at him, screaming mightily until the deer in the little pasture fled in terror. Gard stopped and turned in his tracks, listening. There was no compromise in his eyes.

"Anything you want to know, Ashley! The place'll burn like hell! Cut me loose . . . a chance!" The swearing ripped and crackled without meaning. Just profanity for its own sake, tumbling wildly from the lips of man half mad with fright, each word hastening to get past his lips to make room for the next scorcher.

Gard went back slowly and stood in the doorway. The cabin was brilliant with a shifting glitter of bright fire, but it hadn't yet found its hold on the flooring. He looked at the sweat-streaked, purple face. "Where're the others, Dentzel?"

"Put the fire out! This place'll go like . . . !"

Gard didn't listen. He took a pail of spring water from the table and sloshed out the flames. They died ragingly, hissing their fury, sizzling, and at last sighing in their death throes. He put the bucket down and looked back. Dentzel's face was still twisted in fear, pale and puffy; behind him, his wrists were slippery with blood from straining.

"Dentzel, you've got about a minute to tell me. Horse around and the next time I won't come back. You ought to roast real good, there's enough grease in you."

Dentzel's appalled spirit was looking out of his wide-open eyes. "You'd do it. I can see you would."

Gard didn't nod. "Just give me half a chance and I'll do it yet."

"No," the frightened voice said. "No, I'll tell you. Billings and Snider are shirt-tail relations. Snider's got a little ranch back in the hills behind Missionary Peak . . . over north of Yankton about twenty miles. They . . . took their share . . . and went over there to hide out the rest of the winter. Listen . . ."

"*You* listen! Where's the money?"

Dentzel's fear was slackening, but not his respect for the savage look on Gard's face. He could read the truth in the gray eyes. Ashley would burn him to death in a second. He nodded toward the fireplace. "Up in there . . . in a can. Forty thousand of it, about."

Gard didn't move. "Forty to you, ten to each of the others. You must've been the brains."

"Wait a minute." The fear was coming back to Dentzel. "I didn't shoot him. The . . ."

"Of course not," Gard said dryly. "That'll keep. Shut up and sit still." He turned away scornfully, went to the fireplace, squatted, and reached up inside. There was a small rock ledge; his hand felt a can that moved when his fingers groped for it. Slowly he grasped it and drew it out. There wasn't time to count it in now, so he shoved it inside his shirt, and faced back toward the prisoner. "All right, Dentzel. A lady said I'd shoot you down like a dog. I owe *her* better than that." He went over and slashed the man's ropes, watched him flex his fingers, wild-eyed, and withdrew the outlaw's gun from his belt. "This'll make it legal."

Gard dropped the loaded gun at Dentzel's feet. The man looked down at it longingly, then raised his eyes again, wondering, seeing the tall, hawkish face moving backward, toward the table, the gray eyes intent on his face, then Ashley's head inclined a little. "Pick it up and put it on the bed beside you." They both knew Dentzel wouldn't do that. A sweaty right hand went down slowly, grasped the gun, let it slide back against the palm, then the barrel tilted upward, and the hammer jumped back. Dentzel was still bent over, only his head was raised to show the animal viciousness in the small eyes. Gard's own gun was clearing its holster like a living thing when the killer's gun exploded. The second explosion that rocked the cabin and chased its echo out over the still, gloomy night, was Gard Ashley's. Dentzel came half off the bed, jerked erect, and squeezed off another shot. The eruptions were almost simultaneous. Gard rocked back a little, begrudgingly taking a backward step, glaring his hatred, but Carl Dentzel wasn't seeing. He bent a little, going lower like a mule had kicked him in the chest. Only his legs refused to give way. They stood rigid, stubbornly holding up the bulk of torso that was wilting, then they, too, over-balanced, folded. Dentzel went down in a heap of flesh that seemed to flatten and widen as the breath went out of his lungs.

Gard toed the man with his boot and then went out of the cabin, still holding his gun in his hand, hesitated, turned, and went back, kneeled and took a ragged wallet from Dentzel's pocket, shoved that inside his shirt, also, and went back out.

The horse picked his way drowsily back down the chilly night toward Hurd's Crossing, feeling his rider easing one leg in the stirrup. They stopped once near a clump of junipers while Gard smoked and counted the money, stuffed it into his money belt, and threw the can away. About $500 shy of $40,000. Next, he lowered his pants and studied a swelling hole in the flesh of his upper leg, cursed at the pain in the thing as shock lessened, mounted again, and rode ahead, teeth gritted against the cold of predawn that warned him of the imminence of daylight.

Hurd's Crossing lay, gray and uninviting in the stillness of a mauve world, slumbering in its sickly setting of squalor and confusion and filth. Gard rode like a slow ghost until he was abreast of the Bird Cage Theater. He dismounted, tied his horse, and went up to the barred door. It was a moment's work with his gun barrel for a lever, then the hasp flew off with a suddenly harsh sound, and he was inside. Limping slowly through the cloying, sour odor of the place, he went to the stage, grunted up the steps, turned right into the darkness, and felt his way to the door with the gold star painted on it, knew, without testing, it was locked, and threw his weight against it with an alarming shatter of wood. The panel swung forlornly, saggingly, and he was framed in the opening, wide-legged and motionless. He almost smiled when the drowsy voice came out of the darkness with its edge of deadly purpose.

"Don't move!"

"I won't," he said dryly, tartly. "Just brought

you something." He tossed the dead man's wallet on the floor. "Thought you might like to see it." He reached over and pulled the broken door toward its casing. "Good night, Miss Benton. We're *even* now. Let's see who makes the next score in our little private war."

He went back through the building to his horse, swung up with gritted teeth, and reined back north through Hurd's Crossing until he cut the stage road again, then pushed his horse westward, toward Yankton, not so erect in the saddle as he usually was, and certainly without even a small measure of physical comfort, but, for all that, with a grim smile on his face. Elisa Benton had accepted Buckhorn's challenge and thrown it back in his teeth. Now they were even again. Time and determination would tell whether a woman's wiles or a man's ferocity would win.

He rode slowly over the silent world, uneasy in body but not in spirit, thinking of her face when she saw whose wallet he had thrown down, and, strangely enough, he had a very clear and vivid picture in his mind of the way she would put her knuckles in her mouth and stare, with those large golden eyes, at the broken door, horrified at what he had done. Stranger still, he was perfectly correct; that's exactly what Elisa Benton did, after she had lit the lamp and looked at Dentzel's wallet, and instinctively knew it could only have been taken from the man after he was dead.

IV

By the time Gard made Yankton the sun was high and the back of his throat was dry and hot. He rode into town, went directly to the livery barn, swung down, gathered himself for the effort, and made a lunge toward an old buggy seat mounted on a box, just outside the office door. The day hostler watched him with mounting alarm.

"Put the horse up, pardner. Get me a rig and a driver."

The day man obeyed quickly, recruiting a driver from among the bleary-eyed drifters who were lounging out in back in the shade. He watched Gard's exodus from Yankton from the doorway of the old barn, then hustled over to the doctor's house and told him about the surviving Ashley coming in with blood on the *rosadero* of his saddle, white as a sheet, too weak to ride alone, and hiring a buggy and driver to take him back to Buckhorn.

The sun was a great wet thing of infinite brightness with invisible fingers that reached in behind Gard's eyeballs and scratched at his nerves, making a dull ache that came and went with each beat of his heart, a cyclic rhythm of insistent pain. He saw Buckhorn ahead, recognized the buildings without thinking them real. The heat haze made everything dance a few inches above the ground, as though detached and floating, shimmering.

The throbbing ache increased gradually, inexorably, until the sweat on his body was cooler than the flesh itself. Dimly men were talking. It irritated him that they were asking questions— he could tell by the inflections—but he neither understood them nor felt inclined to answer, then he was floating, like Buckhorn's buildings, floating and bumping and feeling his boots strike solid things indifferently, then an endless sea of darkness with a tiny, almost indistinguishable dot of purple light far down a circling, gently gyrating corridor, took his identity away from him and the darkness blotted out everything.

When Gard opened his eyes, the doctor was smoking one of his strong, black cigars. It may have been the odor that brought him back to consciousness, as much as anything. He looked over slowly because the tiny mallets behind his eyes were still pummeling his nerves with even strokes.

The doctor happened to be looking at him; he smiled. "Well, happy homecoming."

Gard didn't answer. He heard the sarcasm though, through the banter.

"You're lucky, boy, damned lucky. Blood poisoning's a dangerous thing. It's killed hun- dreds with less cause than it had to tote you off."

"How long have I been like this, Doc?"

A shrug of the wispy shoulders. "What's the difference? You're not going anywhere. You hired a rig out of Yankton. . . ."

"I know that."

"Day before yesterday."

Gard studied the wizened face in astonishment. Even the pain in his head was briefly forgotten. "Day before yesterday," he repeated incredulously.

The doctor smiled around the cigar. "My sentiments exactly. Why didn't you stop at the house? I could've cleaned the thing out and maybe saved you a near squeak." He frowned irritably. "By the time I got here, as it was, you looked like a balloon, were as crazy as a hoot owl, and the language you used made me blush . . . let alone Elisa."

"Who?"

"Elisa Benton. Listen, Gard, you've been making a first-class . . ."

"Who brought her here . . . to Buckhorn?"

"Well," the doctor said tartly, "I didn't, but they're still making buggies you know."

"What did she want? What's her . . . ?"

The doctor was shaking his head with a look of impatience on his face, when he broke in. "Mister Buckhorn, I don't understand all I know about this business. I'd been here about an hour or so . . . got here before dark, anyway . . . and was just coming to the house when this rig came flying into the yard like it was carrying the mail. It was Elisa . . . she 'n' my wife are close friends, incidentally."

"Dammit, Doc, get to the point, will you?" The ache was gone, miraculously, but Gard didn't notice. Only the sapping, leaden weakness remained.

"You gave Elisa a man's wallet over at the Crossing. Well, she wouldn't tell me what the devil *that's* about, but the morning after you pulled out, she found drops of blood on the floor where you'd been standing, and drove over here like the devil was after her."

Gard closed his eyes and let the blackness engulf him for a moment, then opened them again. "And . . . I had blood poisoning from Dentzel's bullet?"

"From someone's bullet. I don't know whose. Gard"—the little cigar was dropped in a dish on the bedside table, cold and dead—"Elisa's a wonderful woman."

"Rope it, Doc. I'm not interested. How long'll I be like this? Flat on my back?"

"You know how weak you are, I don't. Until you're able to get around, boy . . . a week, maybe two, three weeks. There's no sure way to tell. It depends on your constitution. Some men are up and around in ten days, some a month."

"Well," Gard said dryly, "I can't lie around here

for a month. Even a week may be too long. News travels fast in the back country."

"What's that got to do with it?"

"Dentzel's dead. Men who know him . . . knew him . . . will hear about it. They'll run for it, more than likely."

The doctor washed in a shiny bowl and dried his hands while he studied the wan, drawn face in the bed. "Something to do with Court's killing, I take it?" He got a short nod, put the towel down, and drew up a chair. Gard knew what he was in for and grimaced; he couldn't run away.

"Listen, boy, you're treading awfully thin ice. It's not like it used to be. A man can't go out and spread his own private brand of gun law around any more. There's law in Dakota Territory and lawmen. They get paid to hunt down killers and bring them to justice. You're using an out-dated excuse for what you're doing. Revenge based on self-defense. You bait these men into drawing, then kill them. That's not justice, Gard, that's unnecessary risk. Suppose you killed one before he got his gun out? It'd be murder, wouldn't it? On the other hand, supposing one of them ambushed you, or beat you to the draw. You'd be dead, and that's worse." He shook his head back and forth, studying the closed lips of the wounded man, trying to catch his eyes and pull them away from the ceiling.

The voice that answered him was as determined

240

as wind in the winter treetops, and as husky. "Doc, you mean well. Just stick to patching up folks. Minding other folk's business isn't in your line."

The doctor arose. "You'd be surprised," he said. "Well, when you get hungry, there's a little bell on the table beside the bed. Ring it. Don't try to get up for at least a week, because you'll never make it. You've lost a lot of blood and don't have the resistance of a puppy. One good chill will fix you for good." He was going toward the door when he turned back, cocked his head a little, and smiled icily. "Of course you know better . . . you Ashleys . . . so you'll do what you please, but at least I've warned you."

Gard's eyes came down slowly; there was a soft twinkle in them. "All right, Doc. You're a good man if you do go pretty far afield for a pill-roller, sometimes."

The doctor went out without another word, and Gard lay back feeling the drowsiness in his limbs when he tested them. There was no particular agony or ache any more, just the lethargic sense of drowsiness, inherent weakness that made each arm and leg feel like it weighed a ton. He sighed. There was a fifty-fifty chance that Snider and Billings hadn't heard of Dentzel's death, or, having heard and not knowing who killed him, might consider it a personal brawl with some friend. But with the passing of each day, the chances of the killers staying beyond Missionary Peak, on their hide-away ranch, lessened. Especially since they had adequate funds for cutting a wide swath. Gard didn't know either of them, but he knew the breed, vicious, restless, unable to conform to confinement, self-imposed or not. He cursed to himself bitterly and moved his limbs again; nothing had changed and he knew it wouldn't have. The same leaden, exhausted sensation was still there.

It made the perspiration come out on his upper lip, just reaching for the little bell, but logic and conviction dictated a possible remedy for his run-down condition. Food and lots of it, gorge on the kind of sustenance that made frontiersmen indefatigable. If it worked, he'd cut his convalescence period in half—maybe less. He rang the bell. If he could do that, there was still an even chance that he might hunt down Court's killers. The big house echoed with the unaccustomed little sound and Gard lay back again, letting his mind carry him over the obstacle of his battered body, up through the deer trails behind the peak into a primeval backlands that had never been completely explored, and where Buckhorn riders went occasionally when the ranch needed game meat. He knew that area as well, almost, as the scattered little clutches of Indians who inhabited it, and he knew about where a hide-away ranch would be, had to be, if there was to be feed for horses, which the murderers certainly would need, having their stock with them.

The door opened while Gard's fancy was threading through the endlessness of the Missionary Peak country, searching out the most likely clearing for Snider and Billings to have their place. He smelled the food and grunted without looking at it. Cookie had outdone himself. The odors weren't the usual man-cooked aromas. There was meat, of course, but there were other streamers of fragrance, too, that hadn't been inside the main house at Buckhorn since the passing of Mrs. Ashley, years before.

Gradually Gard pulled his thoughts back out of the wild country, reluctantly, and turned his head to study this burdened tray with the smells that even tempted a man who was forcing himself to be hungry against the listlessness of his weakened body. The same jolt he had gotten in the doctor's kitchen, but to a slighter degree, held him motionless. His face was turned so that the glance from Elisa's eyes fell fully into his own stare, and held there, imprisoned by his surprise and impaled on the wasted look of his face.

"You! What the devil! Elisa . . . Miss Benton!" He was recovering from the astonishment at seeing her, in his house, putting down the laden tray that she had obviously prepared herself for him, and the reaction was exasperation bordering on fury. Only his condition kept him from shouting at her. As it was, the fingers made fists on top of the counterpane.

There were two high splotches of color in her face, one under each eye. She deliberately set out the food, profile to him, and he sensed the way she was braced against the anger that lashed out of his glare at her. Then he let the air come out past his teeth in a sharp sigh and said nothing. For some inexplicable reason, the way she was bent there, face half averted and unhappy, apprehensive-looking, made him think of a puppy that was afraid of a licking.

"I . . . don't know how much of it you can eat," she said, still not looking his way again, sort of studying the food and hoping it was what he wanted, needed, "but it's all good for you. The doctor said . . ."

"The doctor!" Gard rolled his head and looked at her again. "That meddling . . . darned fool!"

Elisa shook her head gently at him, trying to find something in his face that wasn't there. "Gard, he didn't bring me here. He didn't even think it was wise of me to stay. Don't blame him."

He stared without speaking. She was wearing a cream-colored dress that, if it hadn't been tailored for her, at least fit like it had. He dropped his eyes from her face, saw the uneven, hectic pulsations in the small sunken spot where her throat and chest met, and raised his eyes again. "Miss Benton, why do you insist on making yourself a nuisance?" He saw the hurt come into her face briefly, then fade before a dogged look of perseverance that was blunt and without feeling, a defense she had cultivated against him. "You are nothing but trouble. I told you that once before. Trouble for Court, trouble for Buckhorn, and now trouble for me. Uninvited trouble at that."

"Won't you eat a little of this roast, Gard? It'll get cold, maybe." Each word was a dagger; the defenses were fast weakening. She had to say something, do something—before he saw actually how he was driving her, breaking her, with the knout of his words.

He looked once more at the food. She had worked long and hard over it; it was the kind of food a woman would make. Perhaps it was the all but forgotten look of homemade ice cream that kept his eyes on the dishes, but he didn't look back at her. Naturally she couldn't know that Gard Ashley was making himself admire the food for the strength he hoped to acquire from it.

"Elisa, if you'll leave . . ."

"Of course." She turned once more toward the dishes, moved the table in closer to the bed, and picked up the napkin, pulled it from the ring, flicked it once, and bent over him, keeping her eyes on the jungle of his mussed hair while she

245

tied it behind his neck, then straightened, and walked away,

Gard was too startled to move. He lay there, smelling the fragrance of her, up close, and seeing again in his mind's eye the broken breathing that had tugged at her bosom while she had bent over, tying the napkin. He lay like that for a long three minutes without moving, conscious again of that starved sensation that he had never been able to define or name. He felt it even larger within himself, then he turned savagely, weakly, and threw himself at the food, eating like a man possessed, hardly catching more than a taste, until even the laboriously made ice cream was gone, then he lay back, uneasy in the stomach and uncomfortable.

When Elisa came back into the room, Gard had tried twice, unsuccessfully, to roll a cigarette. His fingers shook and tore the paper each time. He glanced up from the third attempt, angry-eyed, and looked back down again as she crossed the room toward the crowded table. And the paper split again. The vein in the side of his neck was throbbing with suppressed fury, but he said nothing.

She reached over almost timidly, took up the little sack, made a trough out of the paper, poured in flakes, and rolled the thing unevenly, albeit tightly, gave it a lick and a twist and stood there, looking her amazement at the little brown object she was holding. Gard had watched, not sullenly, but with no graciousness, either.

There was a hesitant amusement in her amber eyes when she looked down at him, still holding the cigarette. "I've seen it done thousands of times. That's the first time I ever tried it, though." He said nothing. "Where are your matches?" "Left hand front pants pocket." He watched her stoop and get one. "Shall I light it? I . . . never tried it, though." Gard almost forgot the rancor he bore her at the look of doubt on her face. Under other circumstances it might have been hilarious, the way she stood there like a small girl, eyeing the cigarette in one hand, the match in the other, and looking up from both, beneath long, gently upcurving lashes, awaiting encouragement, which she needed, or discouragement that she would welcome.

"No," he said, remembering seeing a girl get sick once trying to smoke. "Just stick it in my mouth and light it."

Elisa went over, bent again, and the vital closeness and fragrance made Gard's nameless hunger writhe deeply inside of him. She bent lower to put the cigarette in his mouth. He waited, lips parted slightly, then the electric, inexplicable shock of agonizing awareness made them both look up at the same time. It was like the early evening had become static, never getting any lighter or darker for an eternity. Their glances held, frightened and awed. He forgot the cigarette. Her hand went lower, touched his chest, fingers tightening until the paper broke. He said her name. It came out strained, almost in horror. "Elisa!"

"Gard . . . oh, Gard!"

It cost him a lot to lift the right arm and put it up into the soft wealth of her hair at the base of the neck, and press, bringing her mouth harder into his own until little spiraling tingles of pain shot up into her brain, signaling a benumbed, indifferent, otherwise occupied nervous system. Gard could feel the fullness and soft texture of her mouth against his own chapped lips, like new honey. The undefined sensation grew to a hot, pale light inside his head, its appetite appeased but not sated, then she was pulling away from under his arm, and pushing firmly, softly against the bedside, raising slowly to look down at him. The amber eyes were tortured and misty.

"Gard . . . why?"

"I . . . don't know, Elisa." It was simply and quietly said. He was dumbfounded and almost frightened.

"You didn't mean it, Gard."

"Didn't I?" he said, still unable to gather up the scattered ends of his composure. He shook his head. "How did it happen?"

She turned away quickly, grasped the tray, and walked out of the room without a backward glance. He watched her go, saw the erect, unyielding posture, and lost her when the door closed.

The hours went by like winged messengers heralding the night. Gard hadn't moved but once, and that was to sit up and make another cigarette with hands that were, incredibly, as steady as ice. He smoked indifferently, as though preoccupation made traditional stimulus unnecessary. It was like being in another world, foreign and filled with foreboding for the newcomer. She *had* responded; argue as he might, she *had* responded. If there was a purpose for the kiss, though, he didn't know it. All that he knew with certainty was that she had kissed him, and he had kissed her. It had been a long kiss, too, the kind that means something, like a seal or a promise—or something very, very solemn.

The room was misty with shifting patterns that came from scrollwork of leaf shadows cast through the open windows and projected by the weak moonlight, when the door opened softly.

"Gard . . . are you awake?"

He closed his fist over the cigarette and crushed it to death, letting the broken carcass drop to the floor before he answered. There was an odd, unprecedented stricture in his throat. "Yes'm. I'm awake."

"Well . . . I just remembered . . . do you still want a cigarette?"

"Yes'm," he lied soberly. "I'd like one."

She came in, her hair catching the dull moonlight and throwing it back into the room disdainfully, the lithe motion of her body with its sturdy grace and abundance, alive in a natural aura of starlight, then she stopped beside the bed and looked over at him briefly, fleetingly and with embarrassment making high color that he couldn't see. She gravely took up the tobacco sack, troughed the paper with narrowed eyes, and twisted another quirly into existence.

Gard's sardonic, whimsical little smile barely showed in the gloom. "Maybe you'd better light it first . . . this time."

She did, making an awful face, and put it gently into his mouth. He waited, lips parted, looking up into her face, but she avoided his glance by concentrating on the lower part of his features. He inhaled dutifully, took the cigarette out of his mouth, and exhaled without moving his eyes, letting it lie imprisoned and forgotten between his fingers.

"Elisa?"

"Yes, Gard?"

"I'm sorry."

She looked stunned. "The kiss, Gard?"

"No, the things I've said. All . . . those things. The past few weeks . . ." He made an inclusive

gesture with his hand. "About . . . everything."
It ended lamely and he couldn't find the courage
to enumerate the hurts that had flowed so readily
from him.

"I have a confession to make, too. I was partly
wrong . . . in some things, Gard."

"What things, Elisa?"

"Do you remember what I said at the theater?"

He nodded wryly. "Every cussed word,
ma'am."

"Well, you see, I thought Buckhorn was your
first love. I thought you were after Court's killers
for . . . the money they took. Gard, please . . . I'm
awfully sorry, but . . . well . . . that night we all
had dinner. When I went into the office and you
were sitting there so comfortably, with your feet
up and smoking a cigar . . . I got that impression.
Then, later . . . in Hurd's Crossing . . . it seemed
like you *were* Buckhorn, not Gard Ashley, or
even Court's brother."

"What made you change your mind?"

"Something you said that night, at the theater.
You said nothing . . . not even Buckhorn, or
words like that . . . would stop you from finding
Court's killers."

"Elisa, I reckon you were close to being right
that night. Buckhorn's been my life and my
business, so it's also been my world. You . . .
came along in time to make me see it. You said
I was a machine, maybe I was at that. I thought

251

about it." The gray eyes were looking into her face and beyond it. "Court and I never were what you'd call real close. We differed too much for that, but he *was* my brother . . . and maybe you were right when you said he was so different from me because he saw a lot he didn't like. I don't know." Gard shrugged, letting his glance focus on her again. "But . . . whatever else the Ashleys are . . . have been . . . they've always considered family first . . . Buckhorn second."

Elisa put a tentative hand on a chair. "Can I stay a little while?"

He nodded, making a smile that was as shaky as it was sincere. "I'm sorry, please sit down, Miss Benton. If you go now . . . I'll follow and bring you back."

She sat down and looked over at him with a wry shake of her head. "I doubt that very much, Mister Ashley. Even if you wanted to, you couldn't."

The gray eyes were impassive. He knew something she didn't—and the doctor wouldn't have believed—his body was making an incredible come-back. Strength was flowing like water over a parched desert, bringing with it the Ashley stamina and rawhide toughness. It would be better if they all thought Gard was down for several weeks. He had his purpose.

"Gard . . . you really didn't want that cigarette, just now, did you?"

He felt a little guilty. "What makes you think that, Elisa?"

"Oh, a woman's intuition, call it. No, not really. I could smell smoke before I opened your door. I'm not a smoker, that makes a difference."

"That's right, ma'am. I just said that to get you in here. But . . . if you knew I didn't want the thing, why'd you come in to make me one?"

She looked at him soberly for a second, then laughed. It was a fabulous sound, soft and melodious and rich, with a wonderful timbre and alive that washed over him like new health. "We're even, then, Gard Ashley."

He nodded, still remembering the laughter and wanting her to find amusement in something again. But Elisa's mind had swept ahead, to what was nearest her heart. She regarded him with a solemnity in which others might have read significance. Not Gard Ashley of Buckhorn for he knew nothing of women and until this instant had enjoyed this ignorance and disinterest.

"Elisa, there's something that puzzles me. Why? What's your interest in this thing? Like I said before, it isn't Court and it isn't money. What then?"

She arose and smiled ruefully down at him. "And, if you'll recall my answer, it was something like this . . . oh, you damned fool!"

His forehead was wrinkled. "I'll be flogged if it makes sense to me. Tell me, Elisa, why?"

"*You* tell *me,* Gard Ashley, how you found Dentzel?"

"That was easy. I saw your two-gun deputy in the theater when you were singing. He had a girl with him." He shrugged, watching her face closely, mentally wincing. "I . . . bribed her to get the names for me . . . all four of them."

"She told you the names and where the men are . . . or at least where Dentzel was . . . that it?"

"Right," he hurried to tack back with the topic before it got on unsteady ground about Billings and Snider. "Now . . . tell me why you're into Court's killing up to your neck?"

She gave the chair a short, abrupt shove to where it had been, then turned back. For just a second Gard saw that her lower lip had been caught between her teeth, then she was smiling at him, shaking her head. "Good night, Gard."

"But . . . you can't just up and . . ."

"Oh, but I *can.* Good night."

"Elisa, you'll be here in the morning? You won't leave?"

She was going to remind him of the things he had said before the kiss, but didn't, couldn't, not with the anxious, worried look that was in his eyes right then. She couldn't help a little sarcasm though, and made a mock curtsy to him. "With your permission . . . Mister Buckhorn . . . I'll stay the night."

"Elisa, that wasn't fair."

She laughed again, and Gard's final defenses were carried by the melody of the sound. He was smiling at her when she looked back at him, the amber eyes showing that strange, untamed fire that he had noticed long ago, that thrilled him now with the same passionate fervor that once had made him hate her. Now this same passionate streak that looked out of him brought up a wild response that thrilled him with its promise.

"I'll ask Buck . . . no, Cookie, send the cook in will you? The house is his. . . ."

"Thank you, you're a dear. It's already been taken care of, though. You see, I had no intention of leaving until you were up and around, anyway." She grinned again, youthfully and teasingly. "It was a safe thing to do, I think. The doctor told me you wouldn't be able to chase me off for a week at the least."

Humorous acceptance and gratitude swept through him. He smiled at her. "In that case, you don't have to go. . . ."

"Yes, good night, Gard."

"No . . . stay a little. . . ."

"You're a sick man. Besides . . . there'll be tomorrow. Good night."

"Elisa . . ." He said it with a peculiar, gentle sound to it. Neither of them was unaware of what it meant, his saying her name that way. She could feel it go all the way through her, like a fever that burned once, fast, and died away in a heady warmth that drained energy—and resistance.

"No . . . Gard." There was more to come but she held it back with all the control she had—almost.

He didn't say any more. She hesitated, looking down into his eyes, being drawn to him, shaking her head ruefully with a wan little smile. He reached out hungrily.

The kiss was more intimate, more reverent, and less constrained by shock and disbelief than the other one had been. They clung to one another with no pretence of embarrassment. He felt the moisture on her cheeks and the rapid, ragged way her breath struck his upper lip and was deflected. He looked into her eyes suddenly and the meaning of that untamed, savage fire that moved in their golden background was clear to him. She was a volatile, passionate woman.

Her hands were pushing with uncertain, convulsive little gestures to get away. He released her. Elisa went out of the room in a flash, and Gard lay there stunned, worried at this violent reaction to something that—to him—was excruciatingly beautiful and primitively bewildering.

He groped in the darkness of his mind, searching for something that just barely eluded him. The thing was perfect in everything but—something. There was one facet still lost. He could feel it, but never quite reach it. He lay there in the dark, too wrought up to sleep and yet too weary for wakefulness, walking in that pathless world he had felt open before him, once previously that same day—and still he couldn't find the elusive little part that would make this all fit an ageless pattern.

V

When Elisa returned with the breakfast tray, Gard could have gotten out of bed and helped her with it—almost. His recovery was amazing, but he hoarded the secret of it to himself. There was still the certain opposition he would encounter at first mention of continued pursuit of Court's killers.

She pulled up the little chair and smiled wryly at him. "You need a shave. You have no idea how villainous you look without one. Those black whiskers and the sunken places under your eyes."

He hoped she'd laugh but she didn't, just sat there watching him with a wistful, small smile. He ate all he could force down and handed her the tobacco sack with a twinkle. She laughed then, and declined by putting it back on his table. The early morning sun flashed off her white teeth.

"Elisa . . . if you don't tell me why you're doing all this, I'll ride out of here, so help me, and dig up your friends."

"What friends?"

"Snider and Billings."

She shook her head at him. "I doubt it. Not for a while yet, anyway. Besides, they're probably hundreds of miles away by now." She saw the sudden tightening of his mouth and the level, hard look of the gray eyes before he spoke.

"I hope not, ma'am. But that's not why I brought this up . . . and you know it."

"Gard, right from the start, from that night in the doctor's kitchen, I had just one reason. I'm not sure I didn't have a feeling pretty much the same, before that night. It's what made me get into this mess. I had planned to go back East again, take jobs between here and Independence, then . . ." Her eyes widened. "Gard! How did you know their names? Billings and Snider?"

He ignored her frozen astonishment when he spoke again. "Back where, Elisa? Where's your family?"

She didn't answer immediately, then, very slowly, she said: "I don't have any. Originally, I'm from Illinois. Gard . . ."

"All right," he said smoothly, ignoring the urgency in her glance. "Go on. Tell me what that reason was."

She didn't look away from him at all. It was a thrilling experience, those long, somber looks that spoke so eloquently for them. "Gard, you've learned a lot. Why don't you forget these men, let them go?"

"You haven't forgotten, I'm sure," he said very dryly, "that they shot Court . . . in the back."

"No, of course not. Do more killings make it possible for Court to come back? Please, Gard, even Court wouldn't have asked this much."

He shook his head. "You didn't know Court as well as you thought, or you wouldn't have said that. Elisa, we're even. You have Emmons somewhere . . . I'm not going to ask where . . . and I killed Dentzel. There are still two around and I'll get them."

The amber eyes flashed at him. He saw the turmoil and anguish in their backgrounds, and understood it. Icicles raced up his spine, then she was speaking.

"I don't think you'll find Billings and Snider. I tried like the devil, and I couldn't."

He smiled at her, speaking quietly. "I know."

She was startled and showed it. "Gard, you know where they are?" He didn't speak and she didn't care. The answer to her own question had swept over her in that second. "That girl . . . the deputy's girl . . . she told you about them, too, didn't she?"

"No, not exactly, but she gave me the clue I needed. For a while I figured that sheriff of the Crossing might have been in on the killing, too."

"Why did you change?"

He smiled at her. "After finding forty thousand on that unwashed Dentzel *hombre*, I knew Sheriff

259

Rupert wasn't in it, or he'd've had the lion's share, not some coyote like Dentzel."

"Gard . . . I'll tell you why I'm staying in this mess against you . . . if you'll tell me where Billings and Snider are."

"I can't do that, Elisa. I wish I could, but, in the first place there's a darned good chance they aren't there any more, and in the second place I haven't anything but a vague idea where their hide-out is myself. But . . . I'll give anything else you ask, if you'll clear up this other little mystery for me. The one about Elisa Benton's private little hate trail."

"Hasn't it occurred to you, Gard, that I just don't want to see any more killings?"

"Well . . . I can't feel that way. It was my brother they shot down. An Ashley."

"Of Buckhorn," she echoed, with an ironic twist to the ranch name.

He watched her get up, felt the futility of further arguing, and smiled. "Elisa, you're sure beautiful. You've been told that before, of course."

"Of course," she repeated hollowly. "Gard, please, what can I do to make you stay away from those men . . . those killers?"

"Nothing, Elisa. You should be ashamed to ask a man not to hunt down his brother's killers."

Her anger showed then. It wasn't a new sight to him, but surely it was more devastating now because of their intimacy. "You're exactly what

I said you were, Gard Ashley. A damned fool."

He didn't try to stop her when she swept out of the bedroom, but very thoughtfully reached for his tobacco sack and papers, had almost finished twisting the thing into existence when the paper tore. He cast it furiously aside and glared at the closed door for a full minute, then pushed back the covers and edged out on to the floor.

It would take two days of surreptitious calisthenics before Gard felt strong enough to saddle and ride a horse. His heart pounded like a condemned man's the second night after his excursion back into the realm of the ambulatory again. He let the ranch sink slowly into darkness and slumber, before he tried to get up, pull on his clothes, and duck out a bedroom window.

By the time the horse was saddled he had to sit down for a few minutes and dab at the nervous perspiration on his upper lip, then he swung awkwardly into the saddle, grasped the handy carbine butt, below the forks, to steady himself, and rode out of the Buckhorn yard like a man in a stupor.

It wasn't a matter of strength with Gard Ashley. It was the need for persevering in the face of his own Ashley determination. That was what had kept Buckhorn prospering all the years since its founder's death. Determination, that and nothing else, and that was what held him in the saddle now, inherent determination that was without consciousness, bearing him upward and outward, away from Buckhorn's sleeping occupants, with their own indifferent slumbering to the same force that drove him until, just before dawn, in the first wave of trees that hid the back country, like Elisa's eyelashes sometimes hid her amber eyes, he had to dismount and rest.

He watched the sun come up, tremendous and golden, spilling heat down over the cool land, and sat there until the mysterious rays had caught him, warmed the front of his shirt, sifted through and relaxed the muscles in his chest and shoulders, then he knew the first step of the trail ahead was not only behind him, but worth the effort—providing the killers he sought were up there, somewhere.

He let the sun work on his chilled body for a long, delicious hour. Until every taut muscle was slack with warmth, then he fought off the drowsiness and mounted again. Surprisingly it was easier the second time. Feeling better than he had since the day before, Gard Ashley ducked his head and rode a loose rein, letting the horse figure out which of the trails was wide enough. It didn't matter anyway, which trail he took, or how he went, just so long as he kept going northward. That was the direction he had decided back at the ranch he would search first.

Beyond the great, shaggy, old snow dome called Missionary Peak, that would be the first place to strike for, the most likely. Failing there, which he thought unlikely, he'd go westward, toward the mighty plains that broke away from the wild uplands on the far side of the peak's last fringe of virgin forest. There were also clearings westward, but Indians camped there this time of the year. It was unlikely Billings and Snider would have their cabin there, but it was second and final choice.

The sun climbed, but its warmth only seeped through the forested canopy overhead. None of the blasting, searing heat reached the forest floor below. Gard stopped once, when he shot his carbine into a covey of mountain quail, blew one to smithereens, and stunned three others. He ate while the horse grazed languidly along a creekbed.

He felt secure from anything—or anyone—that might trail him. Once into the primitive area, tracking would be beyond the ability of any cowhand trained in the obvious and blunt imprints of ranch animals over burned, sere ranges without underbrush. He made a cigarette, leaned back against a massive old tree, and smiled to himself. Elisa would be dumbfounded. More than that, she would be furious at him. He laughed out loud. The horse twisted his head, looked askance, then ignored the man.

But Elisa was all Gard Ashley thought of, even after he had become hopelessly lost in the tangle of great, endless silences that came stalking in behind him until they filled the whole of this pathless part of the world. Silences and windfalls and feed knee-deep to a mounted man, and endless varieties of game that watched him pass in rigid surprise. Elisa Benton—he said the name to himself as day waned, dropped its almost immediate mantle of darkness over the lost regions as he made a tiny clearing his bedroom, hobbling the horse and lying down with his carbine close, and the handgun in his fist.

Even when the cougar screamed, and his loaded gun tilted up instinctively, aware of the despairing sound to the eerie cry, he was still thinking of Elisa. The smile, the wonderfully musical laugh, the way she looked when she was afraid of his anger—and finally the two kisses. Especially that last one when he had seen the tawny fire in her golden eyes, moving in the background, writhing, hungering for release.

It was close to morning of the third day that he became painfully aware of two things. One, that he was in the country of the little clearings, and two—that Elisa loved him. She must—had to—and he had been so blind, so stupidly, incredibly blind. The revelation made a little of the weakness return. He dismounted, studying the first meadow in the northward chain from his haunches. He didn't go out into it, though, but instead turned back, made a camp, found a spot along the little creek he had stayed close to, where big rainbow trout lay, somnolent and secure, and skewered three with his boot knife before they took fright and fled in a flash of brilliant coloring. He ate the fish slowly.

She loved him. It was a wild and fantastic thought, but she must, otherwise why . . . ? He had it. He knew what she had refused to tell him, why she had refused as well. One followed the other as naturally as day following night. She loved Gard Ashley. Because of that, she didn't want him subjected to the undeniable risk of hunting down his brother's killers. That being true, then she had tried to keep him from the gunmen. That was also why she had come on the run when she knew he was wounded. It also explained why she'd taken his abuse and stayed at Buckhorn when she knew, at first anyway, that she hadn't been wanted—and also why she had tried so valiantly to find the killers before he did. And what followed naturally was that she wouldn't tell him of her love because, well, women just weren't supposed to, that's all. It was a custom—a tradition—that the man must say those things first. Or at least show them.

Gard didn't finish his last fish. He just sat there, staring into the darkness. Of course he loved her, damn it. That's what that funny feeling had been—still was—whenever he thought of her. He was in love with Elisa Benton, and she was in love with Gard Ashley. He sat up, fumbled excitedly for the tobacco sack, and made the belated quirly. Sleep was out of the question now.

The night noises came and went, heard, classified, and unheeded, for hours before he tried to sleep again. Then he saw the amber eyes looking down on him; she was shaking her head gently back and forth, but there wasn't an altogether disapproving look to the hazy features. It was a shadowy expression of sadness, real fear, and unhappiness, too, all mixed.

When the sun was new, struggling to re-establish its supremacy through the reluctant dinginess of the giant trees, Gard crossed the first meadow and the second. He was riding lazily, lost a little in the limbo of his fancy, when he caught an unmistakable odor of wood smoke. He frowned. There still existed close to a mile of forest before he came out into the next clearing. Reining back deeper into the trees, he left the horse, traded spurs for the carbine, and went on afoot, cautiously as he had in the uplands behind Hurd's Crossing, where Dentzel's body probably still lay, undiscovered.

The first thing he saw was three horses, one of which had the dried, matted down hair of recent riding on its lean back. The brands were unknown to him on two of the animals, and the third, an older horse, was rump to him, no brand being visible. The feed was sparse where they were

266

grazing, but they were heading slowly, driftingly toward the meadow northward. He noticed that they acted perfectly at home, too.

Going slower, taking longer periods for study, Gard moved like a lean ghost from shadow to shadow. It was a good hour later that he felt the thumping in his throat from an excited heart. The cabin was ahead, off to his left a little, more than half hidden in the trees and evidently built to blend in as it did. The horses were drifting faster now, as though scenting the lush feed beyond the trees.

Gard got in as close as he dared. The cabin had a decidedly lived-in look. There was no smoke drifting above the stone chimney, but there had been earlier; the entire woods around smelled of a fragrant cooking fire. A small area behind the cabin had been cleared in years past; there was a thrifty little garden growing there. The cabin itself was old and dark from age and weather. Gard feared the occupants would break for their horses at the first sign of his presence, and yet the animals were drifting in such a way that he couldn't get around the house and run them off without being detected. Pondering, he squatted beside a gnarled stump that stood stubbornly out of the tangle of brush and reviewed the best approach, when the door opened and a tall, extremely thin man stepped out under the little overhang and tossed a basin of greasy water onto the well-packed ground, beside the shuttered window to his left. Instantly Gard's gun was up, searching out the target with its single, sinister eye, then the flat explosion tore up the silence with a startling report, and the thin man went sideways drunkenly, jerked off balance, and flung up against the building by the slug's impact through the bottom of the basin. The second sound, that of the pan striking the ground, was small and insignificant by comparison.

The badly shaken man at the cabin's wall pushed himself erect, clawing at the pistol hanging low on his hip. Gard levered the carbine with a metallic grimness that carried in the new stillness, and called out: "Steady, *hombre*, don't make a move!"

The man seemed petrified, uncertain, and frightened, the way his fingers froze around the pistol butt, white-knuckled and unmoving. His face was turned toward the sound of Gard's shot.

"Drop it. Pull it out and drop it!"

The man hesitated. His face was flat and blank with disbelief. No cowardice showed, just a plain blank look of surprise and wonderment.

Gard had his lips parted to repeat the order, then a carbine roared from the back of the cabin and a living fir tree on his left erupted a flurry of dried bark and ancient dust.

The thin man was lunging for the opened door and bringing up his pistol, cocked and held steadily in his hand, when Gard, angry-eyed, threw down easily and ripped off his second shot. The man was almost into the opening when the slug took him like a club in the side of the chest, high, and jarred him backward on wobbly legs, then dumped him off the little slab porch flat on his back. He never moved again, but lay there looking up into the artistic pattern of limbs and needles that half obscured the brassy sky overhead.

The hidden gunman didn't fire again and Gard cursed savagely at his luck. Not pinned down, he nevertheless was limited in his movements because of the narrowed eyes he knew would be keeping a grim vigil for any kind of movement in the fringe of trees and underbrush. There was dour satisfaction in knowing the man in the cabin wouldn't be foolish enough to break out in a run for the horses. Not when he knew death was waiting for him to make such a move.

Gard finally left the carbine leaning against the stump, crept back to his horse, and mopped the sweat off his face, took down his lariat, and crawled back, cursing the underbrush that reached out to delay him, and had to be carefully allowed to go without a quiver. By the time he had squirmed to a sturdy young fir tree, made the rope fast near the ground, and crawled back to the stump with the dally end of the rope in his hand, he was covered with perspiration. His shirt was damp and cool with it and he felt a renewal of the old weakness. Lying face down in the spongy leaf mold, he rested for a full ten minutes, then straightened again, took the carbine up, got settled carefully, and gave the lariat a gradual, snugging pull until he had all the slack out of it, then called out.

"You there in the cabin! Your pardner's dead and you're going to be, if you don't hike out the front door unarmed. You're boxed in, *hombre*. Either come out or get burned out."

Nothing but his echo came back. Smiling slightly, eyes bright, Gard reached down, caught the end of the rope, and gave it a gentle pull. Out of the corner of his eye he saw the distant tree quiver slightly in the motionless forest, causing the scrub brush around to shake, also. Instantly what he was waiting for happened. A carbine snout leaped into view from the rear of the cabin and Gard's shot burst simultaneously with the hidden man's shot. The gun at the cabin swung wildly to the right, arced high with the vicious impact of Gard's bullet, then a brownish shirt was exposed, showing half a shoulder, and Gard's next shot, levered and tugged off in a blur of frantic movement, smacked soddenly into the log siding within inches of the man's back. Gard cursed, knowing he shouldn't have hoped for a hit when he had to fire so fast, but the man jumped at the sound of splintering wood behind him, dropped the shattered gun, and fled from view.

Gard called out again, hoping against hope, but feeling the urgency of immediate action. "This is your last chance to come out alive. Come out the front way now!"

Astounded, Gard saw the door open and a man emerge, black-haired, swarthy-faced, and beady-eyed, his hands held high overhead. He was looking south, toward the direction of the shots, waiting. Instinct alone kept Gard where he was. Centering the carbine on the man's chest he ordered him toward the stump. The soft sound of spur music went ahead of the gunman as he approached. Gard was watching his face. There was something there, half seen, that showed a vein of craftiness struggling with the slack look of defeat.

"That's close enough. Lie down on your face and stay there. Don't move."

The man obeyed, seeing Gard and letting his eyes range intently over the woods around the little fir trees, seeking out other men.

Gard palmed his pistol, cocked it, and used his pigging string to lash the man's hands behind his back, then he crawled laboriously back to the little tree, untied his lariat, and wormed back. The man sat up when a loop dropped around his neck and stared at his captor.

"Where's the rest of 'em?"

"Aren't any more, *hombre*. What's your name?"

The man looked at him, disbelieving. Dark color came into his face slowly. A glitter of fire showed in the bright eyes. "Snider, what's yours?"

"Ashley. It mean anything to you?"

The dark head bobbed once, then the eyes ranged over the forest again, still not sure.

"Get up, Snider." The gunman arose sullenly with naked hatred and humiliation showing in his face. "Move, over to the cabin." A shove started the burly, thin-lipped man walking. Gard kept behind him, watching. When they were at the door, another shove, more brutal than the first, sent the bound killer against the rotting old panel and it flew inward. Snider froze instantly. His voice made Gard look over his shoulder quickly. There was a handsome young Indian girl, very pretty and heavy-bodied, standing with her back against the far door, holding a shotgun hip high and cocked.

Snider's tone was frightened and gruff. "Steady, Tina, steady. It's me."

Gard nudged the man forward. They entered the room almost as one. He saw the shotgun droop a little, and spoke. "Uncock it and let it drop."

Large, black eyes like twin olives dipped in fresh oil saw him and obeyed. Defiance with very real fear was in their depths. Gard breathed softly when the gun was on the floor at the girl's feet.

She stood with her hands behind her, stony-faced and bitter-looking. Gard saw the impassiveness on her face and reckoned her to be in love with his prisoner.

He pushed Snider to a chair, motioned the girl around where he could watch her, thumbed back his hat, and fished for the tobacco sack. He felt the tension go out of him like blood, leaving a drained, almost childishly weak body behind.

"What's that *hombre*'s name . . . out there?"

"Ed Billings. You knew that."

Gard nodded. "I knew one of you was Billings, but I didn't know which one." He smoked silently; the tobacco revived his spirits a little. "Where's the money?"

"What money?"

Gard didn't answer right away. "Listen, Snider, Dentzel's dead. He gave me the same answer." His voice was unconcerned, casual, as though they were discussing a dull topic. "I set a little fire on the floor of his cabin and walked out."

"Yeah?"

"Yeah. He was tied to the bed."

Snider's mind worked on what Gard had left unsaid. Understanding came quickly. It showed in his stunned features. "I don't believe it."

Gard shrugged. He told Snider where Dentzel's cabin was and what had happened. It was convincing, too. Snider licked his lips and shot the pretty girl a nervous, startled look. "You wouldn't do it . . . here. Hell, you'd burn the whole god-damned country down."

"That's not my worry. Where is it?"

The dark, uneasy eyes went to the door. "Billings's got his in a belt under his shirt."

Gard smiled tightly, making a nod toward the door at the girl. "Get the belt off him. We'll see." She did, grunting and keeping a stony expression as she rummaged through the clothes of the cooling body. Then she straightened, went back, and looked up into Gard's eyes, standing flat-bellied and sullen, holding out a sweat-stained, thick money belt. Gard nodded, studying her. "Drop it and get back over by Snider."

There was $8,000 dollars left of the $10,000. He buckled the thing around his own middle, over his pants. "Now yours, Snider."

The gunman licked his lips, staring at Gard. He was cornered and knew it. The very calm resolve in his captor's eyes made it glaringly apparent he wouldn't waste time with his brother's killers. Snider shrugged with a savage jerk of his shoulders. "Under my shirt."

"Get it," Gard said to the girl. She went to work quickly and held the bulging belt out toward him. Gard smiled sardonically at her. "Just drop it." She did and with the same sullen stare. Gard buckled Snider's belt around his middle, too. He didn't bother to count the money. The girl was looking into his face when he glanced up, with a strange expression. He smiled at her slightly. "Go get their horses and bring 'em back here."

She went willingly enough, then Gard yanked Snider to his feet, shoved him outside toward the back of the cabin, and squatted with him there, waiting. When she returned, leading the animals, Gard called her over. Together they saddled up and threw Billings's carcass athwart one horse and lashed him down. Snider, thoroughly glum, was tied to his horse, and Gard turned to the girl, handing her the reins of the third horse.

"Who's horse is this?"

She spoke for the first time in clipped, slightly guttural accents. "It was Billings's horse. He's tied to their pack animal."

"It's a good horse." He was watching her face thoughtfully. She nodded, giving him a bold look but saying nothing. "It's yours now. Take it and ride back where you come from."

She considered this carefully for a moment, still looking into his face, then shook her head with an abrupt, determined little smile. "No, I go along."

Gard was surprised and bewildered. Watching Snider, with treachery stamped in every line of the man, would be hard enough, but watching them both would be extremely difficult, if not impossible. He was on the verge of brusquely ordering her off, when he thought of something else. She could follow them and probably would.

A night of darkness, a knife in the back, and Snider would have his freedom again. Turning angrily away, he nodded. "Go ahead. Lead his horse through the brush along that creek until you come to another horse tied to a pine. Stop there."

Without a word she sprang up. If she recognized his anger, it didn't show. There was a flash of sturdy leg, then she was looking down at him, the black eyes bright with some secret passion, and she smiled again, turned curtly, and started down through the thick undergrowth where the horses had to pick their way carefully and their riders were pulled at, forced to bend almost double against the scratching fingers of the endless branches. Snider, unable to fend off the blows, because he was tied, cursed in a savage monotone.

Gard, who followed on foot, leading the pack horse, got his own horse, mounted, and turned southward. He continued to lead the pack horse with its grisly burden, following the Indian girl's cannily selected little trails, riding directly behind the killer, Snider, keeping his eye on both of them.

They rode until late darkness and gradually Gard passed the familiar landmarks again and chose their night camp in a spot where he had thought of Elisa. It was an enchanted spot to him. Each second he spent there, watching the Indian girl make their late supper with supple, confident arms, took him back to memories of the amber-eyed woman at Buckhorn. He even grinned a little to himself, thinking of his reception when he would ride in triumphantly with the last of his brother's murderers. Elisa had accepted his invitation to war with him, and had lost. Somewhere, she had Hooker Emmons as her prisoner, but Gard had gotten the other three renegades.

His thoughts were jerked back to reality by the Indian girl. She was kneeling in front of him, looking into his face, and responding to his slight smile with one of her own. An open, frank little grin that said he was braver than Snider and Billings because he had fought them together, and smarter because he had conquered them. Gard blinked at the invitation in her black eyes, flushed quickly, and accepted the slab of cooked food without looking at her again. She didn't move, though. He looked up quickly, gruffly, and scowled. "Well, what's the matter?" He looked past her tawny shoulder and saw the venomous look he was getting from the prisoner. "Oh. You feed him." He saw the look was still in her eyes and got off a barb. "He's your man, take care of him."

She caught it but didn't let it bother her. The pretty, full mouth didn't speak, but the ebony eyes did. They said many things, and one of them was that Snider was *not* her man—not any longer, anyway.

Snider ate in baleful silence. When he was finished, he jerked his head savagely at the girl. She shrugged indifferently and went back to the fire, made her own meal, and sat there, cross-legged, eating and raising her round, youthful face every once in a while to glance across at Gard. It made him uncomfortable, because the looks were eloquently frank.

He turned to Snider, saw the cold, unblinking, watchful glare of the man, rolled a cigarette, lit it, and shoved it to arm's length. The outlaw inclined his head, took the thing between his thin lips, and inhaled deeply, narrowing his eyes against the drifting smoke.

"Which one of you shot my brother?"

Snider's mouth slit around the cigarette when he answered without any hesitation. "Dentzel fired first. He was the boss. Ashley was bad hit. He yanked up his horse and started to fall."

Gard could see it vividly in his mind's eye. "Then you all jumped in. Right?"

Snider nodded without speaking. The uncompromising stare held. Whatever else he was, Snider was no coward.

Gard studied the man. Every second they were together he would be watching for an opportunity—not to escape, so much, as to kill his captor. He shifted on the pine needles and glanced at the girl. She was looking at him, too, impassively—all except for the hot, dry look in her eyes. He wondered if she was playing a part. Encouraging him so she could get her hands on his gun. Gard turned back to Snider, stared at the man speculatively, then reached down, dragged the carbine into his lap, cocked it, and withdrew his own handgun, tossed it in the dirt before the prisoner, and motioned toward Snider's bound hands with one hand, speaking to the girl without looking at her. "Untie him." She pushed off her knees with a startled look, and hesitated. Gard nodded coldly. "Go ahead. Untie him."

She moved forward on silent feet when Snider threw back his head and laughed. "No, I'm not sitting in this game, Ashley. You might work it with the others . . . I don't know . . . but not me. Do I look like a damned fool? Listen, cowman, I got a chance in a court. Especially over at Hurd's Crossing where this brother of yours was killed. I'll take my chances there, not here in any damned-fool gun duel like this." He looked scornfully at the narrow space that separated him from Gard. "Couldn't either of us miss at this distance. Maybe you don't give a damn about your chances. Well, I do."

Gard reached down, uncocked the carbine automatically, and retrieved the pistol. Neither Snider nor the girl moved. He holstered the pistol and shoved the carbine away, looking at the gun-man thoughtfully. What the man said was true.

At Hurd's Crossing his brother's killing would have become half forgotten in the wildness and turmoil of that boom town by now. The chances of convicting a man like Snider, with his host of gunmen friends, would be very small. Even bringing him to justice the day of the crime might not have convicted him. The lawless element at the Crossing was strong.

He said nothing, pondering bitterly on the chances of exacting justice, and recalled what the doctor had said, with an acid smile. Maybe the territory had law now, and lawmen, but Buckhorn gun justice was still best, and would continue to be, until places like Hurd's Crossing grew up and men like Snider and the others were cleaned out. Still—he couldn't shoot a man in cold blood. That wasn't the Ashley way, either. He grunted to himself, went over, and lashed Snider to a tree so that he couldn't move more than three inches in any direction, facing away from the fire, then resumed his place, kicked up the fire, and settled back to spend an uneasy night in catnaps, uncertain of the girl's intentions, and afraid to trust even the rope that held Snider.

The Indian girl was watching him with an almost gentle, dreamy look. It annoyed him that he should be so weary and she so wide-awake. He thought of Elisa. It was a subject that kept him occupied for a long time. The night sounds came to the quiet camp. Curious eyes peered from the fringes, reflecting the vagaries of the dying fire. He reached over for some of the wood the girl had piled close beside her. She misinterpreted the movement and bent quickly, both round arms going out to him. Gard jerked back as though bitten and glared at her through eyes grown scratchy from weariness. He didn't say anything, though. She pulled back, wooden-faced, and resumed her vigil. It made him uneasy. He watched her toss two more dry limbs on the fire and stared down the little alleys of flame, seeing Elisa again. She was sleeping. He could see her so very plainly, resting there, then one of her hands was feeling for him, drawing him close.

VI

Gard saddled the horses, made the bent corpse fast again in the saddle, avoiding the face. He could smell food cooking with no appetite for it. There was a tension in the air and a feeling of near tragedy in him as well. He finished with the animals, went back to the fire, and watched the girl stomping out the last of the embers. Snider's bloodshot eyes were more livid than they had been the night before. He knew.

Gard watched the girl's movements, saw the

same animal suppleness when she moved, and understood that she was avoiding his eyes. He made a cigarette, held it tentatively toward the gunman, and received a savage glare for his efforts.

"Not from you, *hombre.*"

He smoked the thing himself, even though it tasted bitter, like alum and vitriol. "All right. Let's go." Snider went past him to the horses. One reassuring glance showed that the prisoner's arms were still secured behind his back. The flesh was purple and swollen badly from impaired circulation. He hesitated when they were close to the horses, then shrugged. He wouldn't take any chances until they were out in the open country again, whether Snider suffered or not. It had to be that way; Snider would never relax his efforts to escape.

The day was a long one, full of tedious twistings and back-trackings to avoid mammoth fallen trees and impenetrable barriers of thorny brush. Gard sweated, feeling warmer than he should. There were complete blank periods, too, when he fell asleep in the saddle, lurching along exhausted in body and mind.

The noon meal was a scavenging affair with the Indian girl coming up with food that was unpalatable to either white man, then they went on again, feeling the slight incline of the land sloping gently downward. Gard pushed them hard. He knew his body couldn't stand another night like the last one. He had to have sleep, hours and hours of it. Days, even.

When the first star came out, they were fortunately nearing the end of the primitive area. Gard saw the sign of venturing cattle and horses within the perimeter of the last fringe of trees. It took his mind off other things that weren't pleasant. Even shook off some of the languor that was riding in the saddle with him.

The Indian stopped and looked back, making the horses behind her stop, too. Her black eyes went over Gard once, caressingly, then she spoke. "We'll camp here?"

"No. Keep going straight ahead. Due south."

"But this is open land, out here. It must be a great ranch. There will be no cover for us."

He wanted to laugh at her perplexity but instead just nodded. "We'll take the chance. Move out."

She was turning, lifting her reins, when Snider spoke for the first time since dawn. "Hell, this is Buckhorn range, Tina. You've heard of the big Buckhorn outfit." She was twisted back again, looking at Snider. The renegade spat lustily before he went on. "This . . . cowman with us, well, he's Mister Buckhorn. Owns the place." Snider's cold eyes stared through her. "Now you know why he wants to push on."

The girl looked past Snider to Gard, appraised

283

him again, but with a new, dawning look of wonder in her face, then turned abruptly and reined out again.

The night was warm and balmy. Stars seemed close enough for a tall man to touch, tiny little prisms of diamond light, clear and brittle and thrilling-looking in their firmament of deep, deep purple. The horses went ahead listlessly, wearily, only one—Gard's mount—showing any signs of knowing the trail wasn't far from ending.

When the girl saw some bulky outlines arrayed in a motionless line across their trail, she reined up quickly and froze fast in her saddle, looking, head high and wary.

Gard saw the shapes, too. Both he and Snider knew what they were. He nudged his horse up a little. "Go ahead. It's only cattle."

She stared a little longer, then turned to face him. "Buckhorn cattle?" she asked simply. He nodded. The black eyes were almost shy now, but he couldn't see it. She leaned forward and started out again. The cattle caught their scent, snorted softly, and threw their tails in the air in a lumbering run of fright. Several cows bellowed frantically for misplaced calves and received assurances in frightened, wavering voices that the youngsters had seen the horsemen, too, and were running from them.

When they struck the little creek that meandered across the burned range, Gard reined over toward it. He knew the water would be polluted from stock, but their horses would drink there. "Come on. Here's a good clear place."

They dismounted in a wide opening where the rushes had long since succumbed to the generations of pawing cattle and given up even trying to grow. The ground was dusty and gray-looking. Snider staggered a little when he got down, but the violence was still deep in his eyes. Gard watched the horses drink first, then turned to the girl.

"Untie him."

She didn't hesitate this time at all. All sense of equality—and more—was sublimated.

Gard faced Snider with his handgun dangling, cocked, from one fist. "If you want to try it, Snider, go ahead. This'll be your last chance. We both know that, too. Maybe you meant what you said about being willing to take your chances in a court. I don't know, and don't care." They were giving stare for stare, like strange dogs. Gard's intentions were plain even in the poor light. He waved the pistol gracefully over the flat, barren land. "You can run in any direction, and I can down you before you get a hundred yards." He shrugged. "That's up to you. Just remember that I'll kill you with less thought about it than I would a wolf."

"Then why untie me? I'm not thirsty."

"No, maybe not. I wouldn't drink that water

anyway. It's because your hands are about twice the size they should be, that's all."

The girl had finished untying Snider. He moved his arms with infinite slowness, as though his shoulder muscles were unused to forward motion at all. Then he stood there, looking at the mottled, puffy hands and wrists, and grimaced. Speaking more to himself than the others, he said: "They're numb. I knew that, but hell . . ." He went forward and kneeled by the brackish creek, sticking his hands into the lukewarm water and looking back at Gard. "I'd be a sort of a damned fool to run with open land like this, and hands that couldn't hold a gun . . . if I had one . . . wouldn't I?"

Gard shrugged. "Yeah, I'd figure it that way, but there's no telling how the next one'll think. You and I don't think much alike. I just wanted you to know, is all."

Snider spoke again while he moved his hands a little, feeling the circulation coming back like bundles of needles. "Oh, I reckon we think a little alike. In some things." He jerked his head sideways without looking up. "About Tina, anyway."

Gard expected him to say more. A close look showed that Snider's teeth were locked against the pain that racked him. He may have wanted to say more, but his physical anguish took all the control he had. He began massaging one wrist, and then the other, withdrawing the hands from

286

the murky water and staring at their tremendous proportions ruefully as he got to his feet and faced Gard. "Well, we might as well get to hell to your place and get this over with. The sooner I see the last of both of you, the better I'll like it."

Gard felt ridiculous, standing there before the man whose hands were nothing more dangerous than great lumps of shapeless flesh with the cocked gun in his hand. He holstered the thing and nodded, walking behind Snider until the outlaw was beside his horse, then he motioned for the girl to help him astride. When Snider was sitting there, looking wryly at Gard, who was fingering the pigging string indecisively, he smiled thinly. "Go ahead, cowman, tie me up again."

It was a taunt that Gard let go by. Very deliberately he took down the lariat again, ran it through the rein holes of Snider's horse's bit, and tossed the loose end to the girl.

"I don't think you're dumb enough to try it, Snider . . . but you're welcome if you want to. That'll give you a chance to rub some life into the hands."

They went ahead again, picking their way slowly, the lanky corpse riding smoothly, head and feet down, on the horse that followed drowsily in the wake of Gard's animal. The land leveled off gradually and became a vast plain that stretched much farther than they could see until it swung rapidly upward and threw itself against an impassive bulwark of high mountains made spiny with heavy tree growth. The four horses and their burdens moved slowly through the darkness. Eventually a Comanche moon, sickle-like and sharp-edged, cast pale, washy light down on them, then the horses began to prick up their ears and quicken lagging steps. Gard knew they were close to Buckhorn. He narrowed his eyes and stared ahead into the night until vague, ghostly outlines of white buildings began to show ahead, like distant icebergs, square and large and formidable.

The girl turned once and looked back. Gard motioned her on into the yard where no lights showed. She rode on slowly, holding her horse back a little while she looked closely at the obvious neatness and affluence of this spacious ranch, then Gard pulled his horse up, slipped down, stretched hugely, and called out in a loud, relieved voice: "Buck! Oh, Buck!"

A door opened softly, warily, and a man carrying a sawed-off shotgun peered out, with tousled head and puffy eyes. "That you, Gard?"

"Yeah. Got some company for you. Come on out."

"In a second," the voice said, lower an octave or two, then the mumbling of other voices erupted sleepily, and someone swore that someone else was always hiding the matches to the lamp, and

Gard smiled wanly, letting his glance wander over the buildings and feeling an almost complete peacefulness within himself.

Buck Gault stumbled out of the bunkhouse, still gripping the riot gun, pants legs looped carelessly inside boot tops, shirt buttons askew, and only halfway buttoned at that, and his sandy hair a tumbled mass. "Who's that? The one tied crossways, Gard?"

"One of the men who shot Court. Name of Billings." A hand flick indicated Snider, who was looking dourly at the other men coming out of the bunkhouse, some barefooted, all half-dressed but fully awake. Moonlight glinted on guns among them, too. "This is Jack Snider."

"Another one of 'em?"

Gard nodded. "Yeah."

"Well," Gault said in a different tone of voice. "Who's *this* then? Not another one of 'em?"

"No. She's Snider's friend."

The Buckhorn riders were staring at the pretty, dusky girl as though they weren't used to seeing women on Buckhorn—which they weren't.

Buck's eyes looked Gard up and down. "You all right?"

"I reckon. About all I need is a gutful of food and a month's sleep."

"This all of 'em, Gard?"

"No, there's another one, name of Hooker Emmons. Elisa's got him locked up somewhere.

There was one named Dentzel, too. I shot him in a cabin above Hurd's Crossing."

Snider snorted. "You told me you burned him up."

Gard wagged his head. "What I told you was that he was tied to his bed and I set the cabin on fire. That's right. He cried like a kid, so I went back, put the fire out, and gave him the same chance I gave you. You turned it down. Dentzel didn't. I killed him."

Snider nodded softly, letting his gaze wander away from Ashley.

Buck was eyeing the money belts. "You get it all back, Gard?"

"There'll be some short. These boys had a high time for a little while, from the looks of things. Most of it's here, though."

Buck shifted the shotgun, letting the mouth point downward. "Well, you want us to take 'em over, while you get some sleep? We can tie 'em in the bunkhouse and take turns watching 'em." He looked up at Snider, read the man correctly in one fast appraisal, then ignored the gunman and faced Gard again. "They won't get away, I'll give you my word on that."

Gard was shaking his head before Buck finished. "You can sure take Snider over, and damned good riddance as far as I'm concerned. Tie him to a chair, but make his arms fast instead of his hands. They're in pretty bad shape." He turned a little and looked up into the black eyes of the girl. "What'd Snider call you?"

"Tina."

"Tina, remember when I told you to take a horse and slope?" She nodded, watching his face as he spoke. He was blushing and thankful the darkness kept her from seeing it. "Well, I don't think I'd've made it if you hadn't come along. I'm thankful, Tina." Snider was looking at him curiously. Gard could feel it. He motioned toward the gunman. "Get down." Buckhorn hands—none too gently—helped. Gard motioned toward dead Ed Billings. "Cut him loose, boys." While they were disentangling the corpse, grown quite stiff now and heavy, Gard looked back to the pretty, dusky face. "Here are three pretty good horses, saddles, and the works. Take 'em. They're yours. None of these *hombres*'ll need 'em any more. If you want more, just say so."

The girl didn't look away from his face. Her small hands were lying relaxed on the saddle horn. "I don't need pay," she said simply, then, gathering up the reins, she lifted them. Gard moved forward quickly and caught the horse's bit.

"Tina, you've got to eat, anyway, and rest. You can't just turn around and go back. Here," he held up a hand, "get down." She obeyed, but without touching the hand. On the ground she was very close to him, straight as an arrow and waiting, looking up into his face. Her voice was so low Gard almost didn't hear the two words.

"I sorry."

He turned away quickly. "Buck, put these horses in a separate corral and give 'em a good feed, will you?" He looked at Snider, saw the man's eyes fastened on the girl with a strange, astonished look in them, and nodded grimly. "And Buck, make darned sure he's here in the morning, when I get up." Then he said: "Come on, Tina." She followed along beside him, just a slight, deferential step or two behind, as they went toward the house.

Inside, again Gard's heart was pounding. He saw the girl stop in the great kitchen, wrinkling her nose a little. He had caught the same disturbing scent and felt the weakness sweep over him again. This time there was shame in it.

"Cookie."

The sound echoed through the big house. Somewhere a man's garrulous voice answered profanely, then a shambling figure came into the room rubbing at sleepy seeds in his eyes. "That you, Gard? Damn, boy. You give us a hell of a . . . well, who's this?" The cook fumbled for a lamp, lit it sloppily, and turned to look at the girl. His eyes shot wide open. She was standing, motionless and impassive, every curve of her outlined in the rich, golden lamplight. Gard followed the cook's glance and felt admiration again.

"She's had a long trip, Cookie. How about some good food for both of us and a spare bedroom for her?"

"Why, hell yes," the cook said, still drinking in the girl's beauty. "Why hell . . . yes."

"Fine. I'll go wash up. Show her where she can get some of the trail dust off her, too, will you? Then we'll eat."

Gard was turning away when he caught the frightened look in the black eyes. He smiled, reached out impulsively, and took one of her hands. "You're at home, Tina. I'll be back in a few minutes."

The uneasiness vanished slowly. She smiled at him. He had never seen her smile before. It was an infectious, appealing smile that even made the dour old cook grin in appreciation. Gard dropped the hand and swung out of the room. Tina looked after him, still not moving, and holding her hand out where it had been when he had let it go.

The house was deathly silent when Gard went through it. He knew which of the vacant rooms Cookie would have fixed up for Elisa and was tempted mightily, but veered off and went to his own quarters first and scrubbed hard and diligently to remove the ingrained dirt. For some mysterious reason he couldn't even guess at, his weariness had dropped away when he had entered the house. It was as though he suddenly didn't need sleep.

Finished with his toilet, Gard studied the freshly shaved face by lantern light, saw with a shock how emaciated and hollow-looking his features were, and consoled himself with the knowledge that, at least, the bitterness was gone. Then he went back through the house to the guest bedroom and knocked insistently on the door. There was no answer, even after the third loud pummeling. His heart sinking, he twisted the knob and looked in. The bed was as neatly made as ever—and empty. Going farther into the room, sick at heart, he looked at the bare dresser, then turned slowly and went outside and stood in the middle of the vast living room, stunned.

The sound of Cookie's muted noises from the kitchen brought him back in a flash. He went directly to the lighted room and saw the girl sitting, eating, at the great, vacant dining room table, and ignored her.

"Cookie, where's Elisa . . . Miss Benton?"

The watery eyes came around slowly and read the doubt and hurt in his face. "Why, didn't you go into the office?"

Gard didn't wait. He let the door close behind him as he swept across the house and shoved impatiently at the closed office door. The room had the same, disturbing scent of her, but it was empty, too. He turned in puzzlement and saw the envelope lying face up on the desk. Despair came over him. He sat down and picked up the paper, held it while he lit a lamp with one hand, then tore open the wrapper and spread it out between his hands on the desk top, like a man would hold a child's face he was peering into, and read the letter.

Dear Gard—

It was more than just the shock that Buck and the others felt, when I found you gone. It was a disappointment, too, and fear. Fear of what would happen to you—inside of you, because you're a relentless man—when you found Snider and Billings.

The disappointment was in you, as a man. You're so awfully hard, Gard, that you're blind. I'm not sure you'll see, either.

Elisa

He re-read the note twice more, searching between the lines until he was sure he understood every thought she had had while framing and writing it, then he shoved out of the chair, groped for a cigar, found one, and lit it and strolled back to the kitchen. Tina looked up quickly at his face when he entered. She was standing beside the empty plates. He saw her, but his mind was going along the trail toward Independence, where Elisa would probably head. He nodded absently.

"Cookie show you a room, Tina?" The black head nodded gently. "Fine. Rest till morning. I'll see you later . . . maybe."

The cook looked at him skeptically. "You're not going to eat?"

"No, sorry, after all your work. When did she leave?"

The rheumy eyes were momentarily perplexed, then cleared. "Oh, yesterday. I drove her to Yankton. Said she'd catch a stage out of there."

"She didn't say where, did she?"

The cook shook his head. "No, didn't hardly say anything, all the way in."

Gard's look of preoccupation settled fast. He turned and went back through the house, smoking. There was only one thing to do. Go after her. Explain that he wasn't blind. Tell her what he had figured out—about them—and bring her back.

Buck Gault heard Gard's call and came out of the bunkhouse, looking at the dim silhouette on the verandah of the ranch house.

"Saddle me a fresh horse, Buck. I'll be down in a few minutes."

Buck saddled the animal and waited. A full hour went by. The only thing he saw was the handsome Indian girl. She came silently across the yard, not seeing him, heading toward the corral holding the outlaws' horses. He stepped out of the deep shadows beside Gard's saddled horse and smiled at her. "Heading out?" She nodded, throwing him a quick, darting glance and walking on. "I'll help you." Together they caught the horses, saddled them, and tied the bridle to a lead rope. Buck handed up the lead rope. "Thanks for bringing him home safe. He's the only Ashley left now."

She looked at Buck frankly. "This other one . . . the one Jack and his *hombres* killed . . . was he handsome and brave . . . and so wonderful . . . too?"

Buck was startled. His eyes faltered, then arose again to the dark, smooth face. "Just between us, no. Not like the one that's left." She hadn't taken the lead rope and Buck held it up again. "Here. I heard Gard say for you to take these horses."

"No. Just this one. It was Billings's horse and he hated me. I'll ride it because of that."

Buck was looking his perplexity. "Listen, ma'am, when Gard Ashley gives you something, he means for you to take it. He wants you to have it."

"That's the way he is?"

"Yes'm. That's the way he is."

She reached down, took the lead rope, and shot a fast, experienced look at the led animals. "Then I'll take these. He wanted me to have *this* anyway." She turned and rode slowly back across the yard toward the great sweep of land beyond without another word or so much as a glance back. Buck stood where he was, puzzled. There had been something in her words that had a double meaning, he thought. Shrugging finally, he went back to the patiently waiting horse. It was the cook's voice that shook him out of his reverie.

"Buck? That you?"

"Yeah. Now what's happened? By God, Buckhorn's changing faster'n a man can keep up with."

"Listen, Gard's passed out on his bed."

"Sick?" Buck asked sharply.

"Naw. He was lying on the bed, reading that letter she left for him, and just seemed to fall over asleep looking at the damned thing. You reckon we ought to wake him? I heard him yell to you for a fresh horse. Maybe he's got . . ."

"Let him sleep." Buck inhaled deeply, looking back over the night where the Indian girl had disappeared. "The darned fool's about killed himself as it is, hunting down these killers of Court. He's just plumb wore out, Cookie. Let's let him sleep."

"Yeah," the cook agreed uncertainly, "but he might be sorer'n a wounded bear if we don't get him up."

Buck Gault shrugged and stomped out his

cigarette. "Well, ain't our fault if he passes out, is it? Let him be."

The cook nodded glumly, still uncertain, turned, and stalked back toward the house.

VII

When Gard awoke, the sun was a giant bowl from which splashed molten waves of heat, spilling down on the writhing land, running into shadowy places, and seeking out green things and scorching them like invisible lava. He was wringing wet and swollen in his boots. Shoving off the bed, he began to undress methodically, letting the knowledge that he had wasted many hours soak in. He took a bath, shaved again, and changed into fresh clothing, then went out to the kitchen. It was empty, so he fried his own ham slabs and washed them down with coffee. He felt immeasurably better than he had the day before. There was no one in the yard, or down by the corrals and barns, either. He went to the bunkhouse, looked in, and found Buck playing solitaire in front of a bunk where Snider was tied. Both pair of eyes looked up.

Buck yawned. "Man, you really slept."

"I reckon," Gard said. "Buck, I'm riding out again. Take Snider into Yankton and give him to Johnny, will you?"

"Sure, right away. By the way . . . that Indian girl . . . she rode off last night. I had a time getting her to take those horses, too."

Gard turned and looked down at Snider. "Does she belong with those bands over beyond Missionary Peak?"

Snider nodded. "Yeah. She'll get back all right." He looked at Gard speculatively, on the verge of saying something else, then looked away, apparently deciding against it. "Don't worry about Tina. She knows that country like the back of her hand."

The silence was loud enough to hear their pocket watches ticking, then Gard headed back out. "I don't know how long it'll be this time, Buck," he said.

The foreman shrugged. "Take your time. Nothing's in a hurry around here. Not for another forty, fifty days, when we'll start the fall gather."

"Yeah, well, keep an eye on Snider when you're taking him in."

Buck nodded dryly and watched Gard go over, rope a horse, saddle him, step up, and lope easily out of the yard, heading east, toward Yankton. The foreman's eyes were narrowed. "Hope he catches her."

Snider twisted his head around quizzically. "Who? Tina?"

"Missus Buckhorn," Buck said enigmatically, then slashed the outlaw's ropes and jerked a thumb toward the door. "Outside, *hombre*. You're starting on your last ride."

Gard made town in record time. His horse was lathered when he left him at the livery barn and stalked up to the sheriff's office. Curtain looked up in profound surprise when he walked in.

"Gard Ashley! Where have you been?"

"Later, Johnny. I just stopped to tell you that Buck's bringing in a man named Snider. He was one of Court's killers. There's another dead one out at the ranch. Better send Doc out there for him."

"That's three," Curtain said. "Where's the other one?"

"Dead. I left him in a shack up behind Hurd's Crossing. There's a deputy at the Crossing that wears two guns. He's got a girl friend . . . little pretty blonde thing . . . who can tell you where the cabin is. She told me, that's how I found this Dentzel *hombre*."

Curtain was nodding. "And Dentzel told you about the other two . . . that it?"

"Yeah. Johnny, have you seen Elisa?"

"Sure, yesterday afternoon. She was taking a coach to the Crossing. We talked for a little while. Why?"

"Did she say where she was going?"

"Yeah. Some little town in Illinois, Gard. I forget the name, though."

"Thanks. When's the next stage leaving here?"

Curtain looked at his watch with near-sighted aplomb and smiled. "Shouldn't be more'n twenty minutes, by my watch and chain."

"Thanks again, Johnny. *Adiós*."

The sheriff looked up, saw the tall cowman whirl and head back down the duckboards toward the Burch House, where the stage stopped. He made his slow, appealing smile, shook his head, and sighed loudly, looking around at the thick little door that separated his office from the two strap-steel cages beyond in the small room that were Yankton's two jail cells.

Gard found the clerk in the saloon section of the Burch House and hustled him back to his cubbyhole office where he got a ticket to Hurd's Crossing. Outside, under the warped overhang, a drummer was already sitting on the bench where Gard dropped down.

When the stage arrived, Gard and the drummer climbed aboard. The cowman settled back and relaxed against the starting lurch, listening to the creak of the body and the grinding sound the steel tires made in the dust, then he leaned out and looked ahead at the horses. The coach hadn't started with its usual head-snapping lunge. The animals were wet and weary. He eased back, wondering why the horses hadn't been changed before they left Yankton, then forgot about it in the tumble of his thoughts about Elisa and the things he wanted to say to her.

They were still about seven miles from the Crossing when the stage pulled up and stopped in a flurry of its own backwashing, powdery fine dust. Gard leaned out, puzzled, and saw the driver swing down, cursing. He got out and walked forward. One of the near side horses was standing hip-shot. The driver saw him come up, threw him a glance of appraisal, and jerked a thumb toward the animal. "I told the bosses at the Crossing it wouldn't work."

"What?"

"Using the same teams round trip." The driver began to swear with a zeal found only among those of his calling and their fellows, the muleteers.

Gard looked at the animal and scowled. "Don't they know a horse's flesh and blood, too? You can't push animals like that."

"That's one of their god-darned economy waves," the driver said disgustedly.

The shotgun guard strolled around to their side of the coach, unruffled, with a cud of tobacco riding rhythmically in his mouth.

Gard probed the horse's favored leg and felt the fever above the ankle, running up above the pastern but below the hock. "Bowed tendon, more'n likely." He straightened up suddenly. This would be a crippling delay for him, too. "Cut him out. He's branded. He'll come home all right."

The driver swore blisteringly and bent to help

303

unfasten the harness. The crippled horse was left standing in the heat waves and the stage went on, but now the gait was alternated between a slow trot and a slower walk. Gard fumed and smoked until the Crossing came into view. Thoroughly angry by the time he alighted and almost defeated in his hope to overtake Elisa, he stormed into the headquarters of the stage company and unleashed a scorching, quietly spoken tirade against the plump, astonished president of the company who reared back in his chair in bewilderment, eyebrows climbing, and took it.

"One more thing. I'll see that your franchise is cancelled in Yankton if you go ahead and pull this fool stunt again. If you doubt my ability, pardner, just look me up over there. Name's Gard Ashley. Now, when's the next stage out for Buelton, east, toward Independence?"

The president's complexion was a ruddy color. He dabbed at his forehead, eyes popping, and spoke in a small, thoroughly contrite voice. "Well, Mister Ashley, I'm sure, if the company's inconvenienced you, we'll see that . . ."

"Listen, I asked you a question. When's the next stage out?"

"Eight o'clock, Mister Ashley, for Buelton. Now then . . ."

"Eight o'clock," Gard said, startled. "Hasn't there been a stage out since before . . . I mean . . . earlier?"

The man was sweating, bullets now. "Well, you see, Mister Ashley, because of some unsettled conditions south of us . . . just above the border . . . we've had our schedules shuffled badly. I'm terribly . . ."

"You mean," Gard said softly, "that anyone who was going out on the morning stage, someone, say, who spent the night in Hurd's Crossing, would still be here? They couldn't leave?"

The pink hands went out, palms downward, deprecatingly. "These unsettled conditions along the border, Mister Ashley, they've upset all the lines. Not just ours. It's terrible . . . Mexicans are raiding. The cavalry from Fort Buchanan's already gone south."

Gard's heart was pounding. Elisa had come to the Crossing yesterday night. She wouldn't have been able to leave, and that meant that, somewhere, Elisa Benton was still holed up in Hurd's Crossing. He had a wild, hard glitter in his gray eyes when he turned back and looked down at the frightened face behind the desk. "Listen, pardner, how much would you charge to hire an extra stage and horses?"

"You'd have to hire the driver, too, Mister Ashley. We never let our coaches go. . . ."

"All right, the driver, too."

"For how long, sir?"

"To go back to Yankton . . . the slowest, longest way."

"Well, that's a new one. Usually . . ."

"I know. How much?"

"It'd have to be on a time basis. By the hour, sort of."

Gard pulled out his wallet and laid three $100 bills on the president's desk. "Use that, pardner. When it's used up, let me know. Now, get that stage under way as fast as you can, and have it parked right here, where the stages always park, and don't let a soul into it."

"Gladly . . . it's something special, then?"

"Darned awful special, *hombre*. A young lady with amber eyes will come along when the stage is here and you be on hand to tell her this is the Buelton stage. Put her aboard and don't say a thing. I'll ride on top, with the driver."

"Amber eyes? You don't mean . . . Miss Elisa Benton, by any chance?"

"That's exactly who I mean. Have you seen her?"

"Well, not lately, but she sang at the Bird Cage a week or so back. Beautiful woman, Mister Ashley, beautiful."

"Amen," Gard said. "You'll get this stage up right away?"

"Yes, sir, immediately."

When Gard was back in the sun again, he had to wipe the sweat from his upper lip. Nerves he hadn't known were a part of him were jumping under his skin. There was a new name featured

306

on the theater's front. He made for the little building anyway, shoved into the coolness of the dingy ticket room, and saw the same little chunky man sitting where he had been on his last visit, and wearing the same fabulous sleeve garters. The manager's head tilted under its derby and his eyes widened.

"You! I heard you was killed."

Gard smiled. "Don't you believe it. Where's Miss Benton?"

The small eyes were sardonic. "Still chasing her, huh? Well, she was in here earlier, after supper, I'd say, but I ain't seen her since."

"Do you know where she's staying?"

The man wagged his head dubiously, then looked up quickly. "You really want to see her?" Gard nodded, feeling for another gold piece. "She's due back here in an hour or so to pick up a portmanteau of stuff she left when she run out . . . after you was shot. You could wait."

Gard dropped two of the small gold coins on the man's magazine and watched him beam. "No, I don't want to do that, but you can do me a favor, if you will."

"Name it, cowboy."

"Tell her the Buelton stage is waiting in front of the stage station. Just don't mention me at all, or that I told you."

"Cowboy, Jock McGuire's a sound man with a secret. Yours is safer here than anywhere. Just

307

tell her the Buelton stage is waiting and forget you entirely, that it?"

"*Bueno. Adiós.*"

Heart thumping, Gard went back to a café near the station in time to see the hired stage wheel in close to the duckboards and stop, the driver using both hands on the brake set before he looped the lines, and eased back to wait.

Darkness was a cousin to the creeping despair in Gard's mind, liquefied with innumerable cups of black coffee, before he saw Elisa walk up to the stage. Almost before she had stopped walking, the chubby president of the line eased out of the station doorway and held the coach door open for her with a wide smile and low bow.

Gard got up quickly, waited until Elisa was securely hidden inside, then, sweaty-palmed, he left the café, walked around the back of the coach, and swung up beside the driver who shot him a questioning look. Gard nodded, leaned far over behind the driver who was unlashing his lines, and waved at the pink face that was turned up toward him.

The animals lunged eagerly. The coach was traveling light and responded to the pull with an abrupt, jolting gathering of forward momentum. Gard made a cigarette and lit it, watching the Crossing drop away behind them like a herd of large, orange fireflies. He waited until the stage swung west instead of east and tensed for the tapping on the roof that meant Elisa had noticed the wrong direction. It didn't come, so he leaned back, letting the miles roll away under the spinning wheels, wondering how he should frame what he had to say.

The driver tooled his stage at a gentle clip, letting the horses set their own gait. He hadn't said a word or looked right or left since leaving the Crossing.

When they were about twelve miles out, Gard leaned over and nodded to him. "Pull 'em up, pardner. After I'm inside, go ahead again."

"Back to the Crossing?"

"No, on to Yankton."

The driver nodded, leaning back slightly on the lines. He was smiling gleefully through the mattress of his beard. Before the wheels had stopped turning, Gard went down beside the boot, swung wide, and dropped to the ground. He went to the coach's door, hesitated just a second, then twisted the handle, keeping his head down, stepped up inside, and closed the door again. Instantly the stage shrugged into motion, gathering an easy, rocking momentum. Gard raised his head and looked across at Elisa. She was frowning just the smallest bit, watching him. When his face came up fully and the pale light shone across its sunken places and bronzed skin, she gasped and jerked erect. "Gard!"

He was smiling, wanting to cross over and sit beside her, but not doing it. "Yes'm," he said softly, "surprised?"

"Yes, how did you get here?"

He shrugged and laughed boyishly. As it had been with Court, Gard's smile and laugh made him appear very young and uninhibited. But as in the dead man's case, Gard's grin was deceiving. "Well, I got back to Buckhorn last night. You were gone. I started out after you then, but fell asleep and didn't get under way until this morning, late. I took the stage to the Crossing and you can guess the rest. There was this stage delay."

"Gard, why didn't you just stay at Buckhorn?"

"You mean you didn't . . . don't . . . want me with you?"

Elisa's eyes were desperate and unhappy. She turned away from him, looking out the side window, watching the march of the land, the way it came up slowly, jerkily, then was flung away to the rear, making way for the next panel of night beauty that jumped out of the near darkness. "It's more than that, Gard. First . . . tell me, did you find Snider and Billings?"

"Yes'm. Up at a hide-away they had this side of Missionary Peak, Old Snowy Butte we call it."

"You . . . killed them?"

"Billings, yes. But I brought Snider back alive and gave him to Buck to take in to Johnny

310

Curtain." He thought of the Indian girl and winced.

Elisa was looking back at him. She saw the uneasy flinching of his facial muscles. "What else happened, Gard?"

"Elisa . . . I'll tell you that, too, but first I want to say something I thought about up there." He leaned forward, reached up nervously, and thumbed his hat back, then began rubbing his palms together, half afraid to look at her as he talked. "I think I know why you've been in this affair since the start. If I'm wrong . . . well, it'll be a hell of a disappointment. Elisa, I think you're . . . we're in love with each other." He kept right on talking, building a cordon of words around those important ones, cutting off her chances of interrupting and not daring to look up to see her reaction.

"You've always said you didn't want me to go after those men because it was bad for me . . . well, you couldn't have meant that in any way but the way it sounds. You didn't like the risk, too, maybe, or something." His head came up then. She was white-faced. Her eyes glowed in the shadowy world they were riding in. "Elisa . . . something else I figured out up there. I love you. Have, too, for quite a spell. Maybe that's why I hated you at the start. Didn't want you to marry Court. Maybe I loved you even then, and didn't know it. There was a funny feeling in me and I'd

311

had it a long time." He looked down at his hands again, flushing russet in the soft light. "Then, up there in the wild country, I figured out it was me . . . in love." Again he looked up, making a caustic little smile, half timid, half triumphant. "So, you see, Elisa, I wasn't really as blind as you thought I was . . . if that's what you meant in the note when you said I'd never be able to see."

She didn't speak for a while. The horses were walking now, pulling the coach like it was a wagon, slowly and ponderously. In a way it was degradation for the racy, light vehicle, but in another way it added to the illusion of floating peacefully, drenched in poignant happiness, that was filling Elisa's mind and soul.

"Gard . . . I don't know what to say."

"Was I right, then. Are you . . . we in love?"

"I think so. I've been in love with you from the start. From the night you walked away from the dinner table and went into your office. Do you remember what I told you that night? That I thought I'd snared the wrong one of the Ashley brothers?" He nodded, recalling, also, his cryptic, insulting answer and writhing with the unpleasant memory.

"Well . . . but I was so afraid I'd fallen in love with a machine. A handsome, successful man, without feelings, without a heart, with no warmth in his blood. Oh, Gard, I was terrified when I

312

thought of you going after those men . . . those killers. Court was dead. I knew they'd kill you the first chance they got. How could one man succeed against three killers?"

"I did, Elisa."

She looked squarely at him. "Yes. To me that possibility existed, too. It meant that, if you *did* succeed, you'd be proving yourself a lobo wolf. Cold and deadly and emotionless perhaps."

"No," he countered slowly. "I don't think so."

She waved a gloved hand. "I'd been wrong once, Gard. Nothing on earth makes me happier than thinking I've been wrong again, this second time." She was breathing with an intensity that thrilled him, the golden eyes flashing a fire that reached out and found a mate in the fiery look in his gray eyes. "But, I loved you, Gard. That was the simple secret I had. When I told you, you were a damned fool, I meant that you were so blind. I didn't hide it, but I couldn't tell you, either."

He nodded. "I understand, Elisa. I thought about that, too."

"But, Gard . . . I'm still not sure about us." She leaned back limply against the seat cushion, regarding him somberly. "What did you do with this killer you brought back?"

"Snider?" he asked. "I told you. I left him at the ranch for Buck to take into Yankton and turn over to Johnny Curtain."

"Oh, yes. I remember now." There was a pause. "Well, Johnny has both of them, then."

He started in his seat. "You mean that's where you had Hooker Emmons . . . all the time?"

She nodded. "Yes. I knew he wouldn't be tried fairly at the Crossing. Johnny agreed to keep him and the secret that he was in Yankton, for me. Before I left, I gave Johnny a thousand dollars to have him prosecuted. He told me there wouldn't be much doubt about justice being done . . . not in Yankton."

Gard blinked at her, then made a short laugh. "Well I reckon I *was* blind at that. I never thought of Johnny's having Emmons."

"Then . . . what was this other thing that happened up there, where you found Snider and Billings?"

His palms were greasy again; he rubbed them slowly up and down the seams of his trousers. "Elisa . . . there was an Indian girl at this cabin where Snider and Billings were."

Her head came around slowly, intuitively. The golden eyes, wide and attentive, read the shame and uncertainty in his face. "Go on."

"After the fight . . . Billings was dead and Snider gave up. I went into the cabin and this girl was there. She had a shotgun." He shook his head irritably, forcing himself to hurdle the desire to evade and get to the facts. "Anyway, she went back with us. The first night's camp was made in a little spot where I'd spent the night before, thinking of you. It was sort of . . . like you were there, with me, that other night. I was tired and used up, Elisa. I kept seeing you there, everywhere, even in the fire. I sat looking into the flames, and saw you down there, too. I reckon the flames put me to sleep." It was becoming difficult to speak. "All right," he said bluntly. "Some time after I was looking into the fire, I fell asleep. I was dog-tired. I don't know how much later it was, but I dreamed it was you."

Elisa was watching him with a strange, intent look. Her eyes had lost their mistiness. Only a wondering appraisal looked across the coach at the lean, gray-eyed man. There was no pity in her look—but a vast sheen of understanding was there that he couldn't have helped but see if he had looked over at her. "This girl, Gard . . . she was there with you?"

He nodded stubbornly. "Yes. She was there."

For a moment no one said anything. The coach was rocking along again in a gentle, swaying gallop and the moon, such as it was, came out from behind a stray, ragged old cloud and shone eerily inside the coach, adding to the dim light from the coach lamps. He looked across at her. There was a log jam of words behind his teeth, but wisely he held them back. Nothing else he said would add or detract to the picture in her mind.

Elisa's full mouth was parted over the even teeth where the light reflected softly. She was letting her head lie back gently on the cushions behind her, staring at him. "Come over here beside me, Gard Ashley." He went, bewildered, finding warmth where he had expected anger. She sighed. "She meant . . . means nothing to you, at all?"

"No, of course not. It was you."

"Gard, kiss me. Tell me just how much you *do* love me."

He twisted a little and reached out, feeling the fullness and vitality of her body coming around to meet him, the passion that he had felt before, flowing out of her and into him. Then she pushed him away enough to speak and the little smile was still there.

"You think I should hate you, don't you?" He nodded. "No, Gard, you're wrong. You're just the man . . . I wondered . . . doubted that you were. Do you understand?"

"No," he said. "Frankly I don't."

She laughed then. The sound was rich and musical and lovely. "It doesn't matter, Gard Ashley. Someday you will . . . maybe. I love you . . . and I was wrong again, which makes me very, very happy."

ABOUT THE AUTHOR

Lauran Paine who, under his own name and various pseudonyms has written over a thousand books, was born in Duluth, Minnesota. His family moved to California when he was at a young age and his apprenticeship as a Western writer came about through the years he spent in the livestock trade, rodeos, and even motion pictures where he served as an extra because of his expert horsemanship in several films starring movie cowboy Johnny Mack Brown. In the late 1930s, Paine trapped wild horses in northern Arizona and even, for a time, worked as a professional farrier. Paine came to know the Old West through the eyes of many who had been born in the previous century, and he learned that Western life had been very different from the way it was portrayed on the screen. "I knew men who had killed other men," he later recalled. "But they were the exceptions. Prior to and during the Depression, people were just too busy eking out an existence to indulge in Saturday-night brawls." He served in the U.S. Navy in the Second World War and began writing for Western pulp magazines following his discharge. It is interesting to note that all of his earliest novels (written under his own name and the pseudonym Mark Carrel) were published in the British market and he soon had as strong a following in that country as in the United States. Paine's Western fiction is characterized by strong plots, authenticity, an apparently effortless ability to construct situation and character, and a preference for building his stories upon a solid foundation of historical fact. *Adobe Empire* (1956), one of his best early novels, is a fictionalized account of the last twenty years in the life of trader William Bent and, in an off-trail way, has a melancholy, bittersweet texture that is not easily forgotten. In later novels like *Cache Cañon* (Five Star Westerns, 1998) and *Halfmoon Ranch* (Five Star Westerns, 2007), he showed that the special magic and power of his stories and characters had only matured along with his basic themes of changing times, changing attitudes, learning from experience, respecting Nature, and the yearning for a simpler, more moderate way of life.

Books are
produced in the
United States
using U.S.-based
materials

Books are printed
using a revolutionary
new process called
THINKtech™ that
lowers energy usage
by 70% and increases
overall quality

Books are
durable and
flexible
because of
Smyth-sewing

Paper is
sourced using
environmentally
responsible
foresting methods
and the
paper is acid-free

Center Point Large Print
600 Brooks Road / PO Box 1
Thorndike, ME 04986-0001 USA

(207) 568-3717

US & Canada:
1 800 929-9108
www.centerpointlargeprint.com